REMAINS TO BE SEEN

REMAINS TO BE SEEN

JIM INGRAHAM

FIVE STAR
A part of Gale, Cengage Learning

GALE
CENGAGE Learning

Detroit • New York • San Francisco • New Haven, Conn • Waterville, Maine • London

GALE
CENGAGE Learning

Set in 11 pt. Plantin.
Printed on permanent paper.

LIBRARY OF CONGRESS CATALOGING-IN-PUBLICATION DATA

Ingraham, Jim.
    Remains to be seen / Jim Ingraham. — 1st ed.
      p. cm.
    ISBN-13: 978-1-59414-653-4 (hardcover : alk. paper)
    ISBN-10: 1-59414-653-5 (hardcover : alk. paper)
    1. College presidents—Crimes against—Fiction. 2. Women police chiefs—Fiction. 3. Policewomen—Fiction. 4. Murder—Investigation—Fiction. 5. Maine—Fiction. I. Title.
PS3609.N467R46 2008
813'.6—dc22   2008010778

First Edition. First Printing: July 2008.

Published in 2008 in conjunction with Tekno Books and Ed Gorman.

Printed in the United States of America
1 2 3 4 5 6 7 12 11 10 09 08

This book is for Slim, Pete, and Stefanie.

I wish to thank Paul J. McCarthy, Chief of Police, Westbrook, Maine, and my sister, Janet Cargill, for helping me understand the ways of Maine.

CHAPTER ONE

Lieutenant Webb Harrington stood on the porch of his Maine farmhouse watching Perci Piper's MG skid into a snowbank as she made the turn into his driveway. He smiled and glanced beyond her down the hill past Stickney's dairy farm and watched three police vehicles moving up Cutter's Road, taking the back way.

Good! They'd have to wait out back there a half hour till the woodroad got plowed out, give him time to show Perci the body exactly as he had found it. He brushed ice crystals off his mustache as he went down the steps, feeling a coin in the left slash pocket of his pea coat, probably a quarter by the size of it. Should have dropped it into the coffee can last evening when he emptied his pockets. Would have when his wife was alive.

A post-storm melting had left a film of ice over everything, and Perci was having trouble getting out of her car, unable to get a purchase on the ice-slick gravel, black-booted feet flying out from under her.

"I don't need your help," she said, waving him off.

He hadn't offered any, hadn't intended to, was just standing on the snowbank next to the driveway watching her.

"I'll get the hang of it one of these days," she said, bent down, slapping ice off her knees with a big blue glove, one hand holding the door handle. "My God, but it gets cold up here!" straightening up, breath misting, cheeks raw red, grinning. "Mercury in that thermometer I bought yesterday? Had to stand

9

on tippy toe and look down the hole to find it." Excited telling him that. She'd been in Maine only a few months, up from Florida on a training program.

She had specks of gold in clear blue eyes, a generous mouth, a small straight nose. For a Southern woman with a Greek surname, her skin was impossibly white and English looking.

He was tempted to say her legs would tire breaking through the crust, wading in deep snow, but he guessed she'd figure that out for herself. And she did. Hardly got into the trees before she was walking directly behind him, complaining about logs and rocks and juniper branches buried underfoot.

"What brought you out here?" she said, voice flat out there in the woods. But a strong voice, lot of self-assurance in it.

"Christmas trees. Get a few for the church this time of year."

"You a religious man?"

"Not especially," he said, walking in tracks he'd made earlier past pillows of snow on sagging hemlock branches.

She went through ice on the brook near the foot of the slope, thin hood of it over running water. Only her boots got wet. It took him a minute to fetch her out, but they reached the clearing before the crime team got there. Strange enjoying the clean forest smells of winter while staring at a frozen dead man.

No footprints except Webb's near the man's body, so apparently no one else had discovered it. Small man tied by the belly upright against a pine tree, arms outstretched, wrists bound to two outspread branches, head held up by a thick ligature bonding the neck to the tree trunk.

Perci stood directly in front of it, staring up at the cold gray face, snow like a dunce cap on the head.

"Tell me what you see," Webb said.

"A crucifixion."

"If that means tied up there is what killed him, I'd question it."

She leaned closer to the body, careful not to step into the untouched snow. "The ligature doesn't go completely around his neck," she said, brushing crystals of ice off her nostrils. "More like he was garroted."

"What about those upward marks above the ligature, just behind the ear."

She peered intently at the head. "Think he was hoisted up by the neck?"

"A possibility," Webb said. "Think he was dead before he got strung up?"

She stepped back, her pretty face a model of concentration. "Be tough to get even a small man like that up there if he was kicking and yelling." She glanced toward sounds of the approaching plow, still out of sight beyond screens of pine and hemlock.

"More than one man?"

"Maybe one strong man could do it, if the victim was dead."

They waded around back through a thicket of witch hazel. The rope on the man's waist and the one around his neck were tied behind him. Ropes holding his arms out were tied in front.

"If a rope was flung over that branch to hoist him up, which seems likely, it'll show when somebody climbs up."

"I suppose," Perci said, "one man could have lifted him, then come around back here and tied that ligature around his neck. Maybe the same rope, looks strong enough, piece dangling down in those branches. Maybe once he was tied to the tree at the waist, the hoisting rope was removed and used to bring his neck into the tree trunk."

"Why go to that much complication?"

"Why string him up like that," she said, "unless you're making a statement? A rope flung over a branch would've spoiled the picture."

"Think it was done in the daytime?"

"One thing seems apparent," she said, looking at him with a trace of apology. "I'll keep an open mind, of course. But the way the snow's on it seems obvious it happened before the storm, which means he's been up there at least two days. And if one man did it, I'd vote for nighttime. Had to take a while to do this. Daylight would be too risky."

"Automobile headlights?"

She nodded. "Another reason for thinking it happened before the storm—no tracks."

He didn't question her opinion, although she apparently thought he might, the way she was looking at him, her expression glimmering on uncertainty.

"What's the way he's dressed tell you?" The man was in a gray suit, white shirt, loosened collar, no necktie, gray socks, black shoes.

"Have to know more about his habits, but I wouldn't think he'd come out here voluntarily without an overcoat. Kind of strange having a suit but no necktie. If it happened when he was home, I'd think he hadn't been there very long. Probably didn't happen after he'd gone to bed. Maybe just came home from work, took his outer coat off. What do you think?"

"Just as you said, we'll have to find out what his habits were. But you're guessing he didn't come here on his own?"

"Would he be dressed like that? It's been awful cold."

"Could have left his coat and necktie in a warm car, got into an argument."

"But being trussed up like this on a tree suggests to me he was brought here for a purpose. Maybe a cult thing, something like that. I know I'm not supposed to reach conclusions, but I'd guess he was abducted."

He watched her take a notebook from her jacket pocket, lean against a tree and devote herself to note taking. She was the first student he'd had under the new federal grant program (which, by the way, had listed her as Persis Piperopoulos, not what she called herself—Perci Piper). He hadn't wanted to take her on when the chief proposed it, but now he was glad he had. He'd never had a woman partner before and was pleased they had sent him a good one—bright, forthright, young face shining with honesty. And naivety, which he didn't object to at all.

"We'll learn a lot more from the forensic examination, but this gives us a chance to look at traumatic asphyxia. You can see it involves a lot more than just finding a rope around somebody's neck."

"That's the technical term for hanging?"

"Any kind of suffocation."

She wrote that, then put the notebook away. "Whatever the truth of this is," she said, "somebody went to a lot of trouble to make this look like a crucifixion."

"I guess you don't recognize him," Webb said as they walked around front. He had thought she might, but the face was discolored and a chunk of snow was obscuring one of the eyes. Because she wasn't a local, she probably thought the question odd; but, good student that she was, she leaned forward, eyes narrowing, peering up at the face.

"Don't think so," she said.

"Look again. You were talking to him ten days ago."

She leaned closer, tilted her head, gave Webb a hard stare. "Is that Samuel Spatz?"

"Looks like him to me."

Samuel Loren Spatz was president of Cleeve College (just up the road a few miles) where, two weeks ago, Perci had investigated a coed's death—a girl named Alicia Umber who had died of infection three days after trying to give herself an abortion. The case had achieved a lot of media attention, some of it nationwide. Perci got caught up in the publicity and was accused by some of the college officials of deliberately bringing

13

attention to her "pro-choice prejudices." President Spatz had been especially offended by comments Perci had made on a local television broadcast. She didn't mention Spatz by name, but shortly after meeting with him, she was caught on camera calling the college administration "backward and bigoted."

After the forensic team had taken the body down and sent out for an apparatus to melt the snow, Perci and Webb walked back up the slope, using the tracks they had made coming down.

"All you got up here is hills," she said. "But it's easier going than wading through a cypress swamp. Here we might scare up a rabbit or a deer. There you worry about snakes and gators and whatnot."

"Panthers?"

"Not many of them left outside of zoos and sanctuaries. I was picturing those signs," she said, meaning signs on campus during a protest march. Apparently, like him, she had made a connection between the abortion ruckus on the Cleeve campus and the way President Spatz had been strung up.

Webb tried to remember her report. "Didn't they accuse him of playing God?"

" 'Sanctimonious Sam,' half those signs said. I guess that went on even before the girl's death. I saw in the paper just two days ago something about him heading up a group called 'Champions of the Unborn.' "

Newspaper stories about Spatz had gone across the country, Webb recalled. Even before Alicia Umber's death, Spatz had got into trouble with his board for bringing what they considered adverse publicity to the college. They wanted him out raising money, not raising hell. And his anti-abortion diatribes, it was claimed, were discouraging recruitment of students. "They go to college to have fun and to learn, not to be preached at," a board member was quoted as saying.

"Weren't they trying to get him to resign?"

"Students were," Perci said. "Nobody on the board would talk about it, at least not to me."

Although she had stopped complaining about the cold, she was obviously glad when they reached the house. On the porch she stamped snow off her boots, then went straight inside to the heat register in his kitchen, took her gloves off, shoved her hands into her pockets and shuddered as the heat rose around her.

He was at the stove making coffee.

"You must miss Florida," he said.

"Oh, I'll get used to this." She was looking around at papered walls, small-paned windows, heat register in the ceiling, probably aware of the plank floor she was standing on. "How old is this house?"

"A hundred and fifty years, I'd guess. Maybe more."

"Down my way that would make it a museum," she said.

Ordinarily her question would have led him into a sales pitch. He'd been trying to sell the house for over a year now—a ghost in every room. But she wasn't a candidate for real estate, scheduled to be in Maine only another few weeks.

"What made you pick Maine?" he asked. "Lot of locations on that list."

"I was originally supposed to go to Providence, but when I saw Cleeve was a host city, I jumped on it. Never been this far north."

Without asking whether she wanted any, he put two slices of Canadian bacon into a skillet, made some toast, fried four eggs in the bacon fat and set a meal in front of her.

"I guess you don't believe what they're saying about fat and cholesterol," she said, nibbling at the bacon.

"Oh, I believe it."

"Well, it tastes good, but this will be my quota for the month. Your wife teach you to cook?"

"She taught me a lot of things, but cooking wasn't one of them—except maybe parsnips. She showed me how to cook them, but I haven't had any since she passed away. Hate the damn things."

"What's a parsnip?"

"Looks like a white carrot, tastes funny."

"She liked different kinds of things?"

"I guess," he said. It didn't trouble him talking about Sarah, who had died of leukemia almost two years ago, but Perci might have thought it did. She didn't say anything for a while, kept her eyes on her plate. A thoughtful woman, quiet most of the time. He noticed she didn't sop up egg yolk with her toast, so he didn't, although if alone he would have. His mother had told him women were more refined than men. He'd believed it until he'd become a cop. But this one was very mannerly. Must have come from a good family.

"I suppose we've got to go downtown now and write up a report," she said.

He smiled. "You don't like that?"

"Once I get my legs around it I don't mind. Guess I'm just lazy."

She was far from that, but he didn't argue. Tapping on the keyboard of a computer didn't hold much appeal for him.

Outside the house while standing on the porch gazing down the long sloping pasture of the dairy farm, she said, "Where's the college from here?"

"Almost due west," and Webb pointed toward some trees north of the dairy.

"So Main Street is southwest of here about two miles, would you say? How far's it to the college?"

"From here? Probably five miles."

"Where would Portland be?"

"That way," Webb said, pointing to his left.

"Hard to get oriented," she said. "All these hills and crooked roads confuse me. Down my way roads are like lines on a compass."

They decided to leave her MG in Webb's yard and take his 4Runner. On their way downtown, he asked about two students she had questioned during her investigation of the Umber abortion case. "Were they her only two boyfriends?"

"I'm not sure, but I couldn't scare up any other names. She was a pretty horny girl but terrified of AIDS, and all the people I talked to said she didn't go out with anyone else, although she flirted with just about every boy she came by."

"High-school boyfriends?"

"Didn't get to check with any. You guys cut me off, remember? But according to those two boys, Crozier and Vinnie Milano, she was a virgin when she got to college. I guess only one of them could know that for a fact—at least I hope so. And I'd guess it was Milano. Son of a bitch sweats testosterone."

"I remember you zoned in on him. Found him attractive, didn't you?" Little smile on his mouth.

"Too crude for my taste. I like Southern boys," she said, laughing.

"They're not crude?"

"Not the ones I go for," she said.

"You still think Milano did it?"

"Haven't ruled him out."

"What kind of home'd Alicia come from?"

"Christian Evangelist, very strict. One of her aunts said Alicia spent half her life stuffed in a closet being punished."

"Well, I think we, or whoever gets this case, are going to have another look at all of that."

"You guess there's a connection?"

"Not hard to imagine one."

"Why do you suppose the body was taken into the woods

right near your house? If that's what happened," she asked.

"I'd guess it was somebody who'd used that woodroad before. Students go in there a lot at night."

"You think it was a student? Some kind of a super prank?"

"It's got the earmarks of one. You know, the chief's going to bring up the Umber investigation, so why don't we go over it a bit, the part that caused all the trouble."

"Me and the television reporter, you mean—Lorraine Lord."

"When did you run into her?"

"At the hospital. She responded to the same call I did. She was there with the cameraman before I got there."

"You think she tricked you into saying those things?"

Perci shrugged. "Some things she said riled me, I guess, about the self-righteousness at the college, but it was just looking at that poor girl lying under a sheet on that table. That's what got to me. Maybe if you'd been there you'd've noticed the camera was on me. I thought it was just me and the pathologist. And I'd been here only a day or so, if you remember. I think working under the eye of the press is one of the things I'm here to learn about."

"Well, the chief might balk at sending you to the campus again. We'll see."

"She going to deputize me?"

"She might. Federal law, as you know, gives you the right to carry a weapon up here, and you can use it under the same circumstances I can."

"But I can't make an arrest."

"That's why Agatha might deputize you. It curdles her milk to see a woman have to get a man to do something for her, like you'd have to get me to make the arrest. What's the literature about this grant you're on say about it?"

"Nothing. The Congress gave the Attorney General some money to spread out to any jurisdictions that wanted to host sworn police officers. What duties and what authority we'd get depends on the host city."

"You sure the death of Alicia Umber didn't entice you to pick Cleeve instead of Providence? It was on national news."

"It might have had an influence," she admitted, smiling.

"How long you been a deputy sheriff down there in Florida? You're still on their payroll, aren't you?"

"A little more than a year. And, yes, they're still paying me. And the government's paying them, just like it's paying you. I guess that's why you're hosting me."

"What you supposed to be studying?"

"Police work in a different environment is what the literature says, and I guess I've hit the jackpot," laughing, kicking up a bunch of snow.

Chapter Two

Big Vinnie Milano sat behind the wheel of his three-year-old Trans Am watching an old Italian woman making her way slowly up the city steps of her tenement building, holding the iron rail in small gloved hands, pausing at every step, probably scared as he was. Scared because no one loved her enough to sand the steps, scared because she was old.

He knew her. Name was Ella Carducci, grandmother of a girl named Gina he almost made it with behind the bleachers at the Dolan Street Recreation Center. Last he heard she'd married a plumber and had a kid. Got knocked up. Happened to most of the neighborhood girls. But who knew it when they came down the aisle with their old man and stood up there with the priest? And who cared?

Everybody does something stupid once in a while. They get past it!

His hands were white-knuckled clutching the wheel as he watched Mrs. Carducci finally get inside her house. Sweat on his hands.

Aw, Jesus, why'd I do it? Lousy piece of ass I could've had anywhere. Why her? Lousy pig! Threw everything away for a pig!

His mother was alive she'd say, "Look what you done now, you moron. When you gonna learn?" Or she'd say that other thing: "When He gave you this body, this face, why didn't He give you a brain?"

She says to Uncle Dom: "So how's he gonna get in college? They let morons in college?"

"If they got an arm like Vinnie's, they do."

And they did. Only it wasn't Notre Dame or Miami or Oklahoma like he'd dreamed. It was Division II Cleeve College up here in Maine. And no scholarship. Uncle Dom had to pay his freshman year. It was before he got all those inches.

He watched an Airedale lapping water from a puddle outside the Mobil station where he used to pump gas for Charlie Twitchell, five-ten high-school senior hosing down school buses back of the garage dreaming he'd be a big-time quarterback. His college freshman year he grew five inches. Guys came from all over begging him to redshirt, go someplace and worry about getting minutes. Hell with that. At Cleeve he was the franchise.

His roommate, Boyd Crozier, sat with NFL scouts in the stands and came back with phrases like What an arm! He can run! He can scramble! He read that defense like a pro! Top ten in the draft! Vinnie could still see his Uncle Dom screaming at Coach Flaherty, Gimme my money back!

"Stop worrying about thousands," Flaherty told him. "You got a kid here's looking at millions."

Maybe a week ago. Not now. And maybe never. Even if they don't blame me.

Why'd I do it? Sitting there with Boyd and two sure things. Then the president's wife, big deal! She walks in, gives me a look and I crawl after her. And the other broad running out there screaming so the whole world heard it. "You're an asshole, Milano!" They'll remember! And they'll tell the cops!

Jesus, I probably lost everything!

He rubbed his palms on his thighs and started the engine. Shouldn't've come back to the hill. People see me here. Should've known Toni'd be at the store.

He drove slowly past yards he'd found Easter eggs in, fences he'd jumped over, hoops he'd thrown a million basketballs at. Turned his head aside going past the Mobil station. Charlie Twitchell standing right there at the coke machine, must've seen him.

Boyd said it was dumb coming here. Stay on campus, he said. Cops'll want to talk to you because you were seen with the man's wife. And all you have to say is she brought you back to our apartment. Nothing else. You don't know anything, Vinnie. She gave you a ride home. Period!

But he couldn't just hang out there waiting to be questioned. He had to come here. Couldn't sleep, couldn't go to class. Had to see Toni, be with her, take her in his arms, suck her mouth—if she'd let him. Hung up on him last night. Wouldn't even talk to him. Hey, this is Vinnie, he said. Bang! What's she sore about? He told her a hundred times he never touched that girl. And this time it was the truth! Honest to God. Okay, she blew him, but what's that?

Down on India Street, just off the wharves, he pulled up against a snow bank across from the store. It said Vito's Variety on a Coca Cola sign over a window filled with pyramids of fruit, bottles of wine and netted cheese dangling off strings, Coors beer sign hard to read behind frosted glass. Toni's old man in his butcher apron was shoveling snow out front—little weasel face, stubble of beard, black woolen hat stretched over his ears, short guy with red-rimmed eyes. Hard to believe he could be the father of a tall beautiful girl like Toni.

"She's in there?"

"She's working. Leave her alone."

"I just want to talk to her."

The man raised his hand in protest, then made a slapping motion in disgust and turned away. Five years ago he'd've chased Vinnie down the street yelling and waving the shovel. Caught him one night behind the back stairs getting Toni's bra off and broke a flashlight on his head.

She was at the sandwich bar behind the counter slicing Italian bread. Made him feel good just looking at her.

"Hey, Toni," he said, coming right up to the gumball machine, hands on the counter, leaning in.

She didn't turn around.

"Come on," he said. "Say hello or something. I come all the way down here just to see you."

She went over to the refrigerator, came back with a tray of sliced tomatoes. Kept her back to him as she laid strips of ham and salami on the bread, strips of provolone, tomato slices, bits of green pepper, dill pickle, chopped black olives.

"It wasn't me, Toni. I swear to God I never touched that girl!"

She put the sandwich on a double sheet of butcher paper, sprinkled salt on it, a little olive oil.

"I had nothing to do with any of that. She was Boyd's girl. What are you sore about?"

"It isn't just her," Toni said, putting tape around the sandwich, marking it, giving him a sharp look as she reached for a paper towel to wipe her hands.

"What else?"

"I can't trust you, Vinnie." Not yelling like he'd expected her to, just looking him right in the face and saying it.

"What'd I do?"

She sighed, glanced out the window at her father. "It isn't anything you did."

"Then what's the matter?"

"I'm here and you're there. That's what's the matter. I'm not like you. I can't go out. I want a boyfriend. I want someone who wants me."

"You don't think I want you? I fucking love you, Toni!"

She took a deep breath, looked at her hands, tossed the paper towel into something under the counter.

He said, "You wanted me to go to college!"

"I didn't know it'd be like this, all right?"

"I don't fool around."

"Aw, Vinnie, stop lying. Don't you think I know?"

"That story was bullshit, I told you that."

"I don't care about that story. I know you, Vinnie."

"Well, I'm young, too."

A man came into the store—tall guy in a long coat, red scarf around his neck, glasses all steamed up. Vinnie turned his back and waited until Toni got a carton of milk for him and a half dozen eggs.

"After work," he said, when the guy was gone, "we go out, have something to eat."

"No."

"Come on, Toni."

"No. I'm through with that. You come here expecting things to be like they were. But I'm alive, too, you know. Not a toy you stick in a closet till you want to play with it again."

"I can't help it. I can't be here!"

"Yeah, I know."

"Don't you love me anymore?"

"Aw, Vinnie." She looked sadly at him, like he was a kid and it was hopeless to argue with him.

"Come on," he said. "After work. I'll wait. We'll go out and have dinner."

The sad look stayed in her eyes as she watched him. "You didn't come down here for that, did you." Not asking him, telling him. "What happened?"

"What? Nothing happened. I just want to be with you."

"You're in trouble, aren't you," she said, like his mother, looking worriedly at him. "You did something."

"What? Come on."

"You did something stupid."

"Come on. I just want to take you to dinner. Morello's. How's that sound? We'll get one of those tables near the fireplace."

Her father came inside, went into the back room and took his coat and hat and gloves off, came back out and said to Vinnie, "You want something here? You gonna buy something?"

"Yeah," Vinnie said. "A salami sandwich, no onions."

Toni's father said to her, "Go in back and take care of that thing I told you. I'll make the sandwich."

Vinnie waited until he'd sliced the bread and put some meat in it before he said, "I changed my mind." Fucking prick. He walked out of the store.

He waited in a place up the street almost three hours before she came out. He followed her yellow Mazda up the hill right into her driveway, drove right up to her bumper. She didn't get out. Wouldn't open the door or roll down her window.

"Don't be like this. Come on," he said, feeling sad because she was so beautiful—jet black hair and blue eyes, skin like rose petals. He had to believe people who said Italian women were the prettiest in the world.

She didn't say anything when she finally got out of the car, just looked at him, went up on the snowbank to get past him.

"What'd I do?" he said, following her, going up the back steps, taking her arm as she opened the storm door.

"Vinnie, I mean it. I'm not your girl anymore."

"You think it was me knocked up that Alicia Umber? It was Crozier. He even told me."

She made a face like she was disgusted, pushed his hand off her arm and went inside and closed the door.

He got into his car. Hell with it. He'd go back to school. All he had to tell the cops was Mrs. Spatz gave him a ride home from the Highwayman. She dropped him off at his apartment. They could ask Crozier.

There was a kid across the street who recognized him.

"Hey, Vinnie! Vinnie Milano!"

He gave the kid a wave, big grin on the kid's face, made the kid happy.

Hey, like Boyd said, what the hell was he worried about?

Nothing's going to happen.

I'm Vinnie Milano!

CHAPTER THREE

Webb pulled into his personal slot next to the chief's Cadillac and was following Perci down the sidewalk past three illegally parked cars, which he imagined were owned by politicians upstairs visiting the mayor.

"Anyone file an MPR on him?" Perci asked.

"What's an MPR?"

He saw a brief flush in her cheek before she turned her face aside. "Thought that's what you called a missing persons report."

"Oh. Sorry. I guess some do. Newspaper talk mostly. Like CI for confidential informant or CW for confidential witness."

He nodded at Al Krupinski who was having trouble getting a scale of ice off the City Hall steps, banging at it with the blade of his shovel.

"It's like the word 'snitch'," Perci said. "Cops I know just say 'source'."

"Right. Why belittle someone who's trying to help you."

As they walked down the long corridor past names painted on pebbled windows, framed pictures of politicians on the walls between office doors, warm stale air blown down from ceiling vents, Perci remarked that she had trouble thinking of Cleeve as a city.

"It's not very big."

"Sixteen thousand five hundred the last I heard," Webb said. "It was chartered a city in 1891."

"Down my way it would just be a town. How many in the police department?"

"Thirty-four sworn officers and four detectives."

"You and Rudy on this shift."

"Al and Pete Haskell on the other," Webb said. "While you're here, Rudy's on a drug detail."

At the chief's office Perci opened the door for him, apparently wanting him to go in ahead of her. It was against his upbringing but he bent to the times and allowed her to enter the room behind him.

Agatha Pickford, police chief for the past four years—smallish woman with a thin face, gray hair cut short as a man's, bright blue eyes—looked up and waved them into two straight-backed chairs in front of her desk, to sit there while she finished reading something. They watched her straighten a few papers, put a pamphlet in a side drawer, take off her glasses and lean back, teasing her lower lip with the end piece of her bifocals.

"Tentatively identified," she said.

"Oh, it's Spatz, all right," he told her.

"And you would know, wouldn't you," she said with the kind of smile his mother had used to remind him of transgressions she hadn't quite forgiven. Did that a lot. Must have known it was irritating. "I don't suppose I have to tell you that Haskell Paine has been here already."

"Doesn't surprise me."

"Thinks I should assign someone else."

"Be all right with me," Webb said, aware that Perci was being left out of this. Maybe she knew Haskell Paine was a top assistant to the state majority leader. And maybe she knew the majority leader was the brother of Claire Edison Spatz, wife of the deceased. But she probably didn't know why Haskell Paine's boss wanted Webb off the case. Maybe, later, he'd explain it to her.

"Well, I don't like pushing you into a storm, but I don't have a decent alternative," the chief went on. "It isn't the kind of thing Rudy can handle, and right now the state police have their hands full with that serial killing. So I'm afraid it'll have to be you. And if George Edison complains, I'll raise me a little hell about not getting the money I've been promised. Do you know he voted his secretary a fat salary boost on the very day he voted to cut the law enforcement budget?"

"Guess that slipped past me," Webb said, not intending any sarcasm, but she looked for some in his face before she turned her attention to Perci.

"As for you, young lady, I don't think it's in the best interest of anything to have you out on that campus again. All those wisecracks you made about the college, getting your name in the paper. I don't like politicians coming into my office complaining about my people."

"I need her," Webb said. "She's made contacts with students I can't duplicate."

"She made enemies, Webb."

"In the administration, not with students. And they know things I'll need to know. You read what they said about her in the student newspaper?"

"Oh, yes. And so did George Edison. If you remember, he's the one wanted this young lady shipped back to Florida. I don't need him as an enemy."

"But I need her, Agatha, and I need your support. She can get close to those students. I can't. Now, goddamn it, Agatha, I know you don't take orders from anyone outside this office."

He hadn't intended sarcasm but she again searched his face for it before she turned to Perci, stared at her a few seconds undecided and finally said, "You think you can keep your personal thoughts to yourself?"

"Yes, ma'am."

"Just do your job?"

"Yes, ma'am."

"Not go traipsing off after things are none of your business? You got a hate for those boys?"

"No, ma'am."

"Well, there's no room for personal feelings in a murder investigation. I'm sure you've been told that."

"I know I got carried away last time."

"I want you to stay away from those TV people. Think you can do that?"

"Yes, ma'am."

The chief studied her a few more seconds, then dismissed the two of them with a wave of her hand.

They spent the next half hour in Webb's office logging notes into a computer. While his Epson was printing out a hard copy, he and Perci stood at the window watching people across the street on shoveled sidewalks hurrying past store windows decorated with Christmas ribbon and plastic Santas. Although it was wintery up here with all the snow, the celebration of Christmas was about the same as in Florida, even though there were no palm trees up here with lights wrapped around them.

"I want you to get as close as you can to those campus pro-choice leaders," Webb said. "Put heat on them while they're still nervous about this."

"I can't make myself believe they did it."

"Don't try. Right now that's not a problem. Don't work a puzzle till all the pieces are out of the box."

"That's Down East wisdom?"

"Webb Harrington wisdom."

"I'll try to remember it," and she laughed.

The president's house was on a small rise in a grove of birch trees just off the main drive into the Cleeve campus. It was a one-story building with a shingled roof and cedar siding on a circular drive. It was less than ten years old, a gift from a local businessman whose father, twenty years earlier, had provided two hundred acres of pasture and woods a mile north of downtown so that the trustees could move the college out of old buildings on Main Street into high ground above the city. You couldn't see much of the campus from the president's house—only the top of the bell tower and the upper sections of two of the dormitories. The other buildings, the big parking lot, and the playing fields were hidden by evergreens.

Webb pulled up a few feet from a snow bank, allowing Perci room to get out of the car. They walked through an aroma of pines around back of the house with a security man. Webb wanted to make sure the president's car was in his garage and there was no snow on it and no tracks to suggest that the car had been outside since before the storm. The car next to it, the wife's dark green, four-door Cadillac, was coated with snow and there were wet tracks on the cement beneath it. There were no keys in the president's car, no indications it had been recently moved or washed. It was locked.

"I'd appreciate it," he told the security man, "if you'd tell your chief to post somebody out here. I don't want this car touched or moved."

The security man immediately raised the antenna of his portable and contacted his base. "Lieutenant Harrington would like Number One to come to the president's house," he said. He lowered the antenna. "I'd rather you told him in person so I don't catch hell for doing something wrong."

"You've been given a warning?"

"I just do my job, Lieutenant."

Webb had known Hank Fowler, security chief at the college, for more than five years. When Hank arrived, Webb led him and Perci into the house where Perci stayed in the kitchen questioning the housekeeper about household routines while Webb went into the front room to see Claire Spatz. He hadn't seen her in more than a year.

She was sitting on a bone-white L-shaped sectional next to a woman he believed was her sister-in-law. She was wearing pale blue slacks and a white silk blouse. She was barefoot. Surprisingly she looked younger than she had two years ago. Her hair was different, still the light brown he remembered, but shorter. Her lips seemed fuller. It wouldn't have surprised him to learn she'd had cosmetic surgery. She was the type—a woman who'd been beautiful all her life now pushing forty and still beautiful.

"I'm not sure I should talk to you before my brother gets here," she said.

Without sitting up she reached a slender arm toward a pack of Virginia Slims on the glass top of a driftwood coffee table, almost knocked over a black African statuette she had bought in a gift shop in Nairobi, the only remnant of a wasted week in Kenya with a man who wanted to be Ernest Hemingway. He remembered her laughter when she told him that story.

"I'd like to express my sorrow about your loss," he said.

Her hand trembled as she touched the flame of a gold lighter to her cigarette. She made a big thing of blowing smoke into the air, then waving it from her face.

"I'm sure that comes from the bottom of your heart," she said.

Her sister-in-law, without a change of expression, moved one cushion down on the sectional, apparently to avoid the smoke.

"Just a few things to find out—if you're up to it," Webb said

"Like where was I when the gun went off?"

"The gun?"

"A figure of speech, Lieutenant."

The sarcasm, the bored impatience, was exactly as it had been when he'd last talked to her. She apparently expected people to think she had seen it all and didn't give a damn what they came there to show her. From what Perci had told him, that pose had given students a lot of laughs.

"When was the last time you saw him?" Webb asked, getting out his pen, leafing for a fresh page in his notebook.

"Tuesday morning," she said. "From my bedroom window I watched him go down the path through the trees."

"And he was going to his office?"

"That's probably where he was going."

"That was about what time?"

"Eight-ten. The administration day starts at eight-thirty. He always got there early to justify complaining when others were late."

She dragged on the cigarette, tapping ash into a blue ceramic tray with long pale fingers slightly trembling.

"Did he come back to the house any time during the day?"

"I wouldn't know. I left around ten in the morning and got back around midnight. He wasn't here when I got back. He was probably at a meeting."

"You know where?"

"He goes to a lot of meetings, Lieutenant. It's part of his job."

"Was his car in the garage when you got home?"

"It might have been. I'm not sure."

"How could you miss it? It's right there next to yours."

"I know where it is. I just didn't notice. If you prefer, I don't remember whether I noticed or not. Is that better?"

"Wouldn't he have taken his car to this meeting?"

"Not necessarily. He doesn't like to drive at night."

Her evasiveness, he believed, was more out of resentment than a desire to mislead. She obviously didn't like being questioned, especially by him.

"Were the houselights on when you came in?"

"The house was dark."

"Mind telling me where you were that evening?"

"I was at the Maine Mall in South Portland."

"With anyone?"

She looked at her sister-in-law.

"I was with her," the woman said.

"For the record, you are?"

The woman frowned. "Paula Stone. Mrs. Paula Stone. Mrs. Everett Stone. You know damn well who I am."

"The president's sister," Webb said. "My condolences."

The woman nodded, looked down at hands folded in her lap, took a deep breath, sitting there like a fixture that didn't belong in the room and could hardly wait to get out of it.

"Did you both leave together?"

"We left the mall together," Claire said.

"And what time was that?"

"I don't know. When it closed—ten maybe, nine-thirty. I'm sure if you called they'd tell you."

"And after that?"

"I stopped for a drink at the Highwayman on the parkway."

"Alone?"

She dragged on her cigarette, didn't answer.

"Did anyone see you there?"

"I imagine so. I'm not invisible."

"Anyone you know?"

"Lieutenant, if the point of this is to establish an alibi, why don't you tell me when my husband was killed and ask where I was at that time instead of dragging me through this dreary itinerary?"

"You're not a suspect, Mrs. Spatz. I don't know when your husband was killed. This is just for the record."

"Ah, yes," she said. "How dull of me."

As though alone in the room, she sat up, poked her cigarette out in an ashtray, ran both hands past her ears with splayed fingers coming through soft brown hair, large nipples roving under the silk blouse. She stood up.

"If you'd care to wait until my brother gets here . . ."

"I have a few more questions."

"I'm sure you do," she said.

A fragrance of roses drifted from her as she brushed past him and walked out of the room.

Haskell Paine came into the house five minutes before the arrival of Senator George Edison. A cigarette in pale lips, a gaunt frame chronically bent forward as though hovering over a cough. A walking advertisement for lung cancer.

"He doesn't want you in the room when he greets his sister," Haskell said.

The offense was typical of Paine and outrageous enough to justify resentment, but Webb simply pointed to the open doorway.

"She's in there."

He had known Haskell Paine since high school, had watched him build a fortune as a bodily-injury lawyer before attaching himself to Edison. He had once been suspended from school for beating up a girl. In front of four others, she had referred to him as a "fag."

"And who's this?" Haskell had given the sister-in-law a brief nod and was looking at Perci, who had just come in from the kitchen with Hank Fowler.

"I thought you had met my partner," Webb said. "This is Detective Piper."

Perci stepped forward, smiling, holding out her hand. Haskell ignored it, ignored her, gave the room a quick once-over and walked out. Self-important, rude son of a bitch! He had known all along who Perci was and had deliberately slighted her.

Hank Fowler slipped Webb an apologetic glance and meekly trailed after the man who, with a word, could get him fired. Perci said the kids referred to Hank Fowler as "Mr. Brown."

Five minutes later Senator George Edison came in, a burly man with thinning gray hair combed straight back. He greeted Webb and Perci with a politician's warmth, gave Mrs. Stone a hug and a kiss, told her how "grieved" he was, then went off in search of his sister.

"I expected a thundering herd," Perci said. "But he was a pussycat. He acted like he didn't even know me."

"I guess you haven't known many politicians. But never mind him. Show me where the keys and the overcoat were."

She led him to the entryway off the kitchen, opened a door and pointed inside a small closet. There was an unexpected odor of cheap perfume in the dead air.

"And when I asked if she had noticed anything unusual, she mentioned the smell. It comes from that blanket on the floor. She said she'd never noticed it before. And that jacket over there? Said it was Mrs. Spatz's and was usually kept upstairs. She also admitted she didn't often get into this closet."

"This is where Spatz usually hung his overcoat?"

"Always," Perci said. "First thing he came into the house, he'd come back here, hang up his coat and put his keys on that nail."

"And his overcoat and keys were where they are now?"

"That's what she said."

Webb examined the lock on the back door, the edge of the door, the doorframe.

"Could anyone pick that lock?" Perci asked. It was a common lockset with a spring latch bolt.

"I suppose so," Webb said. "Don't see any scratches around it."

"When you close the door, it locks?"

"Unless that button's pushed over. Seems to be working okay."

Webb opened the door. Haskell Paine and Hank Fowler were standing in front of the garage doors, breath vapors gusting from their mouths, hands in their coat pockets.

"You have a yellow barrier tape?" Webb asked Fowler.

"I can get you one."

"Please do," Webb said. "And seal off the garage door on the president's side. Also run it front to back on the inside, close it off from the wife's side." He couldn't imagine how Claire could have driven her car into the garage and got out of it without noticing whether her husband's car was there just a few feet from her elbow. An uncooperative witness. She must have been a hateful child. She probably decided at an early age that people didn't respect her and was now making everybody pay for it.

"Do I see a contradiction?" Perci said, pulling the door closed to make sure no one was within earshot.

"Wait till we leave," Webb said. "And don't fix too many things in your mind. We've got a lot of looking to do."

"No problem," she said. "The housekeeper said his bed hadn't been slept in. They use separate bedrooms. D'you know that?"

"Doesn't surprise me." He opened the back door again and stepped outside, looked around, ignoring the two men who were staring at him. "Wouldn't be a bad place for an ambush. Nobody would see you back here."

Walking off the porch, Perci asked, "We're not waiting to talk to the senator?"

"Not unless we find out he witnessed something. Don't worry, we'll see plenty of him. Right now I want to talk to Spatz's secretary."

As Webb drove up Campus Drive past the frozen reflecting

37

pond and the hundreds of cars in the student parking lot, he said,

"Now what was it seemed a contradiction?"

Students with book bags on their backs were moving single-file on a walk not yet plowed between the classroom building and the gym. Far to the left of them, three girls were in the doorway of the library and a man was shoveling snow down by the administration building.

"She said her husband wasn't home when she drove in around midnight," Perci said. "The house lights weren't on, but his overcoat and keys were in that closet."

"Maybe not until after she was in bed. We still have an hour before it started to snow. He could have come home."

She shook her head. "Doesn't make sense. A woman like that'd take an hour to undress and grease her face and stare at a mirror before she got to sleep. Even if she hadn't actually seen him, wouldn't she have said she heard him come in?"

"You don't think a man would voluntarily leave his house even to go off in someone else's car without carrying his keys?"

"Would you?"

"I guess not if he wanted to get back in," Webb said, "unless whoever he was with had keys."

"Who would that be? Not his wife."

"You don't think he got home after she did?"

"Well, it's possible. It just doesn't seem natural that she wouldn't have heard him come in."

Webb noticed Christmas decorations in the windows of the student union and wreaths on most of the doors. There was a snowman in front of the library.

"Maybe she did and just didn't tell us," he said.

"Well, that doesn't seem natural."

Webb laughed. "A lot of things about Claire aren't natural."

"Her sex life, you mean?"

"You heard those stories."

"I couldn't believe half of them."

"Well, she is an unusual woman."

"If he had been snatched from the house before she got there, would the house lights have been off?"

"You do ask good questions," Webb said, tempted to pat her knee but afraid she might find it patronizing. She was sensitive about things like that. Besides, he had no business tapping a woman's knee.

CHAPTER FOUR

Vinnie stopped at the Cumberland Farms store on Pride Street near the off-campus housing project where he and Boyd Crozier had shared an apartment since their freshman year. He got a half gallon of milk, a quart of orange juice, and two Snickers bars. When the girl dropped change into his hand, she said,

"This guy just in here said the Greeks did it, says Spatzie busted up a party Monday night. I know you college guys are crazy, but they wouldn't do it for that, would they? I mean, kill him?"

Vinnie shrugged. "I don't know." Didn't want to talk about it. "Gimme a scratch ticket," he said. "One on the left, that green one."

When she turned, he noticed a worn circle from a snuff can on the back pocket of jeans that hugged her ass tighter than skin. Her face had little pits in it and her nose was too big, but the rest of her was great. When she got back to the counter, he noticed a button on her shirt had come open.

"I'll bet when they were stringing him up he wished he'd never heard of abortion." She laughed. "Maybe my ex did it. That's the night he left me."

Vinnie's gaze lingered on her chest while he put the ticket in his shirt pocket. He carried the two plastic containers and the candy outside.

It was going to be like a couple of weeks ago, only worse. Everybody talking about it. In class tomorrow all he'd hear was abortion and President Spatz. Kids yelling and waving their hands, and Ms. Steinberg saying, "That's not the issue!" What the fuck does that mean?

He dug gray coating off numbers on his ticket. Not a winner on it. He tore the ticket in half and pushed it into his ashtray. Couple of girls outside his off-campus apartment house gave him a lot of arms as he drove past.

"Come over tonight," one named Silvia yelled. "Lennie's got a keg."

Boyd said she'd drink till it squirted out her ears but wouldn't get on her back. Scared of AIDS. Like nobody else was.

Boyd's Toyota wasn't in the parking lot. Shit! Vinnie wanted to find out if anything happened. But maybe Boyd just brought it back to his spot on campus, said he would when they got the spaces cleared. Liked to keep his car in the commuters' lot near the classrooms. Better security up there.

Boyd was asleep on the living-room couch with the TV on, a can of Miller on the floor, a pizza crust on a rug near a pile of laundry. Vinnie laid a hand on Boyd's warm back.

Boyd's blue eyes opened wide. "Hey!" he said, throwing off a breath that smelled of onions, arms up, rubbing both eyes with his knuckles. "Thought you were gonna stay down there."

"Toni's still pissed off," Vinnie said.

"She'll come around."

"I wish you'd call her, say it wasn't me knocked up Alicia."

"I told you, Vinnie, she'd just say I was trying to help you. Stop worrying. She'll come around."

Boyd was almost as big as Vinnie, maybe five-eleven, two hundred pounds of bone and meat, a weight lifter. Thinning blond hair, probably be bald in five years. He wanted to be Vinnie's manager, but the coach said, "You out of your mind? Don't worry about it. We'll find you a manager."

People always telling Vinnie not to worry, like he was some

kind of a dummy.

In the kitchen he said, "I gotta talk to Mrs. Spatz."

"Just be careful what you say. Remember, I wasn't over there. You don't know what happened after you ran off. I was asleep when you got here. I didn't know anything until I saw it on TV."

"I'm not stupid, Boyd. I won't mention you. I just wanna know what she's gonna tell the cops."

"I told you. She'll say she brought you here. And that's all you have to know because that's your story."

Boyd was sucking orange juice from the container Vinnie had picked up at the Cumberland Farms. Didn't like drinking after anybody, but didn't want to hurt Boyd's feelings. He took a couple of mouthfuls, put the container in the refrigerator.

"What if she tells them a different story?"

"Like what? That you were banging her when he busted in? She won't do that."

"But what if she says she dropped me off at the store and we say it was here?"

"Look, Vinnie." Boyd put his hand gently on Vinnie's shoulder, looked at him like you would a little kid. "She's got to admit she picked you up at the Highwayman. Half the people out there probably told the cops by now. All she'll say is she gave a student a ride home. They'll believe her."

"I'm really scared, you know. This could fucking ruin everything."

"I know that. I'm in it same as you. You're just making up things to worry about. We'll say she brought you here. If it's different than what she says, they'll just think you're protecting her."

Vinnie stood at the sink looking through the little window at white fields across the street, red cedars sticking up through the snow, screen of trees in the distance, the campus bell tower above the trees.

"I wish it never happened," Vinnie said.

Being up here, playing football, hanging out with college kids—it was so beautiful! Everybody liked him, liked being near him, even important people like the mayor, like Senator Edison, like NFL scouts pumping his hand, grinning at him. All over campus people yelling at him. Hey, Vinnie! Yo, Vinnie Milano! Girls, happy laughing kids jumping in his lap, calling him up, coming over in wheels like you see in beer ads. All he had to do was smile and they're upstairs on their backs. A paradise up here!

And I threw it all away for ten minutes with a forty-year-old broad who thinks she did me a favor.

"But it did happen," Boyd said, "and you can't change that. It's like on the field, Vinnie. You gotta forget what happened and think about what's coming. It's taken care of. I'm telling you the truth. It's covered. Not in a million years they gonna connect you with what happened."

"But what if they do?" Vinnie said.

"Then you and me are both dead. It ain't just you, Vinnie. You lose your cool and we're both gone."

"Yeah, I know. I know I owe you, Boyd."

"You keep feeling sorry for yourself you're gonna fall apart and say things they don't have to know. It's just like on the field, Vinnie. Think about losing, you're gonna lose. Think about winning."

"Yeah, I know."

"I didn't have to get rid of the evidence for you, but I did. I stuck my neck out. I didn't even have to go over there. But I did. We're in this together. Now you gotta protect me."

"Yeah, I know. I know I owe you, Boyd."

Boyd scrubbed his fingers through Vinnie's hair like you would a dog's. "Come on, let's hit the gym, do some hoops."

"I don't know. I don't feel like it."

"We'll shoot around. Got this new Shaq move I want to show you."

There was a girl at the supply desk in the Rec Center Vinnie had always wanted to meet at a party. She was a forward on the basketball team. Most varsity women were gorillas, but this one was sleek, smooth creamy skin, great face.

"Hey, Cindy! How come you're not working upstairs? Thought you worked upstairs."

"Coach sent me down here," she said. "He wants to see you, been asking all around where you are, said it was important."

Vinnie shot a glance at Boyd.

"Say what it was all about?" Boyd asked.

"Yeah, like he tells me all his little secrets," Cindy said, throwing a cold look at Boyd.

Vinnie didn't know why she hated Boyd except he was always coming on to her. He was dumb about women.

Going upstairs to the coach's suite, Boyd said, "If it's about Spatzie, say you don't know anything. Don't even admit you were with his wife last night."

They could see Coach Flaherty through the window from where his secretary told them to sit—chairs against a row of office lockers, hard oak chairs like ones his cousin Mario made down in Portland where he'd be sucking up sawdust if he wasn't here.

A lot of coaches have thin slitty mouths, Vinnie noticed. A stubble of beard and no lips, skin with a lot of veins showing. Coach Flaherty was like that. Stocky guy liked to stand with his feet apart, sizing you up. Bald on top with the side hairs trimmed close. The way he looked, he couldn't be anything else—a cop, maybe, or in the army. Two of the fingers on his right hand were broken from when he was a minor league catcher.

"You," he said, pointing one of the crooked fingers at Boyd, then at the door. "Out!"

"I gotta right to be with him."

The lips disappeared. Eyebrows went down hard over the eyes. He moved a finger like cutting a throat. "Out!"

For a few seconds Boyd had this look like something died in his eyes. He got up and patted Vinnie's shoulder, went over to the door, stood there like he couldn't decide to open it. He finally opened it and went out.

"I wish you'd dump that parasite," the coach said, leaning back in a leather-padded swivel chair, hands folded over his New York Jets belt buckle. "He is certified bad news, Vinnie. A leech. I really wish you'd move back on campus, get away from him."

Vinnie went over to a hard chair near a trophy case, sat down, forearms on his spread knees, staring at the floor.

"When you getting your phone fixed?" the coach said. "I tried reaching you this morning."

"I was over at the store."

"The phone?"

"They said they'd come over. I don't know when."

"You heard about Spatzie."

Vinnie looked up, nodded, prayed he didn't look scared.

"Well, they're already here—cameras, newspaper people, just like before. And that same policewoman. She's here."

"The one from Florida?"

The coach nodded. "The one that kept bugging you. I guess she hasn't caught up to you yet."

"I haven't seen her."

"Well, you can bet she'll find you."

"Why? I don't know anything."

"You're news, Vinnie. This kind of story, the way Spatzie was put up on that tree, it'll go national. She'll love that, get her face on every TV screen in the country. There's no way you'll be kept out of it."

"But why? What's it got to do with me? I didn't do anything."

"They don't care, Vinnie. It's an opportunity. They'll use it just like they did last time. Only it's bigger. What I want to do is keep you low profile in this. Tell them you don't know anything. Don't talk about that Umber girl. They'll try to bring that in."

"I had nothing to do with it!"

"You don't have to be nice to them, Vinnie. Cut them off. Walk away. It's got nothing to do with you. Keep out of it."

"Why would that woman want to question me?"

"People like that don't need a reason. They just want their name in the paper."

"I won't tell her anything."

When the coach walked him to the door, he put a hand on Vinnie's shoulder and said,

"Just don't feel you have to be nice to these people, Vinnie. It's their job to get a story, but it's your job to keep out of it. The National Football League doesn't like to draft players who've been involved in scandals. You gotta protect yourself. Those people don't care anything about you. They just want a story."

Downstairs Cindy told him Boyd was in the varsity locker room. "I wouldn't let him have a towel. He's not supposed to be in there."

"Yeah, I know," draping a towel over his shoulder, walking away.

"You're too nice to people," Cindy said.

Vinnie didn't like Boyd using the varsity lockers. It took away the honor somebody using them who didn't earn it. But he didn't want to say anything. Let somebody else kick him out.

"So what'd he say?" Boyd asked, sitting on the bench in front of Vinnie's locker, tying laces on his sneakers.

"Nothing. He doesn't want me talking to reporters."

"What'd he say about me?"

"Nothing."

There was all kinds of Boyd's shit in the locker. Vinnie knocked over a can of hairspray reaching for his Reeboks.

"All he wanted was for me to stay out of trouble like last time."

"He blamed that on me?"

"He didn't talk about you," Vinnie said, annoyed. "That cop? The one from Florida. She's back."

"You saw her?"

"Coach told me. Said I shouldn't talk to her."

"She comes around, send her to me. See the tits on her? Man, I'd love to get me some of that. I think she's got the hots for me."

"She comes around, what do I say?"

"Nothing. You don't know anything."

The door opened and a kid came in and went over to the urinals.

"Hey, this is varsity!" Boyd yelled at him. "You ain't supposed to be here."

"Up yours," the kid said.

Boyd laughed. To Vinnie he said, "So get your wheels on and I'll show you this move. Like a triple pivot I seen Shaq do on television."

"What you need that for?" Vinnie said. "Nobody guards you."

"They guard me."

"They see you shoot, they run in for the rebound."

CHAPTER FIVE

"Looks like a calendar picture," Perci said, standing at a window in the Administration Building looking past the Student Union at snowy rooftops below them in the village. "That a lake over there?" Big flat stretch of snow in the distance.

"Skunk Pond," Webb told her. "My father had a cottage there years ago."

"Sold it?"

"Lost it in a poker game. One day my brother and I were out there pitching horseshoes, and this guy drove up in a truck and told us to get off his property."

"Your father didn't tell you?"

"Ashamed to, I guess. It wasn't worth much, but still—"

"Lieutenant Harrington?"

The girl with the soft voice and the smile for all occasions led Perci and Webb into a windowless office where they met the president's secretary, a bosomy white-haired woman who told them, among other things, that President Spatz on Tuesday had left his office around five and had no scheduled appointments for that evening.

"Any that were unscheduled?"

"Senator Edison mentioned this morning that he had had dinner with the president last evening."

"He was here? Before he visited his sister?"

"That I don't know. He got here around ten."

Webb knew that Edison was on the Board of Trustees and

doubtless had legitimate concerns about the effect on the college of Spatz's death. He also knew that he was more active in college affairs than board members usually are. Yet it seemed odd that he hadn't gone first to visit a sister whose husband had just been murdered.

"What did he want here?"

"He met with the provost and the vice-president for student affairs. I think he was concerned about student reaction."

"Has there been any?"

"Nothing organized that I'm aware of. I'm sure the students are upset."

"Have classes been cancelled?"

"Just for today. Finals are next week, and we can't postpone them. It would push us right into the Christmas holiday."

"You keep logs? Of visitors? Incoming calls?"

"Not unless I'm asked to," she said. "There was nothing unusual about Tuesday . . . except of course. . . . I mean it was otherwise a very ordinary day—a staff meeting in the morning, several letters to get out, a meeting with parents, nothing exceptional."

"Been any student protests lately?"

"About what?"

"The abortion issue."

The woman glanced at Perci. A coolness came into her expression. Not a subject she wanted to talk about. "That hasn't been on anyone's agenda since that girl. . . ."

"Alicia Umber?"

"Since that entire episode."

"Things have been in the paper."

"Yes, trying to stir things up. But the president. . . . Well, not any of those protest things."

"Was he asked to lay off?"

"I wouldn't know," she said, eyes hardened and cold.

"I understand Senator Edison didn't like what the president was doing."

"I can't comment on that."

"Was there a board meeting on the abortion issue? The president's role in it?"

She took a deep breath as though to fortify herself against what was becoming a tedious ordeal. "There were several meetings just after Miss Umber's suicide."

"Suicide?"

"That's what the president called it." And she wasn't going to gainsay the president. "I didn't attend any of those meetings, Lieutenant. I don't know what was discussed. We've tried very hard to let that issue fade into the past."

"That include the president?"

Her eyes seemed to flatten inside the big glasses. She didn't answer.

"Has he received any threatening letters, phone calls, anything like that?"

"Not to my knowledge."

"And you don't know anything about a meeting he might have attended that night?"

She shook her head. "There was nothing scheduled."

"Just a couple more questions. Did the president wear his overcoat to work Tuesday?"

"I believe so."

"The suit he was wearing, you remember what color it was?"

"If it was Tuesday, it was his gray tweed."

"He always wore the gray tweed on Tuesday?" The corpse on the tree was wearing a gray tweed.

"He had five favorite suits, Lieutenant. One for each workday. He was a very methodical man."

"And very predictable?"

She seemed puzzled. "I suppose in some ways."

"But he commonly followed routines?"

"That was his way, yes."

"If he went home from here, would he have walked?"

"Usually he brought his car to the office only when he expected to go off campus during the day."

"So," Webb said, "if he had walked to work on Tuesday, he probably went home from here before going to dinner with the senator."

"That would be my assumption, yes. Unless, of course, the senator met him before he got home."

"Did he?"

"Not that I know of."

Out on the sidewalk, turning up his collar against a bitter wind coming off a grove of pines that separated the playing fields from the rest of the campus, Webb suggested that Perci locate some of the student leaders she'd met during the Umber investigation while he went back to the president's house to talk with Senator Edison.

"Suicide!" Perci exclaimed, the word bursting from her mouth in disgust. "Alicia Umber gave herself an abortion because she wanted to live! Who the hell would try to commit suicide by jabbing a wire into her vagina? Does that make any sense? If that girl had wanted to die, she would have stayed pregnant, dropped out of college and gone home to live in shame inside that tight-lipped puritan house she was trying to escape from. What's the matter with these people? They twist everything around!"

Webb wasn't about to get into an argument. He listened while she vented her anger. After a while she stopped talking, although it was clear she didn't want to.

"I won't shoot my mouth off if I go down there with you," she said.

"I know that. I'm just trying to save time."

"But don't you agree with me?"

"That it wasn't suicide? Yes."

She wanted a discussion but didn't press for one. Probably remembered her promise to the chief.

Actually Webb didn't know how he felt about abortion. It was legal in Maine so he didn't worry about the morality of it. If pressed, he'd probably say the state should stay out of it. The question had never come up in his marriage. Sarah had wanted children, had become pregnant three times but hadn't been able to carry a pregnancy to term.

"What I'd like you to do right now is find those activists before they've had time to invent alibis and excuses."

"Could I ask one question? Why'd you ask about the clothes?"

"Just wondering whether he went home before or after he had dinner with the senator."

"Won't you find out from him?"

"The senator? I'm sure I'll get his version of it."

"Think that wife of the president's ever cooked for him?"

"Claire? I doubt she knows how."

"They ever care about each other?"

"Have no idea."

"Kids said he couldn't get it up. Said he drank a lot to hide his impotence."

There was a lot of fun in her eyes when she said that, baiting him. Office talk said she referred to him as a "straight-laced New England prude." He didn't like hearing women talk about sex, but he didn't think he was a prude.

He was walking toward his car when she said, "While you're talking to the senator, would you find out whether he. . . . I mean, if they went to dinner in his car, did he drop the president off at his front door? Doesn't seem likely he'd've gone around back."

"I'll ask," Webb told her. He suspected she was working on a theory. Not a good idea at this stage of things, but he'd let her be. "Where you going to look for those kids?"

She pointed at a square brick building over near the student union. "The library. Newspaper office's in the basement. That kid, Tennyson Smith, the editor? I think he's the best one to start with."

"Okay. I'll find you there or downstairs here in the security office. Maybe you can find out whether security noticed Spatz going in or out or doing anything funny around here Tuesday evening."

"You know," Perci said, "I've been thinking. If they had dinner at a normal hour, say before eight, that would give them a long time before midnight. Suppose they did anything else during that time?"

"I'm sure we'll find out. Go see what's going on with the kids."

Webb pulled up behind a black Cadillac in the president's driveway just as Senator Edison was coming out of the president's front door—important man moving briskly down the steps wearing a soft gray fedora and a Harris tweed raglan topcoat.

The driver's door of the Cadillac was open. Haskell Paine was in the passenger seat.

"Glad I caught you," Webb said.

Clearly Edison wasn't. He affected an impatient frown. "It'll have to be quick, Lieutenant."

The voice, the facial mannerisms came from that old movie Gone with the Wind. He even sucked in his cheeks like Gable, made that little crooked line with his lips. Only thing missing was good looks and a mustache.

"Just a couple of questions," Webb said. He already had his

notebook and pen out, turning pages, noticing Haskell Paine getting out his side of the Cadillac, poking his head over the roof.

"Those people are waiting, Senator," Haskell said.

Edison ignored him—important man watching Webb leafing through his notebook.

"I don't want this turned into a media circus like that last episode," Edison said.

"Had nothing to do with me," Webb said.

"But you brought that Piper woman back. That doesn't exhibit very good judgment."

Webb wouldn't argue about that. looking into the senator's eyes, he said, "I understand you were with the president Tuesday evening, had dinner with him. Mind telling me where?"

"The Heritage Club. We're both. . . . I'm a member. He was a member."

"And what time was that?"

"When we ate?"

"You picked him up here, at his house?"

"We went in my car, yes. We left here I'd say around eight, maybe seven-thirty."

"And you brought him back here?"

"Some time around midnight."

"Go anywhere else except to the club? That's a long time sitting at a table eating dinner."

Edison gave the question some thought.

"It's important," Webb said, "that I account for every minute of his time that evening."

"I'm sure it is. He was with me continuously between the time I picked him up here and the time I brought him back. Four, four and a half hours."

"Did you go anywhere with him except to your club?"

A sigh. "Well, as a matter of fact, we stopped for a few

minutes at someone's house."

"And who was that?"

"I'll vouch for the person we visited," Edison said. "That person had nothing to do with his murder, I can assure you."

"Who was it, Senator?"

"Let's just say that if this inquiry gets to the prosecutor's desk, I'll reveal the name to Jerry."

Webb knew he couldn't squeeze the name out of him, not at this stage in the investigation, not without getting into trouble with the people upstairs.

"Needless to say, I have little faith in your discretion, Lieutenant."

Webb brushed off the insult. "You remember what clothes Dr. Spatz was wearing? When you first came to his house was he wearing a suit?"

"I didn't notice."

"A gray suit?"

"I suppose it's possible. I really didn't notice."

"Well, did he have to go upstairs to change? Anything like that?"

"I truly don't remember," affecting boredom and impatience.

"Did he bring his overcoat when you left for dinner?"

"Yes, as a matter of fact, I recall his going through the pockets for something before he gave it to the attendant."

"When you dropped him off, did you go into the house?"

"No."

"Were there lights on in the house when you got here?"

"I don't really. . . . No, I don't think so. That small light over the entrance." He pointed at a white globe above a black mailbox next to the door. "I remember watching Sam bent over, having trouble, apparently, getting his key into the lock. The light isn't very bright."

"You see him actually go inside?"

"I believe so. I'm not sure."

"But you actually saw keys in his hand?"

"Oh, I don't remember. I just have this image of him the way a man leans over fitting a key into a lock. I may have seen the door open."

"Did you notice any cars parked along the drive?"

Webb glanced across a cluster of junipers to check whether the garage could be seen from where they were standing. He could see only a few inches of the door on the right side, Mrs. Spatz's side.

"I just came here, dropped him off and left. I didn't notice anything unusual. No stray cars."

"You didn't notice whether Mrs. Spatz's car was here?"

"As I said, I noticed very little and certainly nothing unusual."

"And you went straight to the club from here?"

"That's right, Lieutenant. We were both hungry, as I recall. He said he usually had dinner around six-thirty, and here it was at least an hour past that."

That was interesting. "Why'd he wait?"

"Because I called, I think, around five-thirty and asked him to."

"Then I guess this dinner wasn't just a casual social get-together."

"Well, we had things to discuss."

"Mind telling me what?"

"College business. Nothing sinister, Lieutenant. Nothing happened while we were together that could be remotely related to his death. Do you know, by the way, when that was?"

"No idea," Webb said. "When you finished eating and visited this other person, what time was that?"

"Oh, I don't remember. I'll try to summon up a lot of these details and catch you later, okay? Right now I've got to run."

There was a triumphant smirk on Haskell Paine's face as his

head ducked out of sight. Webb watched the two men wrap themselves in seatbelts. He stood on the salted brick sidewalk and watched the car make the turn around a clump of rhododendrons and move slowly down the drive.

He wanted to go into the house and talk with Claire, but she would think he had deliberately waited until the senator was gone, and that would weaken his position. Besides, he wanted to find Perci before she got into trouble. This was going to be a tough assignment for her. She blamed President Spatz for what had happened to Alicia Umber, and sympathy for Alicia was a powerful motive for her interest in this case. There was no question in his mind that if the two cases had a connection, Perci'd ferret it out. She was persistent.

Chapter Six

Around six that evening Webb and Perci were at the bar in the Highwayman. The bartender had just taken their order. The long room smelled of air freshener and whiskey.

"So tell me again why you think this guy Tennyson Smith isn't involved," Webb said, studying the cartoon Perci had handed him as they were leaving the campus. It was a drawing of President Spatz nailed to a cross. No caption. The initials TS were in the lower right corner.

"He's too timid," she said. "He writes, he draws pictures, he's the editor, but he's no killer. And he's not strong enough to have lifted that body up the tree."

"And when did this appear in the school paper?"

"Two days after Alicia Umber died."

"When you go back, get a copy of the whole issue. And the following two issues."

"I guess all this proves," Perci said, "is that whoever put Spatz on that tree wasn't necessarily an original thinker."

Webb was watching the door at the end of the bar, wondering how long they'd have to wait before the manager came out.

"So what'd you learn?" Perci asked, running her forefinger through condensation on the side of her glass, clear blue eyes absently watching her finger, thoughtful expression, a lot of kindness there.

She had ordered a Sprint with grenadine. Webb had ordered coffee.

"Can't stand colorless drinks," she said. "Remind me of water. Up here the water's good. Down home it's like drinking from a swimming pool." She glanced around the large open room. "These places are all alike, no matter what part of the country you're in."

Webb said, "You're sure that gateman didn't see Spatz leave the campus?"

"They don't see anyone leave. The way the gate booth is made, they care only about cars coming in. And only at certain hours. Commuters coming in for night school, fans for athletic events, they don't pay any attention. The guy just sits there. If you ask for something, he slides back a little window and talks to you. Otherwise nothing."

"So they don't know when Edison came in?"

"The man saw him around midnight. Didn't see him earlier when he picked Spatz up."

"At midnight, Spatz was with him?"

Perci nodded.

"And Claire?" Webb asked. "They saw her come in?"

"Around eleven-fifteen."

"Anyone with her?"

"Didn't see anyone."

"So she was at the house more than a half hour before he got home."

"And there's no way I'll believe she didn't hear him come in," Perci said. "Somebody's lying."

The "happy-hour" crowd was thinning out. Two guys in black silks were on stage setting up music gear. There was a couple talking at the end of the bar. A few kids were laughing in booths along a wall under cartooned sporting murals, didn't look twenty-one, the legal age for drinking.

"Starts picking up again around nine-thirty," Perci said. "You come too early, you have to drink. You lose control. What's the legal age for drinking in Maine?"

"Twenty-one. I thought that was the idea."

"For guys, maybe. For girls it's get the cheap drinks after five, go back to the campus and hang out or sleep for a couple of hours, then come in for serious drinking."

"Every day?"

"End of the week."

"So, tell me," Webb said. "I'm still not clear why you blamed Spatz."

Perci rubbed her finger through the little pebbles of sweat on her glass. "Wanted to assign blame, I guess. Seeing Alicia, so young, knowing what she must have gone through all by herself didn't seem fair. She was all alone in that field when she pushed a wire through her uterus into the wall of her stomach.

"He wouldn't let her get into the clinic! If he'd left her alone, she'd've had it done safely. You remember what happened? She went to that clinic around eight in the morning, hoping to get in before anyone saw her. Spatz and the crazies were right there with their signs and bullhorns; and he recognized her, wouldn't let her go in, some of them right up there yelling in her face."

Tears came into Perci's eyes and she looked away.

"Funny he'd recognize one out of . . . What is it, three thousand students?"

"Kids probably pointed her out."

Webb's attention was caught by a small dark-haired man in a bone-white jacket approaching them from beyond the bar, a kind of proprietary air about him. Probably the manager.

"Don Summers," the man said with a pink mint protruding from his lips. Pale features delicate as a girl's, glistening black hair combed straight back like a 1920's playboy. He held out a thin, pale hand, very warm. He nodded at Perci.

"Sorry I kept you waiting," he said, climbing onto the stool next to Perci, a smile on his face that said I know you enjoy looking at me and I enjoy looking at you.

"No problem," Webb said. "It's about this past Tuesday."

"Oh, boy." Summers drew back, wiped a hand over his mouth. "I was afraid it was. I mean . . . It's about the crucifixion, isn't it?"

"The what?"

"That's what TV's calling it—Spatz up in that tree."

"Did something happen here Tuesday night?"

"Well, she was here—his wife. And there was that blowup."

"You know Mrs. Spatz? She comes in here a lot?"

"This past couple of weeks. That guy, Vinnie Milano, the football player? Big, good-looking Italian guy?" He bent toward Perci, looking past her at Webb. "This is confidential? I don't want people thinking I gossip."

"I'm sure no one would think that," Webb said. "What about him?"

"Well, they never sit together, and they don't leave exactly together. But for a couple of weeks, she comes in, no bra, tight pants, boots, like a kid, you know? She sits at the bar, orders a drink—wine cooler, something like that—takes a couple of sips. Two or three minutes later she walks out, he doddles out after her."

"This has been happening regularly?"

"Last couple of weeks. Middle of the week, things are slow. Him and another guy in a booth over there with two girls. The one with Milano freaked out. She ran to the door and screamed at him. I mean he was buying her drinks, laughing it up, leading her on; then suddenly he chases Spatz's wife. The girl went crazy, smashed a glass on the floor, screamed 'You bastard!' Ran right out in the parking lot. Could've heard her in Chicago."

"You're sure it was Mrs. Spatz?"

"Without a doubt. How many times you see her on TV? Kids

said it was her. Acting like a bimbo, but it was her. She's got a reputation."

"About what time did this happen?"

"Things were in full swing. Ten thirty, ten forty-five."

"Sure they left together?"

"I didn't see him get in her car."

Webb asked what happened to Milano's car.

"The other guy, I guess. They came together."

"Know the other guy's name?"

"No, he's always with Milano."

"Fairly tall?" Perci asked. "Thinnish blond hair, muscular?"

"Sounds like him."

"He stayed with the girls?"

"They stomped out. He stayed a while. After the girls left he came over to the bar and started hitting on a waitress."

"Why do you remember that?"

"Because that waitress was bitching about guys hitting on her. Threatened to quit."

"She bitched that night?"

"No, but I was watching to see if she was leading him on."

"You know the names of the girls Milano was sitting with?" Perci asked.

"I can get them for you."

Webb handed him a card. "Get me names, addresses, and phone numbers. Call it in."

He thanked the man and he and Perci went outside to his car.

Perci asked, "We going back to the campus?"

"Not tonight. We'll pick it up in the morning. But first I gotta bring you to my house to get your car."

"Don't clues begin to disappear after the first forty-eight hours?"

"After the first forty-eight seconds," Webb said. "But easy does it. We'll get there."

CHAPTER SEVEN

Vinnie wrapped a towel around his waist and went into the kitchen wishing he had the salami sandwich he'd ordered at Toni's. But he'd saved a frozen Salisbury steak dinner in the freezer; and, though he hated frozen dinners, it would hold him while he was at the lake with Mrs. Spatz. Didn't expect to do much there except talk, but you never knew.

Except it wasn't in the freezer.

"Hey, Boyd! You eat that dinner?"

"What dinner?"

"The Salisbury steak I was saving."

"Oh, yeah. I didn't think you wanted it."

"What'd you think I left it for?"

"Hey, I'm sorry. I got hungry."

Like you never aren't, Vinnie thought, deciding to pick up a sandwich at Amato's on his way out, eat it in the car.

When he'd shaved and combed his hair and sprayed his armpits and patted cologne on his face and chest, he put on the lavender jockstrap he'd picked up in New York, put on fresh jeans and looked around for the pink shirt he'd got back from the cleaner. After searching the room, he found it on the floor next to Boyd's cot, a splotch of red wine on the sleeve.

He angrily carried it into the front room where Boyd was flat out on the sofa watching a cartoon on TV, almost shoved it in Boyd's face.

"Why you have to wear my shirts? Whyn't you ask me? What

if they can't get the stain out?"

"I was gonna get it cleaned. I forgot," Boyd said. "What you so jumpy about?"

Vinnie went back to the bedroom and put on a shirt his mother had given him for Christmas, a blue one he didn't really like but wore once in a while out of respect for her. He thought about what Boyd did for him Tuesday night. Okay, Boyd was there when he needed him, but he was a slob.

"So remember," Boyd said, when Vinnie came back to the front room. He was sitting up, making little circular movements with the heels of his hands pressed to his eyes. "What we gotta know is if she saw me. That's number one."

"Number one what?"

"It makes her a threat, Vinnie. She knows about me she can do a lot of damage. She could've been looking out a window. But don't offer it. I mean, don't give her ideas. Just say you came back here. If she wonders where I was, say asleep. If she gives you a funny look, maybe she saw somebody. But she couldn't know it was me. If I was in bed, it couldn't've been me, right?"

"Who else would've gone out there?"

"Who cares? Could've been a security guy. Could've been some of those abortion freaks."

"But if she thinks I came back and did it?"

"She won't. Just say you didn't. The story is you came back here and I was in bed and you went to bed. Period."

"What if she don't believe it?"

"Why won't she? All you gotta do is play dumb. I'm telling you, Vinnie. There's nothing to worry about."

"Don't keep saying that. I'd be stupid not to worry."

"Take it easy. All you gotta do is say you came back here and I was asleep. But don't even mention me if she don't ask."

Boyd thought he could outsmart everyone. But fooling teachers was one thing. Fooling cops was something else. The kind of questions they asked, you never knew what they already knew. They could trap you.

"What you suppose she did?" Vinnie asked. "I mean, just go in the house? Leave the body out there?"

"If she didn't want to get rid of it or get somebody else to, what else could she've done? In the morning when they found it, she'd just lie, say she didn't know what happened."

"But what if she doesn't? What if she tells them about me?"

"She won't. For Christ's sake, stop worrying. No reason for anyone to think anything happened in the garage. She knows that. She knows you're both off the hook—thanks to what I did. The only thing she don't know is how the body got to the woods. And we don't want her to know."

The road leading to the lake off the highway had been plowed, but stretches of it were icy. Twice he rolled up the banking and had to fight his way back onto the icy gravel. Headlights shining on big fields out there, bushes like black wires sticking out of the snow. He slowed as he got close to the professor's cottage— little A-frame down near the frozen lake. All he could see through a screen of fir was a panel of light on the snow from one of the side windows and a pale rectangle of lighted window next to the entrance.

He pulled up behind Mrs. Spatz's dark green Cadillac. When Mrs. Spatz opened the door of the house, throwing a blanket of light over the snow, he noticed two sets of footprints leading from her car. There wasn't supposed to be anyone else here. For a second he thought of taking off.

"Come in," Mrs. Spatz said, eyes lowered, like she couldn't look at him, like she didn't know him.

She was in a ski jacket with a white scarf around her neck, same tight-fitting designer jeans she'd worn the other night, only white boots instead of those black ones Toni drooled over in a store window, probably cost a fortune. She stepped back when he entered the house, again not looking at him.

There was no warmth in the house.

"I just turned up the electric heat," she said. "It'll be warm in a few minutes. There's no wood in the stove."

It had one of those Norwegian woodstoves on a stone hearth, huge granite chimney behind it, big model of a sailing ship on a stone mantel. It belonged to a professor who was on leave in Europe. President Spatz sometimes used it for meetings of his "Champions of the Unborn." Because Mrs. Spatz always knew when these meetings happened, she felt free to use it in between times. Vinnie had been here only twice.

"Who else is here?" Vinnie said, looking around—all kinds of books on the walls, an open kitchen back of the chimney.

"I brought a friend, Vinnie. We've got to talk."

"What friend? You said it'd be just me and you."

A skinny guy with slightly stooped shoulders came out of a doorway in back. Vinnie didn't know his name but he'd seen him with Senator Edison.

"What's there to talk about?" Vinnie said. He hadn't planned for anything like this. "You said we'd be alone."

"I was a last minute addition," the man said, little know-it-all smile on his face.

"So who the fuck are you?"

"I don't think that's one of our problems," the kind of big slick who thinks only what he says is important, expects you to stand there with your mouth open while he explains things to you.

"Please, Vinnie. We have to talk," Mrs. Spatz said. She looked scared, not the free-swinging woman she was when they were alone together. Now she looked like a president's wife like when he first saw her at the head table with the governor at that thing when they honored the football team. She was smoking one of those foreign cigarettes, looking bored, like sitting with the governor meant nothing to her, like her whole life was boring. Even from way back in the hall, before the team came up and shook hands with everyone, he could see she wished something exciting would happen. It was all over her face looking at him.

"You never said there'd be somebody else here."

"Would you close the door?" the man said. "We have a lot of talking to do."

Vinnie didn't realize he'd been holding the door open, frigid air coming in. He closed the door. Didn't like the man, but there was something important enough about him to make Vinnie at least want to hear him out.

"Why don't we all come over here and sit down," the man said, taking charge, going to a little circle of chairs around a low glass-topped table.

"You want me to stay here, you tell me who you are," Vinnie said. Boyd would call him stupid for not finding out who the guy was and what he wanted.

"I'm Mrs. Spatz's attorney."

Vinnie shot a hard glance at Mrs. Spatz. "What'd you bring a fucking lawyer for?"

In a softer tone than he had used before, the lawyer said, "Why don't we all sit down and discuss this quietly."

Vinnie waited until Mrs. Spatz and the lawyer sat down before he lowered himself onto the fat arm of a chair opposite them. The door was right behind him. He could get out any time he wanted to.

Mrs. Spatz got a pack of Virginia Slims out of a black bag, fitted a cigarette to her mouth, then fussed nervously in the bag for her lighter.

"Don't light it," Vinnie said. "I don't like breathing smoke." He didn't want to breathe the same air with her. Not now.

Why'd she bring a lawyer?

She gave him a long look, shrugged, put the cigarette away, sat back and looked down at her fingernails, ashamed to look at him, he believed.

"I'll keep the smoke over here," the lawyer said as he put a cigarette to his lips and moved it into the flame of a cheap lighter. He pulled smoke deep into his lungs like he was getting a fix. Idiot. How could anybody be smart and pollute their lungs like that?

"What we know, Vinnie . . ."

"You got a first name? What am I supposed to call you, Al or something?"

The lawyer looked up, surprised. He shrugged. "Mr. Milano." He dragged on his cigarette, seemed to swallow the smoke, little wisps of it leaking out his nose. "What we know is that you and Mrs. Spatz were in her garage when President Spatz came in, surprising you. We know you responded by attacking him, knocking him backwards where he struck his head on the end of a workbench. It was, at worst, involuntary manslaughter, a serious enough offense but far less serious than murder, which is probably what you think you're guilty of."

"Who said I'm guilty of anything?" Vinnie looked at Mrs. Spatz. "That what you told the police?" No wonder she looked ashamed.

"No, Vinnie. I told my brother. I had to. I didn't know what to do. We're trying to avoid—"

"You're trying to fuck me is what you're trying to do!"

"No," the lawyer said. "We're trying to help. We're hoping the police won't discover what happened in the garage. You don't need it. We certainly don't need it. But we can't plan a strategy unless we know how the body got out of the garage. Who took it? Who brought it to the woods?"

"How do I know? I went back to my house. I don't know

what happened." What'd she tell them? Whyn't she just say she didn't know anything?

"With all due respect, Vin . . . uh, Mr. Milano, that's hard to believe. You killed a man, ran off in panic, then just went to bed? Left all that evidence back there for the police to find? What about your roommate? Was he there?"

"What about her?" pointing his chin at Mrs. Spatz. "What'd she do?" Why they mentioning Boyd?

"She didn't lift the body. She didn't put it into a car. She didn't hoist it up into that tree. It took a strong man to do all that."

"Maybe she got help from somebody. How do I know?"

"Vinnie," Mrs. Spatz said, like she was going to cry. "Please . . . don't make this difficult."

"You told the cops all that? Maybe it was a security guy or something."

"What motive could they have?"

"How do I know? Why couldn't you just say you dropped me off at my place? Why couldn't you say you don't know what happened? Why couldn't you say it must've happened out there in the woods? Why'd you have to tell them about me?"

"I haven't told the police anything, Vinnie."

"Please!" the lawyer said. "This is getting us nowhere."

"Well, I don't know what happened," Vinnie said. "And if the police come over, I'll tell them that, and maybe get my own lawyer. You're trying to fuck me."

"Could we backtrack a little?" the lawyer said. "Could we go back to the Highwayman? Witnesses probably have already told the police you left there with Mrs. Spatz. We can't effectively deny that. It is undeniable that you were with her."

"Yeah, I know that."

"Then you must know we have to account for every minute after that. And, as you said, we don't want to include anything about the garage. But before we can decide what's best for us, we have to know exactly what happened. We have to know who else is involved. If you didn't move the body, who did?"

"Why do you have to know if you're gonna say you don't know?"

"We don't want any surprises. Can we backtrack a little?"

"I'm supposed to think you're here to help me? You think I'm stupid?"

"If you're implicated, Mrs. Spatz is implicated. We don't want anything to come out beyond the fact that Mrs. Spatz gave you a ride home from the Highwayman. But we have to know what happened."

"Just say it," Vinnie said, too nervous to keep sitting down. He got up and shoved his hands into his pockets. "Just say you don't know anything about what happened."

"But we have to know," the lawyer said. "I believe your roommate's name is Boyd Crozier? That is his name? Please sit down, Mr. Milano. We have a great deal to talk about."

"My roommate?"

"He was with you at the Highwayman, I believe. I really wish you would sit down, Mr. Milano."

"Just say what you gotta say." Fucking asshole. Why's he talking about Boyd? Did she see him?

"It could all just have been an accident, Vinnie," the lawyer said, smiling like he was giving Vinnie a present. "It could be that it happened merely as an understandable response to your having been startled. If it is determined by the police that the accident happened in the garage, what actually went on in that garage just prior to the accident doesn't have to be mentioned. You were sitting in the car with Mrs. Spatz. Her husband came in. He made a certain assumption. He physically attacked you. In the course of the struggle he fell backward and hit his head. No crime, just a tragic accident."

"The worst that could happen to us," Mrs. Spatz said, eagerly leaning in, "is an embarrassment for having been indiscreet." A weak smile flitted across her mouth. "I don't think that will shock anyone who knows either of us."

"It's perfectly plausible," the lawyer said.

And goddamn it, like a ton of cement had been lifted off him, that is what happened! That's exactly what happened. It was an accident!

"Where was your car?" the lawyer said.

"When I got to the house?"

"Was it parked there?"

Vinnie nodded, his mind racing through the possibilities, heart pumping. Was he going to get out of this? Was everything going to be okay? Lawyers! He no longer hated this guy. The guy's a genius!

"And your roommate's car. It was there?"

"He leaves it on campus."

"Ah . . ." That seemed to be an answer the lawyer wanted. He sat back and dragged on his cigarette and gave Mrs. Spatz a look like they'd just won the lottery. He got up, reached out to give Mrs. Spatz a hand.

"For now," he said to Vinnie, "I see no harm in your telling the police, if they question you, that Mrs. Spatz dropped you off at your apartment. Maybe later we'll have to modify that, but neither of us can get into any serious trouble saying that's what happened. I assume that's all right with you?"

Vinnie didn't know whether it was all right or what the hell it was, but it's what Boyd wanted.

"If you say it, I'll say it." It was like he was standing a foot off the ground. He couldn't believe how free he felt! He didn't murder anybody! He wasn't going to jail!

"Good enough," the lawyer said. He stuck out his hand and, without thinking, Vinnie shook it, even grinned at the guy.

71

"I think we have good reason to believe that nothing very bad is going to come of all this," the lawyer said, opening the door, waiting for Mrs. Spatz to turn off the lights, turn down the thermostat. "One word of caution. It would not be a good idea for you to have any further contact with Mrs. Spatz. She has agreed to that."

"That's okay," Vinnie said. He never wanted to see her again anyway.

"And one other thing."

Vinnie was outside, half way to his car. He turned.

"Meeting here this evening will be our secret. Okay? We don't tell anyone we've had this meeting."

"That's okay with me," Vinnie said. "I won't tell anyone."

He couldn't wait to get back to his apartment to tell Boyd!

It was an accident! It wasn't my fault! I didn't murder anyone! I'm free! I'm one hundred per cent fucking free!

I can't believe it! I can't believe it!

When Vinnie pulled into the parking lot outside his apartment, he thought about how happy Boyd would be, getting this news. He went up to the apartment two steps at a time. The door was locked. Damn! Boyd probably had a chick in there. He rapped hard on the door. No answer. He put his key in the lock and went inside.

Boyd wasn't there. His shorts and jeans and a wet towel were on the floor in the bathroom. He was probably at some party. Vinnie was disappointed, but his news could wait.

He was starved. There was nothing to eat. He was too happy just to go someplace by himself. He checked his watch. That chick at the Cumberland Farms would be closing up in a little while. If she had nobody waiting for her, he'd take her out, get some Italian food into her, maybe find out how smooth the flesh was under those tight-fitting jeans.

CHAPTER EIGHT

They were in Webb's office. Perci was standing at a window looking down on Main Street. She was in a long skirt and soft-topped boots, a sweater and something like a vest under a loose-fitting jacket, not dressed like a policewoman. It must have cost her a lot for clothes, coming up here from Florida in the winter. He didn't know whether she had private money, but she sometimes acted like she did. He didn't know what her salary was, but it couldn't be more than she needed to support herself.

One time, in response to something the chief had asked, she said she'd been raised by a man named Piperopoulos. The way she said it suggested that the man wasn't her father or any other kind of relative, which maybe explained why she didn't look Greek.

Speaking about the forensic tech, Webb was saying, "Well, he bought a house from a man named Harold Tucker," offering Perci a sugarcoated cruller, amused when she turned it down, making a face. He sat back, gave himself a chance to look at her.

"Don't know how you can eat things like that," she said, "all that sugar."

"This Tucker," he went on, "lowered the price to a figure Charlie couldn't resist. So he bought the house even though Tucker's daughter refused to move out. She'd been born in it and said she'd live there until she died. Of course Charlie could have had her evicted, but all his things were up here from New

York just waiting in a rented truck that was costing him money. And he had no place else to go. So he moved in. Told her she was welcome to stay as long as she was quiet and mannerly."

"How long'd she stay?"

"Well, that was twenty years ago. She's still there."

"They got married?"

"I never asked, but they've got five children."

"Why'd he come here from New York?"

"Likes it in Maine, I guess. Said he came here as a boy. All I know is we're lucky to have a man with his training. Not many places this size have the big-city forensic sophistication he's given us."

When Charlie Putnam, the man they'd been talking about, came in, Webb noticed Perci giving him a strong once over.

"Didn't know they still made those," Charlie said. He didn't take the cruller. He shook hands with Perci. "I've heard of you."

"Guess I've heard about you," she said.

Puzzled him, but he just went over and sat down. He wasn't much taller than Perci, maybe five eight, maybe a hundred and forty pounds, dark thin hair, a kind of Humphrey Bogart face, a kind of Humphrey Bogart smell of whiskey on his breath that mingled with odors of disinfectant wafting into the office when he came in.

"So, what have we got?" Webb asked.

"Not a whole hell of a lot," Charlie said, tilting his chair back against a wall under a picture of Larry Bird that Webb's wife had given him the Christmas before she died. "Afraid we've got miles to travel before we can come up with anything you can use."

"Cause of death?"

"Asphyxia. But remember, that's a very broad term. It doesn't have to mean homicide." He put a finger in his mouth to pick at a back tooth. "Asphyxia's a hard thing to pin down in the best of circumstances, but when the body's been out there freezing for a couple of days . . ."

"Time of death?"

"From pathology? Don't know. Superficially, from how much snow was on him and when he was last seen alive—"

"Hell, I can do that, Charlie."

"And you probably did," Charlie said. "Give me a day or two and maybe I'll be more exact. It would help if you could find out where he was killed."

"It wasn't out there in the woods?"

"It wasn't up on the tree, I can tell you that. And that ligature around his neck didn't do it."

"Was he hanged?"

"Don't think so. And sure as hell not the way we found him. Lividity's all wrong. He was on his right side quite a while after he was dead. Maybe in the trunk of a car would be my guess. Soon as Janet finishes going over his clothes, we'll know more. She says on the side of the right knee, the right arm and shoulder of the jacket there are fibers she thinks came off one of those mats commonly used in car trunks. I'd say he was transported after he was killed. But these findings are preliminary. Get us the car and we'll be more definite. Give us the place of death and we'll know more about the cause of it."

"Marks on the body?"

"I'd guess he was in a fight. Some pressure marks on his chest. There's a contusion on the left side of his jaw and inside his lip. A laceration on the back of his head. He might have been knocked unconscious. Not a clean wound. So it could have come from a fall. Lot of dirt, wood particles, bits of metal stuck in it. You ever hear of burking?"

"I have," Perci said.

Both men looked at her, making her blush.

"Isn't that when years ago they killed people to make cadavers to sell to medical schools?" She looked at Webb as though apologizing for knowing such a thing. She seemed to dread being thought a know-it-all.

"That's right," Charlie said. "First they got their victims drunk, then they sat on their chests and smothered them. Didn't leave many marks. And that's what we've got here—a corpse without clear signs corresponding to what we think killed him. And the exposure in freezing weather doesn't help."

"But you think he could have been smothered when he was unconscious?"

"No evidence to prove that, but it's high on my guess list." He gave Perci a little grin, thinking she'd be amused by the expression, which Webb had heard a hundred times. She gave him a courtesy smile. "There were no broken fingernails or other signs you'd find if he'd fought off being smothered."

"But you said there was a fight."

"What I mean is the marks on him—on his chest, on his wrist, the back of his head—are not typical of someone fighting off an assailant. That's why I think he was knocked out and then, possibly, smothered. I say 'possibly' because the signs that are there, like hemorrhages around the eyes, tend to lose their importance after a little decomposition has occurred."

"The lividity you mentioned wouldn't have happened unless he was dead?"

"Right. When the blood stops circulating, it settles. He died of suffocation after he got that blow on the head. I just don't know how. What I'm trying to say," and he looked at Perci, not wanting to exclude her, "is that this death could have come from any one of several causes. An embolism can cause asphyxia. But I'd say he died of suffocation. It does not appear that he was strangled. That ligature did a lot of damage, but it was post mortem. His death may or may not be a homicide."

"What would you guess?"

"Homicide. I just can't prove it."

"Any possibility of suicide?"

"Suicide by smothering? I don't think so. It's pretty rare. I've never seen it."

"Well, we'll go on the assumption that this was a homicide."

"I would," Charlie said. "You gonna bring Portland up here?"

"Agatha says no."

When he was gone, Webb suggested that he and Perci go out to the college.

"Let's see if we can find out where Spatzie went after he and the senator left their club."

"Think Mrs. Spatz knows?"

"She said she thought her husband was at a meeting. Must have known something to say that."

Webb drove right up to the garage behind the president's house. Although the yellow ribbon was around the locked garage door on the president's side, they didn't find a man stationed there. The driveway had been shoveled. The ramps leading into the garage on both sides had been scraped clean. Mrs. Spatz's car was in the garage, and the door on her side was locked.

When the housekeeper, Marie Rigotti, responded to Webb's knock on the back door, he asked whether Mrs. Spatz had used her car this morning. The woman kept her head down when she mumbled an answer, saying she didn't know.

"Is Mrs. Spatz up?"

The woman nodded, stepped back to allow him and Perci in. She didn't look at them. "I don't know anything," she said, frowning as she closed the door.

"Have you been told not to talk to us?" Perci asked.

Fright leaped into the woman's eyes. She vigorously shook her head.

Perci glanced at Webb. The woman was lying.

"Whatever you might have been told," Webb said, "you are to answer any questions Detective Piper asks you. You understand that?"

She peeked up at him, eyes moistening, nodding.

He left Perci with the woman and went into the room where yesterday he had talked with Mrs. Spatz.

She was lying on the chaise in what he believed were called Capri pants. She greeted him by holding up a glass. He could smell the booze in it.

"As I told you on the phone," she said, after taking a sip, lowering the glass to the table next to her, shaking a cigarette from a pack, tapping the filter end of the cigarette against her thumbnail. "I'm in no mood for an extended interrogation."

But not because you're incapacitated by grief, he told himself, watching her fingertips roving over the silk blouse, lightly massaging her breast.

"I assume this is about the Milano boy. I'm told that's the latest wrinkle in the unfolding saga."

"Among other things," Webb said.

"I didn't mention him, Lieutenant, because I saw no point in involving him in this. I can't imagine how my giving a student a ride had anything to do with your investigation."

"Maybe it doesn't. Mind telling me why you picked him up?"

"I gave him a ride home. I didn't 'pick him up.' He asked me. I think he was trying to get away from a girl."

"You sat at the bar," Webb said. "You ordered a drink, caught his eye, got up and walked out. He trailed after you. That sounds like a pickup to me."

"And whose story is that?"

"A reliable source."

She gave that a small laugh, picked up her lighter and waved the flame across the end of her cigarette as though to demonstrate the lightness of her mood. There were dark smudges under her eyes and a kind of grayish hue to her skin. She looked tired and seemed to be trying hard to appear at ease. She didn't seem drunk, but the blood alcohol was probably working on her.

As she took a long deep drag on her cigarette, Webb went to the nearest cushion of the sectional and sat down a full eight feet from her. He rubbed his fingers on the nubby bone-white fabric and looked around at a lot of expensive, impersonal-looking furniture

"This may not be important," he said. "Probably just an oversight, but from what I understood yesterday, the house lights weren't on when you got home, and that was around eleven-thirty, I think."

"We're back to that?" She dragged so hard on the cigarette he could see fire crawling through the paper toward her mouth. Her eyes were narrowed in concentration. "Why? You think they were on?"

"I think the light over the front door was on."

"And that's important? We leave it on when one of us is out of the house."

"And you left it on for your husband?"

"He doesn't enjoy stumbling in the dark."

"You left it on?"

"We do share the same house."

"So even though you didn't notice whether your husband's car was in the garage, you knew he was not home."

"The light was on and I left it on. I didn't run over and shut it off. What does that prove?"

Webb smiled. "You're not in the habit of turning it off when you come in?"

"As I told you, I thought he was at a meeting."

"His secretary didn't have him scheduled for one." He was tempted to say the senator hadn't spoken about a meeting, but mention of the senator could trigger her into ending this whole conversation.

"It was something other than college business. You think I'm lying? Are we going back to that?"

"I'm just trying to find out what happened. I'm not accusing you of anything."

Three years ago she had had his brother, Chick, fired from his job as baseball coach because Chick had refused to have sex with her after she had chased him all over campus for more than a month. When Webb had raised hell about it, Senator Edison had tried to get Webb fired.

At a hearing in the mayor's office, Webb displayed copies of buried police reports citing three instances of Mrs. Spatz's having been caught at a local drive-in having sex with a male companion. When Webb threatened to bring the reports into court, the senator backed off. Of all the things he had accused Mrs. Spatz of, lying was what she resented most. "Believe me, Lieutenant," she had said, flat out, "you're the liar."

He looked at her now with possibly the same accusation in his eyes. "You have a reminder calendar in the kitchen," he said. "There's nothing in the space for last Tuesday. If he had been scheduled to attend—"

"Oh, for God's sakes!" she said, sitting up. "Marie!"

The housekeeper hurried in from the kitchen, wide-eyed. "Run upstairs. There's an envelope on Sam's dressing table with a postmark from Whitney, New Hampshire. Please get it for me."

She gave Webb a look of disgust, sat there gazing at Perci who had come into the hallway. Perci put her hands behind her back, came quietly into the room and perched on the edge of a chair opposite Webb.

"And what did you learn snooping around in my kitchen?" Mrs. Spatz asked, angrily poking out her cigarette, immediately getting another from the pack on the table.

In a chilly silence they waited for Marie to come down from upstairs. When she did, she handed Mrs. Spatz a white envelope and hurried back to the kitchen.

"I don't normally go through my husband's correspondence, but I'm as interested in where he was as . . . I found this."

She had taken a note from the envelope. She tossed it onto the table. Webb had to get up to reach it.

It was an invitation from a Pro-life group asking Dr. Spatz to attend a meeting and "to say a few words." It was signed by a Mrs. Olga Vance. He leaned across the table and handed the note to Perci.

"I remember his saying something about a meeting when he was looking through his mail last week," Mrs. Spatz said.

There was no point mentioning that the senator had said nothing about a New Hampshire meeting. He watched Perci lean across the table and lay the note in front of Mrs. Spatz.

"I'll ask you to hold onto that," Webb said. "We may need it for evidence."

As he and Perci got up to leave, Mrs. Spatz said, "I'm as anxious as you are, Lieutenant, to find out what happened to my husband."

"I'm sure you are," he said.

Perci looked up at him, searching for sarcasm, he suspected.

Chapter Nine

"She dresses young," Perci said, outside getting into Webb's car. "Those tight-fitting pants. How old is she? Forty?"

"Probably works out, wants everybody to see the results."

"So where now?"

"The Heritage Club. Then maybe to Whitney, New Hampshire. It depends."

"On who's been lying?"

Webb nodded. "Just because Spatz was invited, doesn't mean he went."

"How long would it take to get there?"

"If Spatz went to dinner at the Heritage Club when Edison said he did, there's no way he would have been a speaker that evening in New Hampshire. And he sure as hell wouldn't have got back to his house by midnight."

"She could have thought he went there."

"I suppose," Webb said, "but we haven't got much truth out of her so far."

They crossed the iron bridge at Stickney's Corner and were driving past those two grain elevators in the Grand Trunk railroad yard when Webb asked what Perci had learned from Marie Rogetti.

"She said Spatz had put on some pounds this past year and his shirts didn't fit. So the first thing he did coming into the house was loosen his collar and take his tie off."

"What'd he do with the tie?"

"Well, he usually went upstairs and changed into old clothes. Guess he took his tie up there."

"She remember which tie he wore?"

"Said she couldn't tell. Whole mess of them on a rack up there."

"Well, last Tuesday, if he went upstairs after hanging his coat up, I guess he didn't change clothes."

"At that time of night why would he? Wouldn't he just jump into bed?"

"Not with his suit on."

Perci laughed, gave Webb a playful slap on the knee.

"She notice any signs of a struggle?" Webb asked.

"I asked her that. She said no. Not downstairs or up."

"You remember seeing overshoes in that closet?"

"On the floor under the coat. What she said was he never sat around in a suit unless he had company, and he'd had company there'd've been dishes in the sink. You remember that blanket? It wasn't in the closet this morning and neither was that jacket. Had to be Mrs. Spatz took it unless Marie is lying, and why would she? You remember that smell? Couldn't figure out what it was? Suntan oil. Came off that blanket, Marie said. She thinks the blanket was in Mrs. Spatz's car."

"And she just now, in December, brought it inside? To be cleaned or laundered or something?"

"Marie doesn't know. Nothing was said to her about it."

"And the jacket?"

"Upstairs in the closet where she usually kept it. What seemed strange to Marie is that Mrs. Spatz never picks up."

"So you think it has to mean something?"

"Well," Perci said. "It's curious."

The Heritage Club was three blocks off Congress Street on the west end of town, a one-story brick building hugged by rhododendrons. There were frosted fir wreaths and holly branches on the door, a small wreath like a target ring around a brass door-knocker.

Pulling on a fat brass knob, Webb opened a wooden door and ushered Perci into a kind of lobby that smelled of cigars. They were met by an elderly man in a gray jacket with a red and black coat of arms emblazoning the left breast pocket. Voices down the hall somewhere, men's voices.

"May I help you, sir?"

Webb showed him the badge. "We'd like a few words with the manager."

"Certainly. Would you wait here, please?" He sighed and moved slowly down the hall as though regretting a fate that made him work in a place like this.

"You call a guy like that a 'concierge' up here?"

"I don't," Webb said.

"What do you call him?"

"Damned if I know. A doorman, I guess."

Perci seemed to think that funny. She shook her head for some reason and walked over to look at pictures on the wall, old pictures of sailing ships in old frames

A roar of laughter came from one of the rooms down the hall as an elderly waiter in a white jacket came out a doorway. He disappeared into another. A faint odor of burnt steak drifted toward them.

The manager came out a doorway and walked quickly toward them. He was a smallish bald man with the tiniest hands Webb had ever seen on an adult. All the time he talked, he kept rubbing them, maybe thinking constant massage would make them grow. They were pinkish white and hairless.

"Oh, dear, yes," he said. "Of course I remember. I was standing right here with Reginald reading the morning paper and I said, 'My goodness, he was here that evening'. They were sitting. . . . Come, I'll show you." He started toward the dining room.

"That's all right," Webb said. "Anyone with them?"

"Not that I remember."

"They got here about what time?"

"Oh, eight o'clock, sometime around there."

"And they left?"

"We stop serving at nine-thirty. It couldn't have been after ten at the latest. There were no complaints about dawdlers. Waiters complain, you know."

"Is the waiter here who served them?"

"I'd have to check, if you don't mind waiting."

Still rubbing his hands, he hurried down the hall, came back in a few minutes and said a Carl Stebbing had been their waiter and wouldn't be in until evening.

Perci wrote the name down as Webb handed the man a card.

"Have him call the office for an appointment. I'll want to talk to him."

Outside Perci asked why have the waiter come downtown.

"It's a better place to find out if he overheard what Spatz and Edison talked about. Everybody has a code of behavior, you know. Here he's a waiter; down there he's a witness."

On their way back to the office, they stopped at Bigelow's on State Street. They each had a bowl of chili and a small salad. They didn't talk about the investigation until later when they were in his office. She took the chair under the picture of Larry Bird, hooked her heels over the front stretcher and leaned back against the wall.

"Careful that doesn't come out from under you," Webb said.

She grudgingly acknowledged the warning. He believed she was more than willing to accept advice on police matters, in fact was eager for it. But on little things like breaking her neck, she intended to go it alone. Touchy about things like that.

"Where's your notebook?" he said.

She lifted her bag off the floor and got out the small notebook she always carried with her. She slowly leafed through it to a new page.

As though dictating to her, although he didn't expect her to take down every word, he said,

"From eight-twenty-five Tuesday morning until around five," watching her hand move across the page, "unless someone gave him a ride, Spatz appears not to have left his office even for lunch. He apparently didn't tell his secretary he was going anywhere that evening. His wife thinks he was going to a meeting but he didn't tell her he was. Maybe it was important for her to know when he would be out of town. Maybe her social life revolves around such times."

He paused, giving Perci time to catch up. "I'm inclined to think Edison learned about the meeting and that's why he wanted Spatz to have dinner with him. Anyway, it looks like Spatz got home around five-thirty and thought the meeting with Edison important enough to wait around the house for two hours. We know he didn't change clothes."

The pen paused over the notebook. Perci said, "It was Lorraine Lord, remember, who told Edison about me and got me kicked off the Umber case. If she found out Spatz was doing something the board objected to—like going to that meeting—it might have been she who told Edison."

"That two-hour wait," he said, "pretty much killed any chance Spatz'd get to New Hampshire to give a speech. Think we'd better call up that Olga Vance and find out whether Spatz cancelled or just didn't show up. Be nice to know when he cancelled." He watched Perci's fingers move across the white page. "I want you to talk to her. A woman's voice is less intimidating."

"What do I say?"

"Just say you're a member of Spatz's Champions club getting facts together for a report. What time did he cancel? Did anyone else from here call her? Things like that. Don't scare her."

He got the phone number, punched it in and handed the receiver to Perci, then rolled his chair back almost to the wall and listened.

"Olga Vance, please," screwing up her face in apology for the lies she was about to tell. She stayed on the line for about ten minutes, listening more than talking. When she restored the handset, she said,

"Spatz made two calls, one at seven forty-five, another at eleven. The second call was from a 'Champions' meeting at someone called Eleanor's house. Didn't get a last name. Then there was another call right after Spatz's second call from a woman at the meeting who blamed Edison for getting Spatz to cancel, said he was more interested in protecting the college than protecting babies. I got the impression this Eleanor was publicity shy."

"If it's the Eleanor I think it is, she wouldn't want anyone to know she's connected to a cause like Pro-life. Let me find out."

He left the office, went down the hall and talked to a woman named Harriet Parch, a civilian who had worked in the police department for more than thirty years and knew just about every human being in the county, especially the string pullers.

Perci was at the window when he got back to his office. He asked her, "When you were poking around in this stuff before, did you come across the name Tezzetti?"

"Don't think so."

"Well, Eleanor Wilde Tezzetti my source thinks is the money behind the Champions of the Unborn. She owns the news-paper, the TV station, half the politicians in both parties; and if she refuses to talk to us, there's nothing we can do about it. I'll bet even her editors don't know she supports that Pro-life group. And she's made a public promise to give a fat endowment to Cleeve College is probably why they went over there."

"How does a little burg like this afford a TV station?" Perci asked.

"It doesn't. The studio is here because she owned the land they put it on. But it broadcasts all over southwestern Maine and parts of New Hampshire."

"So what's your take on all of this?"

"Off the top of my head, I'd say Edison talked Spatz out of going to New Hampshire, then the two of them left the Heritage Club and went to Eleanor Tezzetti's to smooth her feathers."

"But the woman I just talked to didn't act as though Eleanor's connection with the Champions was a big secret."

"Because you told her you were part of the group," Webb said.

"We gonna talk to her?"

"I'd rather do Senator Edison a favor. Let's tell him we'd like to keep Eleanor's name out of this scandal."

She laughed. "That's sneaky."

"Oh, no, no. It's called police work in a political environment."

But a phone call to Edison's office revealed that the senator was out of town and wouldn't be available until morning.

"How'd you like to prowl around the campus for a while?" Webb asked. "I've got things here to catch up on."

"What I'd like to do is talk with Vinnie Milano. Want to know why?"

"Because you hate him."

"I don't hate him. I just think it's the proper next step."

"Go ahead."

"If she had a stud like Milano in her car and thought her husband wasn't going to be home. . . . It's only a short walk through the woods from his apartment to her house. And there wouldn't be any tracks because it hadn't started snowing."

"You think she dropped him off and he hiked over there through the woods?"

"She wouldn't want the gateman to see him. Spatz was a very jealous husband, one of the first things I found out about him."

"Yes, I know."

"That he was jealous, or that I found out? You had a run in with him once?"

Webb didn't answer. "Why don't you call this Milano, make sure he's there."

"I did. His phone isn't working."

"Well, just don't tell him any more than you have to. If we close in on him, it'll be details that trip him up. Don't give him any. I know you think he was responsible for Alicia Umber's pregnancy and you'd like to see him punished, but that's not what you're there for."

"I'll be professionally circumspect," she said.

"Like you were when you called him without checking with me. Just remember, there are a lot of people protecting him. Don't give them excuses to get you taken off this case. I need you."

Twenty minutes later he was on the phone with the waiter from the Heritage Club. All the waiter could remember about Edison and Spatz was that they had left a smaller than average tip and one of them poked out his cigar in the mashed potatoes. Webb didn't think it worth his while to bring the man in.

Chapter Ten

The minute he heard the front door open, Vinnie ran out of the kitchen. "Hey, Boyd! You'll never fucking guess!" grinning at Boyd who stood in the open doorway gaping at him, hungover, needing a shave, eyes like he'd been staring into a hurricane.

"Believe what?" Boyd closed the door, went over to the sofa, sat down and put his face in his hands. "I feel like dog shit."

"She had this lawyer."

"Who did? Jesus, don't yell."

"Spatzie's wife. Last night. Where the hell you been?"

"Who remembers? What about her? Oh, yeah. You went there last night."

"She had a lawyer said it was an accident. I didn't do nothing! It was a fucking accident!" He was shaking both fists over his head, grinning, waiting for Boyd to cheer.

But Boyd just uncovered his eyes and stared up at him. "What'd you tell him?"

"Nothing. She told him. I didn't tell him anything. He said the worst could happen is they find out I was screwing her. And Spatzie ain't around, so who cares? I'm in the clear! It's over! It's nothing!"

Eyes wide now, Boyd said, "What'd you tell them? They must've asked how he got in the woods?"

"I said I didn't know. I said you were asleep."

Boyd almost jumped off the sofa. "You mentioned me? You told them about me?"

"No. Take it easy. The lawyer asked when I got home where my roommate was. I said asleep."

"Why'd he ask about me? You told him you had a roommate?"

"She knew it. Come on, Boyd. I'm not stupid. Why would I mention you unless they did?"

Boyd didn't answer. He sat there, mouth half open, staring at the floor. He put his hand on his stomach, got up and hurried across the room into the bathroom and closed the door. He stayed in there a long time. Vinnie thought he could hear him throwing up. When Boyd came out his face was pale. There was vomit on his sweatshirt, a sour smell on him. He dropped onto the sofa, lay back holding a wet facecloth on his forehead.

"Oh, Jesus. Never again," he moaned. "Get me an aspirin, will you. Head's killing me."

Vinnie got him two aspirins and a glass of milk, had to step around spills of vomit on the floor.

Boyd said, "Why'd she have to tell anybody?"

"She got scared. You know that lawyer we see with Edison all the time, skinny guy? It was him. He won't say anything unless the cops find out."

"A lawyer? I'm supposed to trust a lawyer? Find out what?"

"Where it happened?"

Making a face against the pain, Boyd pressed fingertips into his temples and made little circular movements to stretch the skin. "Son of a bitch. Just exactly what did you tell them? No bullshit now."

"Nothing! I said what you told me: she brought me home. I went to bed."

"Nothing else?"

"He knew what happened. She told him."

Boyd shook his head, put his face in his hands. He didn't look up for several seconds. "You sure you didn't say anything?

You told them I was asleep?"

"Yeah. All they're gonna say is she dropped me off and went home. I told you. Nobody saw me under that blanket." Why's he have to make it so complicated?

"Sure as hell they're gonna bring the cops over here," Boyd said, getting up, heading for the bathroom.

"Jesus, Boyd," Vinnie said. "I thought you'd be happy for me."

An hour later Vinnie was in the kitchen trying to decide whether to live with the smell until Boyd got up, make him clean up his own mess, or go in and wipe the vomit off the floor around the toilet.

The doorbell rang. He froze. Cops?

He ran into the bathroom, leaned over the sink and, staring at his image in the mirror, told himself to settle down. It was probably somebody selling magazines or something. He went out through the living room and opened the door. It was the detective, Perci something, the one from Florida. There was nobody with her. She was holding a badge in his face like he didn't know who she was.

He just stood there like a dummy staring at her.

"May I come in?"

If he let her in, he'd have to talk with her. But he couldn't shut the door in her face. He stepped back, closed the door behind her when she came in. He wished Boyd was up.

"Must've been a big party," she said, meaning the smell.

She was dressed like a teacher, Indian colors in layers of different things and a long skirt and floppy boots. Didn't look like a cop.

"Not me," he said. He pointed toward the bedroom. "He's in there sleeping it off."

Like she expected to stay awhile, she went over and sat on

the sofa and looked at the posters over the TV—Michael Jordan, Drew Bledsoe, a girl with a lot of bush leaning on a palm tree, one of Boyd's.

"You know about the president," Perci said, patting her hands on her knees, smoothing her skirt.

"I saw it on TV."

"Well, we'll be talking to a lot of students. Thought I'd better come see you. Maybe you've got some idea."

"Me? I don't know nothing. Why me?"

"Among other things you're pretty friendly with his wife. You were with her Tuesday night, weren't you?"

"Tuesday night?" He couldn't control his face. He knew she could tell if he lied. Why the hell did she have to come over here? Why couldn't she leave him alone?

"At the Highwayman," she said. "It caused a little stir out there when you left."

"Oh, yeah. She gave me a ride home."

"Come on, Vinnie."

"What? She gave me a ride home! What's wrong with that?"

"You've been meeting her in that bar for the past couple of weeks. She came in, sat there until she caught your eye, then you followed her outside and drove off with her. It wasn't just for a ride home."

"She's an old woman! What would I want with her?"

"You tell me. She's an old woman you've been seeing a lot of. And she came there just to find you. You and Boyd had two other girls, but you left yours and hurried off with Mrs. Spatz. Think a jury would believe she came there just to give you a ride home?"

Color drained from his face. "A jury?"

"It could come to that. You were with a man's wife the very night he was murdered."

"All I did was go home with her!"

93

"Her house?"

"No. I mean she brought me here. Ask Boyd?"

"He was here?"

"Yeah. He was asleep."

Her eyes seemed to widen when he said that. Made him nervous the way she looked at him. He remembered last time, talking with her about Alicia Umber. He must've told her ten times it wasn't him knocked Alicia up.

She said, "He was asleep, with all his clothes off? In bed?"

"Yeah."

Little laugh on her mouth as she looked at him, the same laugh when he said he never touched Alicia.

"What's funny?"

"Vinnie. You left the Highwayman before he did. He sat at the bar for a while talking to a waitress. If you came straight here, how'd he get home, get undressed, get into bed, and fall asleep before you got here?"

It's what Boyd said. It's what he told Mrs. Spatz and the lawyer. But he knew now it was stupid. "I don't know. I thought he was asleep."

"But he was in the bedroom?"

"Yeah. I went in there. I thought he was asleep."

"Then you didn't come straight home, did you."

He took a step toward the door, then turned around. He didn't know what to do. He could feel sweat in his armpits. He threw books off the overstuffed chair and sat down, a chair they had brought up from the cellar. It smelled like rats had been living in it.

"All I did was ride home. That girl I was with? I wanted to ditch her. Ask Boyd. She was a dog."

"We have several witnesses to what happened. You didn't just want a ride. Come on, tell me what happened. I'll find out. Are you trying to protect Mrs. Spatz?"

"I'm not trying to protect nobody. I came here and went to bed. Why you getting me involved in something I didn't do?"

"Vinnie, if Boyd was here when you got here, you had to have been doing something besides just riding home. Where'd you go with her?" She leaned forward, forearms on her knees, boring in on him, eyes like guns. "She didn't think her husband would be home. She thought she had the whole night ahead of her. She went to the Highwayman especially to find you."

Too nervous to sit still, he got up and went over to the door, grabbed the cold knob, stood there, felt like an idiot but couldn't turn around.

"If Boyd was here asleep when you got here," Perci said, "a lot of time had elapsed. Did you sit outside in the car with her?"

Without turning, he said, "Yeah. We sat out there awhile."

"Was your car there?"

"I don't know. I didn't pay attention."

"She was clocked into the campus at eleven-fifteen. You left the Highwayman around ten-thirty. The Highwayman is no more than forty minutes from here."

He couldn't look at her. Couldn't just stand there with his back to her. If it was an accident, why not just tell her?

But he couldn't.

"Did you come here and then walk over to her house through the woods?"

"No."

"This is a murder investigation. The man whose wife you were with was murdered."

He finally turned around. "What's that got to do with me?"

"Hopefully nothing. But you haven't been telling the truth."

"She gave me a ride home. I came up here and went to bed."

He didn't care what she believed. He wanted her out of here, but she just sat there looking at him, waiting for him to admit something.

"Believe what you want," he said. "That's what happened. I wasn't anywhere near her house. I don't know why you're after me. I didn't do anything. All I did was take a ride home."

Perci lifted her bag off the cushion and got up. She took her time, fitting straps of the bag onto her shoulder, staring at the floor like she was worried. She finally looked at him. "The newspaper knows what I know. They'll blow it up like they did last time. You can't hide anything."

"I'm telling you the truth. Think what you want to think."

"I want to think you're bright enough to realize that hiding the truth is only making things worse for you."

"I told you what happened."

As she walked toward him, he said, "I was tired. I told her I was tired. I couldn't do nothing."

"Well, when you get tired of lying, come see me."

After she was gone, he went back to the bathroom and stared at his image in the mirror. The goddamned smell of Boyd's vomit sickened him. He strode out of the room and slammed the door, put on his leather jacket and went outside. He looked all around for the detective, but she was gone. He went over and got into his car.

He had to see Toni. Maybe if he went down there again she'd talk to him. Maybe if he told her.

Ah, shit! Everything's falling apart. Why'd this have to happen?

CHAPTER ELEVEN

Vinnie put ten gallons of super into the Trans Am at a Mobil station, went inside and, while the woman was running his Uncle Dom's card through the machine, went to the phone behind the beer coolers and called Toni's house.

Her mom answered in that deeper voice than Toni's, like she had a sore throat. First thing she asked was why he didn't come up the stairs yesterday.

"Toni's mad at me, I don't know. I'd like to see her."

Mrs. Costa told him Toni was at her aunt's house on Cumberland Avenue. He thanked her—a really nice lady, the kind that when you go there always makes you eat. Made this napkin for him once with his name on it, folded it like a hat and put it in front of his plate when he came over. Toni's father ripped it in half and threw it in the fireplace because of that time he caught him and Toni under the stairs.

There were a lot of old houses where Toni's aunt lived, two- and three-story tenements, separated from each other by narrow driveways and little fenced-in yards. In her house there was a For Rent sign in the window on the second floor where an old man used to sit and look down at the street.

Vinnie ran wheels into a snowbank behind Toni's Mazda. Little stickers on her back window—Save The Whales, Save The Earth.

He could barely remember Toni's uncle. He died when Toni was in high school. Even then Toni's aunt couldn't take care of herself. Something made her walk funny, a stroke or something, couldn't do housework. There were plenty of nephews and nieces but Toni was the only one who came over, washed the floors, cleaned the bathroom, took out the laundry.

She came to the door with her hair wrapped in a bandana. She wasn't surprised to see him. Probably her mother phoned her.

"What do you want?" she said, like it made her tired just looking at him.

She was wearing one of her aunt's aprons, wiping her hands on it, her knuckles red. She'd been doing dishes.

"Aw, come on, Toni. Be nice." She looked so good, even in a sweatshirt and jeans, sleeves rolled up, face sweaty. He could've dropped to his knees and wrapped his arms around her, buried his face in her belly.

"If you want to come in, take off your shoes," she said. "I just washed this floor."

When he got his hikers off and set them on the newspapers, he tiptoed across the linoleum and lifted himself onto the counter next to the sink, wood creaking under his weight. There was a faintly female odor on her as she stood next to him lifting dishes out of soapy water, rubbing them with a dishcloth, dipping them a couple of times, putting them into a wire drainer. He closed his eyes and breathed her into him.

Just looking at her made him feel good. Even if she didn't talk to him, he liked being with her. Now that his mother was gone, hanging out with Toni was the closest thing he had to being home.

"You ever taste dishwater?" he said.

She gave him a look like what kind of a dumb question is that?

"I mean," he said, "people always say something tastes like dishwater. How do they know? Maybe . . ."

"What do you want, Vinnie?"

"Why're you mad at me?"

Her face didn't change as she let the soapy water run down the drain. She put the drying rack into the sink and filled a glass with hot water and rinsed off every dish.

"Come on, Toni. Be nice."

She lifted the rack out of the sink, watched water drip off it, then plopped it on his legs, splashing water all over him.

"Hey!" He grabbed the rack and squirmed off the counter.

She wrung out the wet towel that had been under the rack and wiped soapy water off the counter. She took the rack from him and put it on the towel.

"Aw, what'd you do that for?" he said, looking down at his pants.

"Take them off," not laughing or anything, like a mother dealing with a little kid. She wiped her hands on the apron, watched him lower his pants, watched the red welts on his thighs. "Wait here." She left the kitchen and came back with a bath towel. "Wrap this around you."

She went over and laid newspaper on the radiator and draped his pants over the newspaper.

"If you just wanted to get my pants off, Toni . . ."

She shushed him, raising a finger to her lips, eyes scolding. She pointed toward the bedroom. When she had cleaned up the spill on the floor, he said,

"How much more you gotta do?"

"Why?"

"I want to take you to lunch."

"I had lunch."

"Can we go someplace and talk?"

"You know your Uncle Dom's looking for you?" She lifted his pants off the radiator, turned them over, put them back. The steam coming off them smelled funny.

"What for?"

"I don't know. He called my mother, said he'd been looking all over for you."

"I don't wanna talk to him," and a look came into his face that scared her.

"You did something," she said, like a mother who always knows when something's wrong.

He stared at the floor, didn't want to tell her but knew he was going to. He raised his eyes, feeling like a little kid when he said, "It was me hit the president."

At first she didn't understand. She worriedly searched his face. Then her eyes widened. "Oh, my God, Vinnie! The college president? You hit the college president?"

"It was an accident. I didn't mean to."

In a very small voice, her face drained of color, she said, "You killed him?"

"He hit his head. It was an accident. Honest to God, all I did was give him a shove."

"But you killed him?"

"I couldn't help it! He grabbed me and I shoved him away and he hit his head. I didn't mean to hurt him. It was an accident."

"But he was smothered, Vinnie. That's how he was killed. It said on the radio he was smothered."

He didn't know what she meant.

"That's what the radio said, Vinnie. This morning on my way over. It said he was smothered."

"Who said?"

"A doctor. The police doctor."

"How?"

"I don't know. But that's how he died."

She raised her finger to her lips and glanced toward the other room. She went over and lifted Vinnie's pants off the radiator and told him to put them on. She got her coat and boots off the washing machine in the hall. He put his hikers on and followed her down the steps holding the clammy front of his pants away from his skin, knowing his thighs would be chafed. But he didn't care. He had Toni back!

They drove to a Cumberland Farms store and got a morning paper. It was on the front page that President Samuel Spatz had been asphyxiated while unconscious.

"They don't know where it happened, but it didn't happen in the woods."

Toni read the whole story to him.

"Then I'm in the clear!" he said. "I didn't kill him!"

"Tell me exactly everything that happened," she said, holding both his hands, searching his eyes. "Don't lie to me."

He lied. He said he was just sitting in the car with Mrs. Spatz when the president came into the garage and grabbed him.

"Like he was crazy, yelling at me get away from his wife. All I did was get out of the car and shove him away. He hit his head on the workbench and fell on the floor. I thought he was dead. I ran down the woods and got Boyd."

"And he took him out to that tree? He hung him up on that tree? He didn't call the police? He didn't help you?"

"He helped me. He figured . . ."

"He didn't help you, Vinnie!"

His Uncle Dom was a little bald-headed guy who ran a body shop on Mitton Avenue. On the roof of his building there was this sign: Avalone's Body Shop. Dom wasn't rich, but he made enough to let his sister live rent–free in the house on Cumberland Hill. Every month he sent Vinnie three hundred dollars spending money. He said he'd get it back when Vinnie went pro.

He was inside his office talking with a woman customer, and

Vinnie and Toni had to wait outside in this big room that smelled of car exhaust and auto paint. They could hear guys working down in the bays, yelling at each other.

They waited fifteen minutes before Dom came out with a woman and a ten-year-old girl with a brace on her leg.

"It ain't something we paint on," Dom was telling the woman. "Those are decals from the factory. Take us only a few minutes. Come by any morning."

"I need an appointment?"

"Naw, I'm always here."

He led them to the outside door and opened it and patted the little girl on the head as she limped past him.

"Break your heart," he said, gesturing Vinnie and Toni into his office. "Bright little kid like that limp the rest of her life. It ain't fair."

He went behind his desk and got a cigar out of a drawer, bit the end off it, spat into a wastebasket.

"You're more beautiful than last time," he told Toni, igniting a kitchen match on the underside of the desk drawer. It took him twenty seconds to get the cigar lighted the way he wanted it. He leaned back in the chair and blew smoke at the ceiling. "So what you been doing?" he asked Vinnie.

He got the answer in the look on Vinnie's face.

"Aw, shit!" he said, sitting dead still in the chair. "What you done now?"

Vinnie told him.

"So what you doing in the garage with the guy's wife? You crazy?"

"Nothing. Just sitting there. She gave me a ride home."

Dom looked at Toni, see if she agreed he was lying. Then this disgusted look came on his face.

"When you gonna learn? Before it was that Umber broad whatever the hell her name was? What's the matter with you?"

"I wasn't doing nothing!"

"You think she believes that?" Dom pointed his cigar at Toni. "What's the matter with you? You stupid?"

Vinnie put the folded newspaper on the desk in front of his uncle. "It says he was smothered. I didn't do that. I never killed him. All I did was give him a shove."

"He needs a lawyer," Toni said.

"He needs a kick in the ass. What's the matter with you? You got everything! The world's out there like a fucking platter. Why you gotta do stupid things?"

"I didn't kill him!"

"He needs a lawyer," Toni said.

Dom just sat there staring at Vinnie like he couldn't figure him out. A dozen times a year he looked at Vinnie that way.

He got the cigar out of his mouth and set it on a metal ashtray and picked up the phone.

"I'm beginning to understand what killed your mother," he said, rubbing ash off the cigar with his little finger. "Hello, Raymond. How you doing? Fine. Yeah, me too. Listen, my nephew over here's in a little trouble. You got a few minutes?"

CHAPTER TWELVE

Standing in the doorway of his office, Senator Edison was momentarily transfixed by the chocolate-colored glow of flesh eight inches up the thigh of the intern across the room on the ladder dusting books. He had been told her name was Eliana Barstow. She was easily the prettiest of the four girls the college had sent him this semester. His secretary had said she was intelligent, apparently in the belief that that was of some interest to him.

One of the new paralegals at the far end of the office, noticing his admiration of Eliana's thigh, seemed disapproving. Another instance of that and he'd turn her over to Haskell, who enjoyed firing women, especially ugly ones.

He told his secretary, "I'm not in the office, Winona."

When the girl on the ladder looked down at him and grinned, he rewarded her with a wink. Granting these internships not only enlivened the office atmosphere but also enhanced his reputation with fellow board members at the college, none of whom, so far as he knew, had designs on the presidency.

Inside his office he strode past framed photographs of politicians he had posed with, all of them Republicans. He had known few of them personally, but when alone he often strode from picture to picture, as in an art gallery, reliving the moments with Nixon, Bill Casey, Senator Dole, telling himself he was as capable as they of holding high public office

"So what do you think of the plan?" Haskell said, coughing

104

into his hand, then wiping something off his palm with a white handkerchief.

"Go through it again for me," Edison said, lowering himself into the leather-padded chair behind his desk.

"Well, first of all, they were in his garage. She was on his lap facing him . . ."

"I don't want that. I mean your reasoning. I assume you think there's enough to get a warrant."

"To search, you mean."

"The car, Haskell. What the hell are we talking about? Crozier's car."

"Yes, but I think we ought to sit back a while. Webb Harrington will figure out the same thing. It's better to let them stumble onto the evidence without any prompting from us. The last thing we want is their suspicion that we're pushing this off onto those boys."

"But what led you . . . ?"

"It had to be a car that was already on campus," Haskell said. "Otherwise the gateman would have seen it come in. Presumably Crozier drove Milano's car to their off-campus apartment when he came home from the Highwayman."

"And you think he took one of those paths through the trees and got his own car."

"That's my guess. We know the body was never in Claire's car. We'll allow an inspection if they want it. In fact, we'll welcome it. It's damned unfortunate that she had the car cleaned."

Edison frowned. " 'Pubic hairs' she said. Something she saw on television. That damned back seat is probably upholstered with pubic hairs. But to hell with that. Getting the car cleaned doesn't prove anything. Couldn't Milano have lugged the body off through the woods? Couldn't he have got the help of someone else whose car was on campus?"

"Too complicated, George. There wasn't time. Milano said he went straight home, and I believe him. Claire said he panicked. I assume you're talking what happened, not what the police might conjecture."

"Don't get cute. I'm trying to understand our position. I want to believe the police will have a solid case against the two boys so that Claire is not implicated. But putting pressure on Crozier worries me."

Haskell shrugged. "Why? The Mayfair incident? You don't know that Crozier had any knowledge about what happened out there."

"But that pimp Stewart knows I was there with Alicia, and he was at the bar talking with Crozier."

"You sure it was Crozier? It's pretty dark there. And you were where? At the desk?"

"I know it was Crozier," Edison said. "He was Alicia's boyfriend. Three nights a week he picked her up at the office. You saw him there. But why was he at the Mayfair? I don't buy coincidence. He followed me. Why was he talking with Stewart?"

"I wouldn't worry about Stewart. We got enough on him to bury him."

"And he's got enough on me to ruin me."

"Maybe," Haskell said, "but I could take a ride out there, find out what, if anything, went on between him and Crozier. I just don't think there's any substance to it. When the girl died and there was all that hell raised about Sam, why didn't Crozier say something? Let's say he did follow Alicia. Let's say he knew she was there with you? Why didn't he do something then? You said she was a virgin. How come he wasn't screwing her? How close could they have been?"

"He didn't say anything because he didn't want her involved in a scandal. But she's not around now to give a shit. We try to

106

pin something on him, he's going to talk."

"If you'll forgive my saying so, George, that's paranoid. And, besides, we're not pinning anything on him. The police are. Your little girlfriend from Florida is."

"That bitch."

"Look, why don't I take a ride out to the Mayfair and put a thumb up Stewart's nose."

Edison laughed at the image. "Okay, but be careful."

"Am I ever anything but?"

Edison was pacing the floor, rubbing sweaty palms together. "All right," he said. "Let's get back to Milano. How do we point the cops at him without showing our hand?"

"We don't. They'll find out he was in the garage with Claire. He'll cave when they move in on him. If you're worried about the sexual indiscretion . . . it's secondary unless you want to make the ludicrous suggestion that Sam thought his wife was being raped. Sam grabbed the kid. The kid knocked him against the bench and then smothered him."

"Why?"

"Panic. He didn't want to get kicked out of college."

Edison nodded. "The smothering. They're definite about that?"

"Charlie said that's how Sam died. Not definite but probable that he was smothered while unconscious. A jury will never doubt that the guy he was fighting with is the guy who smothered him."

"And Claire will testify that that guy was Milano."

Haskell shook his head. "We can't count on that. She's in love, for Christ's sake. But she's got to say she was with him. Dozens of people saw her pick him up at that roadhouse."

"What did Claire actually see?"

"We can't say she saw him hold his hand over Sam's nose and mouth. Anyway, she'd deny it. Even if she did say it, we'd have a problem explaining why she didn't call the police."

"So why didn't she?"

"Maybe the most obvious reason in the world," Haskell said. "Or maybe she actually saw Milano do it. We'll probably never know. But to get the point across, we don't have to say she actually saw anything except that the two men were fighting. It disgusted her and she went into the house. She had no idea her husband was being murdered out there. She went up to her room and locked the door to avoid arguing with a jealous husband. She went to bed and fell into a sound sleep."

"Will it hold up?"

"Why not? Everybody knows how jealous Sam is . . . or was. There've been public demonstrations, for God's sake. That part doesn't worry me. And what I like is we don't have to accuse either of those boys. We let the prosecution come up with their own version of what happened—murder, misprision of felony, manslaughter, temporary insanity, anything they want. We convince Claire we're not trying to hurt her boyfriend. Besides protecting herself, that's all she cares about."

"You sound pretty confident."

"How else can it go? Your sister will come out looking a little dirty, that's all."

"Yes," Edison said, "And the college will look even dirtier. And that's Sam's fault—all that damned foolishness about abortion. What the hell got into him anyway? He knew it was bad for the college."

"Maybe it was a reaction to Claire's philandering, a kind of substitute thing."

"And maybe it was hypocrisy," George said. "He was no saint. And he knew she was a nympho when he married her. It's what turned him on."

"Maybe he just liked the publicity, a man with a cause, a True Believer. But if it's any consolation, maybe this will be the end of the bad publicity, a kind of balloon payment.'"

George dwelled on that a few seconds, toying with a letter opener someone had given him years ago. "What other reason could there have been for mounting him up like that? Why did those bastards want to hurt the college?"

"I don't think it was that," Haskell said. "I think it was just a clumsy way to place the blame on that group of kids who've been hitting on Sam."

"Any way they could be in on this?"

Haskell shook his head. "I can't imagine how. There wasn't time. You saw Sam alive at midnight, and measurements of the snow on his body suggest that he was on that tree at the beginning of the storm. That means it all happened in about an hour. Even if there had been time, those people wouldn't implicate themselves like that. The boys had to get the body out of there. Why would they call in witnesses? No, they were alone on this."

"But is Milano bright enough to think of it?"

"I think Crozier is. After the Umber thing, I had a long talk with Coach Flaherty about him. He called Crozier an 'ambitious parasite', apparently sees Milano as a meal ticket."

George seemed unconvinced. "That's why he did it? Protecting his future?"

"It's an acceptable theory."

George leaned back, hands clasped behind his head. "But hang him on a tree? How would that help?"

"I don't know."

George laughed. "This is going to break a lot of hearts."

"Sam's death?"

"Vinnie Milano. The local hero in prison for murder."

"More likely manslaughter. But how bad will that impact on the college?"

"I'm sure we'll survive it," George said. "We've been in this city a long time."

"I suppose we can say it's lamentable that our star athlete attempted the seduction of the President's beautiful wife. And tragic that the President died a hero trying to defend her."

"Sounds good to me," George said.

Haskell got a cigarette from his jacket pocket, sat there tapping the filter end on the half-empty pack. "By the way, I might be able to get a line on who made that call to New Hampshire. It's not far-fetched there are traitors in the Champions."

"Forget the Champions," George said. "As far as Cleeve College is concerned, that organization no longer exists. I'm sorry Eleanor got spooked over this, but we probably would have lost her support anyway. She knows how the Board feels about what Sam was doing."

"Well, it isn't her contribution I'm worried about," Haskell said. "I figure we've lost that. It's what she might do to oppose you succeeding Sam."

George thought about that. "You're right. When I get a chance I'll go over and pump her glands up. But don't go prowling around the Champions. I don't want anyone else mad at me."

Before Haskell went outside to catch a smoke, he said, "Did Winona tell you that Piper woman called?"

George scowled. "What the hell does she want?"

"Whether we have a policy that only upper classmen get internships here."

"Why'd she want to know that?"

"Just guessing, George. But Alicia Umber was a sophomore, if you remember. Every other girl's been a junior or senior, including the crop you've got out there now."

"All of them?"

"I checked. And there's a letter to that dean Sam fired, waiving the requirement in Umber's case. Maybe we'd better freshen up that file."

"All right, but be careful how you handle it."

"Another thing," Haskell said. "While we're on this, I'd like to suggest again that we let a few male interns in, just to keep it honest."

"What the hell you mean? It is honest!"

"Oh, I know that. But for appearance's sake."

"Goddamn it! Can't you get that Florida bitch out of here? All she does is cause trouble."

"I'm trying," Haskell said. "I've been putting pressure on Agatha, but she doesn't scare as easily as she used to. And with the Democrats in City Hall . . ."

"Then try a bribe."

"Well, she does want a hookup to AFIS."

"What's that?"

"Computerized fingerprint system."

"Promise it to her."

"That budget's overloaded now. No way she'll get it."

"Who cares? Just make the promise."

CHAPTER THIRTEEN

Perci momentarily glanced out the car window past the girl's face at wisps of snow skittering across the frozen surface of the playing field. The winter sun, pale behind distant tree branches, pushed shadows like witches' fingers across the cold shiny white field. It would soon be dark. They had been sitting here at the edge of the campus for more than an hour. Perci had heard enough. It was time to go.

"Just something we had to check out," she said. "I couldn't go back to headquarters without saying I'd talked to you."

"You believe me?"

"No reason not to."

"Even if we could—I mean, even if we were capable of it, we wouldn't kill anyone. They're the violent ones, not us. Our whole thing is showing people we're rational and law-abiding. It would be crazy!"

"I know," Perci said. "I don't think anyone suspects your group. We're questioning everyone."

"Including the so-called pro-lifers?"

"I talked to Wanda for an hour, asked her the same questions I asked you."

"Did she accuse us?"

"No." As Perci eased the car back onto the asphalt, she asked, "Where'd you find out Spatz had gone to see Alicia's parents?"

"Tennyson told me. I don't know how he found out. But it's why he was so pissed off."

"That's why he did that cartoon?"

"I think it's why he decided to print it."

"A lot of people know about it? All I knew was her parents came on campus, they had a big argument, and she ran out of the dorm crying. When'd you find out?"

"Sunday," the girl said, "this past Sunday. At a party. You know, nobody hated Spatz because he was against abortion. A lot of people are. Who cares, you know? But grabbing her outside the clinic, lecturing her in front of all those people? And going to her house? Telling her parents? I mean, he was supposed to be a president!"

"It says a lot about him, doesn't it."

"Why'd he do that?"

"I don't know." It was a question Perci would give a lot of thought to. It certainly wasn't the kind of thing expected of a college president, no matter how strongly he might feel. With three thousand students on campus, it couldn't be all that uncommon for one or two girls to get pregnant. Was there something special about Alicia Umber to make the president go to her home?

She asked, "Does Tennyson live on campus?"

The girl nodded. "Shares an apartment over on Dunne Street. His phone number's in the book. Don't tell him I told you about this."

"I won't."

She let the girl off at her dorm and drove back to the city. Webb wasn't at the station. She considered driving to his house, but this time of evening it could look like she was expecting to be fed. She drove up the hill to Gorges Street and pulled into a plowed-out empty lot next to a Chevy station wagon. She got a quart of milk at the IGA across the street and walked up the cold staircase behind the photographer's studio to her two-room apartment.

The phone rang while she was at the stove heating a leftover chicken casserole. It was Webb. He had just been called into the chief's office. Somebody had leaked to the media that Spatz had been smothered before being tied to the tree. He wanted to assure himself that it hadn't been she.

"Somebody accused me of that?"

"I have to ask," he said.

"Well, you figure out your own answer." She felt like hanging up, but she didn't. Why'd he have to ask? Didn't he trust her?

"I didn't say I thought you had leaked the information. I'm sure you didn't. But I have to ask. Agatha will want to know whether I asked you."

"How much does it hurt us? The leak, I mean."

"It doesn't help."

"Think it was Charlie?"

"Not according to him."

"You trust him?"

"Not completely. Are you busy right now?"

"I was just fixing something to eat," she said. "Want some?"

"Sure it's no trouble?"

"No trouble at all."

By the time she went down the dimly lighted steps to open the door for him, she had given herself a bath, toyed with her hair, put color on her face and was in sandals, a sweatshirt and designer jeans.

He followed her up the stairs and stood in the middle of her living room with his hands in his pockets, inspecting her rented furniture, gazing quietly at the unframed poster of a snowy egret she had bought in a gallery on Captiva. He was wearing the same tie, jacket, and slacks she had seen him in that morning.

"You like turkey burgers?" she asked, going into the kitchen.

"What are they?"

"Like hamburgers, only made with turkey. That's what we're having, that and home fries and corn-on-the-cob."

"Sounds good," he said.

"There's beer in the fridge," she told him, "and a couple of cold glasses in the freezer door. Help yourself and pour me one."

This was the first time anyone had visited her apartment, and visitors made her nervous. At work she was comfortable with Webb. He was the best boss she'd ever had, rarely critical. But until they were seated at the small kitchen table munching burgers and nibbling corn, she was unable to ignore a nagging uneasiness. It had a lot to do, she believed, with having been raised in foster homes. She hadn't had much experience having a place of her own.

Over coffee, seated across from him in the living room, she told him about her afternoon prowling around the campus.

"I didn't ask for it, but I was talking to a girl about Spatz, and she told me he paid a visit to Alicia Umber's parents the day before she went into that field. That's why they came to the campus. That's why she ran out of the dorm. I also learned that he didn't usually attend protest meetings like that one at the clinic. Kids in the pro-choice group think he was there especially to find Alicia. How'd he know she'd be there?"

"Don't know," Webb said. "But you sure it was just this afternoon you learned these things?"

She nodded, puzzled by the question. "Why?"

"Well, there was another reason the chief called me in. She wanted to know why you contacted Edison's office about his interns."

"Oh."

"Goddamn it, Perci, you were supposed to stay away from all that."

"I just wanted to confirm a suspicion."

"About what?"

"I just think it's strange that Edison went out of his way to get Alicia Umber into his office. She was only a sophomore. I also asked the registrar's office whether a sophomore could get credit for an internship and they said no. I didn't ask and knew I couldn't find out whether Alicia had been given credit for hers. But she clearly was given special treatment, and I'd like to know why."

"Unless you can tie it in with the case we're working on," Webb said, "I want you to leave it alone." After an uncomfortable silence, he added, "I don't know the extent of it and don't want to know, but Edison's in some kind of trouble with his own party. He's lost favor in Augusta, and he's spoiling for trouble. If he gets to the mayor, the mayor can have you shipped back to Florida. I don't want that to happen."

"I just find it hard," Perci said.

"I know, and I'm not asking you to stop thinking. If you come up with a defendable tie-in, we'll go to the chief with it. But don't go looking for it. She didn't issue you a fishing rod."

"I'm sorry."

He gave her a quiet, almost fatherly smile that said he wasn't angry at what she had done. It was patronizing, and that annoyed her. But he meant well.

She asked, "You ever hear that Edison has the same problem his sister has?"

"What problem is that?"

"Sex addiction. The girls tell me he's never had a male student intern."

"And that means . . . ?"

"Nothing, I suppose. But don't you think it's funny? They say boys don't even apply anymore."

"I suppose it could mean something, but you'll only get hurt looking into it."

"And they have to be good-looking," she added.

While Webb was quietly shaking his head and she was trying to suppress her annoyance at his stubborn unwillingness to hear her out, she went into her bedroom and got the three copies of the student newspaper he had asked for. As she was handing them to him, the phone rang.

It was the chief. She wanted to know whether Perci had any idea where Webb was.

"I might be able to find him," she said. "You tried his house?"

"Just tell him to come to my office. And maybe you'd better come in with him."

She wanted to ask what it was about but didn't dare.

"I think I'm in trouble," she told Webb. "She wants you to call her."

"I talk better standing in front of her. Better put on your leather jacket. It's cold out."

"Yes, dad," she said.

Webb laughed as he urged her out of the apartment ahead of him.

"I have to lock the door," she said, pushing him out of her way.

Predictably they went in Webb's 4Runner, which smelled vaguely of burnt oil, vinyl cleaner, and old seat cushions.

Stopped at a red light, Webb said, "The chief knows somebody made inquiries about Eleanor Tezzetti. She didn't say so, but from the context I gathered it came from Edison."

"She know it was us?"

"Don't think so, but it'll probably come out. We've got to justify questioning the old lady, but the chief brought her name into it, so that lead's been handed to us. I wouldn't worry about anything. I just hope the mayor doesn't get into it."

"What's going to happen?"

"Let's wait and see."

"Think I'll get sent back to Florida?"

"I doubt this has anything to do with you. Stop worrying."

Like I can. She was sitting upright on the seat, both hands clasped about her knee, arms tense, eyes staring at oncoming headlights and red reflectors and frozen slush under parked cars, her mind staring at eighteen more car payments, a twelve-hundred-dollar balance on her Visa card, and less than four hundred dollars in a savings account.

God, I hope it's not that.

"The mayor tough to deal with?" she asked.

"If I went over the chief's head to get to the mayor, Agatha'd fry me on a front burner. Stop worrying. I don't know what kind of pressure Agatha's under, but she's fair. The last thing she'd want is to hurt your career."

Probably to take her mind off herself, he said, "Something that didn't get leaked is what they found around Spatz's head wound. Indoor debris, Janet called it—motor oil and metal filings and wood fibers. Said she could find no evidence that the wound, when blood was running, had been in contact with the ground. She thinks he was knocked out indoors somewhere."

"Motor oil? Think it happened in a garage?"

She had offered that so suddenly, he said, "You've already been thinking that?"

"Just trying to make sense of what we know."

"Let's hear it."

"Well, I'm sure Vinnie Milano was with Mrs. Spatz for some time after she got home. The house lights were out, and Spatz's car was in the garage, which meant either he had gone to New Hampshire in someone else's car or was upstairs in bed. Either way, why should she give up a chance for sex? I mean she went out of her way to pick Vinnie up."

"So she took him into the garage?"

"Why not? What I'd like to know is why's a woman like her drive a four-door Cadillac unless she uses it for things other than transportation? Wouldn't you expect her to have a sports car, convertible, something like that?"

"You figure they went into the garage?"

"And kept the motor running and the heater on," Perci said. "That garage isn't heated. Means the garage door would be open and a plume of exhaust flaring into the back yard. We know that Spatz came into the back hallway to hang up his coat. He could have heard something. Could have gone out to look. Charlie said there was a fight. I think there'd be a fight if he caught Vinnie and his wife going at it, don't you?"

"Too bad that's not enough to get us a search warrant."

"That's not reasonable cause? All we need is blood out there somewhere."

"And," Webb said. "to get Janet to find it, we need something more compelling than speculation."

"But it makes sense."

"Making sense isn't enough. But one thing it does do: If true and he knows about it, we've found a good reason why Edison's so nervous. Something like that happening on campus is a hell of a lot more damaging to the college than if it happened in the woods."

As they pulled into the police parking lot, Perci felt a tightness in her stomach. Please God, put the chief in a good mood. I don't want to be sent back to Florida.

CHAPTER FOURTEEN

There's nothing emptier than a public building after hours, Perci thought, listening to their footsteps echoing down the long deserted hallway, trying to keep her step in sync with Webb's but unable to match his long strides, disturbed somehow by the uneven patter of sound. At the far end of the corridor there was a man with a mop leaning over a bucket, the source, she imagined, of a faint odor of ammonia.

Webb opened the door to the chief's outer office. No one was there, but the inner office was fully lighted and a man was saying, "He came here of his own free will."

The chief's voice, sounding tired or bored: "I'm well aware of that."

Perci leaned nervously on the secretary's desk trying to figure out who the man was, felt a paperclip under her finger, turned, put it into a small receptacle. She watched Webb open the door to signal the chief that they had arrived.

"Come in," the chief said. "Is Detective Piper with you?"

Perci's heart turned to stone. As she moved toward the open doorway, the chief said to someone, "I'm afraid you two will have to wait outside. Not enough chairs in here."

God, how many were here?

A tall beautifully featured girl with flowing black hair came out the doorway, followed by a short, bald-headed man.

"We'll stay here, Toni," the man was saying. "We can hear everything out here."

The girl barely glanced at Perci, but the man gave her an accusing look. Who was he? Did he know her?

Confused and nervous, Perci followed Webb into the inner office where two men were sitting in hard wooden chairs in front of the chief's desk. One was a white-haired, handsome man in his sixties. The other was Vinnie Milano.

"Thanks for coming," the chief said to Perci.

No reprimand? No hostility? This is about the investigation. Not about me. Her involuntary sigh of relief caused Webb to turn, smile, tap her hand.

"You two sit over there," the chief said, pointing at a bench along the wall. Addressing Vinnie and the older man, she said, "This is Lieutenant Harrington. And you know Detective Piper," she added, looking at Vinnie.

He raised his head, big shoulders bowed. He was leaning forward, forearms on his thighs. He looked pale, shaken, tired, and scared.

"Mr. Raymond Aiello is Mr. Milano's attorney."

The white-haired man gave Perci a briefly searching glance, neither friendly nor unfriendly. He nodded at Webb, whom he apparently knew.

"Mr. Milano has told us it was he who struggled with President Spatz and knocked him unconscious," the chief said.

"But I never killed him," Vinnie said, looking defiantly at Perci. "I came here to tell you so you wouldn't keep after me."

The lawyer put a restraining hand on Vinnie's arm.

"I'm just telling her," Vinnie said. He looked hurt, a man used to being praised, didn't deserve what was happening to him.

"I want you to listen to a tape," the chief said. "Apparently you talked with him?"

"At his apartment," Perci said. That caused this?

For about ten minutes they listened to a rambling confession, interrupted occasionally by questions, occasionally by cautions from Aiello. It ended with a strong protest of innocence. "I never killed nobody! It was an accident. All I did was push him away."

"I've told Mr. Milano," the chief said, "that we do not intend to charge him with anything at this time but that he will be subject to further investigation." She looked at Webb. "If you have questions?" She looked from Webb to Aiello.

"Within reason," Aiello said.

Webb asked how Vinnie got past the guard when he came on campus with Mrs. Spatz. Vinnie said he'd hidden under a blanket on the floor.

"Would you do that if, as you said on the tape, there was nothing illicit going on between you?"

"What's that mean?"

"If you weren't doing anything wrong."

"She wanted me to. People been lying about her. You know."

"Anything unusual about the blanket?"

"It stank. Made me gag. Some kind of perfume."

"And when you were in the car, in the garage, you weren't having sex with her?"

The lawyer seemed offended. "I don't think that's . . ."

"We were just talking," Vinnie said.

"But you said on the tape President Spatz accused you."

"He started yelling. Yeah, he pulled me out of the car."

"And you struggled and he fell and hit his head on the workbench."

"That's what happened." His manner was hesitantly defiant. He gave both Perci and Webb a challenging look, then stared at the floor.

Perci was listening so intently she didn't realize she had interrupted until she heard herself asking, "Isn't the workbench in the center against the back wall of the garage?"

She looked apologetically at Webb. He motioned with his hand for her to continue.

"Between the two cars," Vinnie said. "When he grabbed me, he fell against the other car, and I gave him a shove, and he hit his head back there."

He avoided looking at his lawyer, and Perci suspected it hadn't been the lawyer's idea to come here. She knew how headstrong Vinnie could be.

Getting an okay from Webb to continue, Perci asked, "Out at the Highwayman the girl followed you into the parking lot."

"What girl?"

"The one you were with."

"She's crazy. All I did was buy her a beer."

"Mrs. Spatz was in her car, the engine running, waiting for you to get in? Is that when you got under the blanket?"

"No. We stopped. There's a little store just . . ."

"With you under the blanket she drove onto the campus?"

Aiello put a hand on Vinnie's arm, looked at Perci and said, "We've been over this."

Vinnie ignored him. "That's right," glaring at Perci.

"And once you got into the garage, what happened?"

"What do you mean?"

"You just started talking?"

He nodded.

"While you were under the blanket?"

"No. She . . . I . . . I got in the front seat."

"And that's where you were when the president found you?"

He nodded.

"She had been driving. Did she move over?"

"No, I . . ."

"If she was behind the wheel, the president must have reached across his wife, and you must have crawled over her to get where you said the struggle took place."

Vinnie's mouth came open. He stared at her, stared at his lawyer. It was exactly the same expression she had seen at his apartment when he had fumbled the question about Boyd's being asleep.

"I don't think we have to work out these details right now," Aiello said, putting a cautioning hand on Vinnie's arm. "I don't think it's necessary."

"I'd like to hear the rest of this," the chief said, nodding at Perci to go on.

"Vinnie, I don't think—"

"I wanna say what happened! I never killed him. I don't want anyone thinking I did." He glanced at Perci. "Okay, I forgot. We were in the back seat."

"She got out of the car on her side, which is at the center of the garage, opened the door to the back seat and got in. Is that what you're saying?"

"She got in the back with me, yeah. She didn't want to twist her head around, you know?"

"But when President Spatz pulled you out of the car, she must have been across from you, on the inside toward the wall. Why did she get over there if you were just talking?"

He lowered his face into his hands and said nothing.

"The whole world knows you're right-handed, Vinnie. Don't you always want the woman on your right?"

"That's enough," the lawyer said, putting his hand out, this time gripping Vinnie's arm. Vinnie twisted around, looked at the door Toni Costa had walked out of.

"We were just talking," he said. But his whole expression said he was lying. Tears filmed his eyes as he looked at Perci. The lawyer had put his hand against Vinnie's face. Vinnie pushed it away. In a near whisper, he said, "Okay, I was fucking her. But I never killed him. All I did was push him away."

The lawyer stood up. "There will be no more questions."

"He's not being coerced," the chief said.

"No more questions. You say nothing more," the lawyer told Vinnie. The implication was clear: you say anything more, you get another lawyer.

There were many questions Perci wanted to ask, but she knew that asking them could jeopardize the value of what they had already learned. She had hoped to have him admit that Mrs. Spatz had taken off the tight-fitting pants Perci knew she was wearing. And the boots.

She watched Vinnie walk ahead of his lawyer out of the room, head hanging. For the first time since she had met him, she felt sorry for him. It seemed to her that if he had been able to convince his lawyer that confessing to the argument with Spatz was in his best interest, he had to know he was innocent, and so did the lawyer. But maybe that's naïve.

When the outer door closed and the chief was settled in her chair behind the desk, the chief said to Webb, "You know Aiello. This some kind of a trick?"

"If so, Milano didn't play his role very well."

"How much of it do you believe?"

"Up to where they went into the garage. We knew everything except about the blanket. And he described the blanket pretty well."

"The one you found in the closet you weren't supposed to look into?"

"The maid opened the door. Everything in there was in plain sight."

"Well, that'll be the DA's problem. You think Milano's trying to protect the lady's reputation?"

Perci and Webb both laughed.

"Ok," the chief said. "So they were in the back seat having sex. What does it signify?"

"The management of the Highwayman," Perci said, flipping

through pages of her notebook, running her finger down a page, "said she was wearing tight-fitting pants and boots. You don't get those off very easily, especially in the back seat of a car. If they were doing what he said, she would have had to take her clothes off, boots first, then pants. That would have taken a long time, and it would have taken even longer to put them back on."

"If she did."

"It was eighteen degrees Fahrenheit. I can't picture her running bareass across that yard into the house."

"And the point?"

"She was in her car while the fight was going on. She must have been there when her husband was unconscious. If Vinnie ran when he said he did, she was alone. She could have smothered her husband. Would she just leave him in the garage and go to bed? If Vinnie did it, why didn't she call the police?"

"Maybe she was so busy pulling her pants on she didn't know what happened."

"But even if Vinnie had killed him, he would have been gone. Spatz would have been on the floor. Whether she thought him dead or unconscious, would she just have left him there to freeze?"

"Something to think about," the chief said. "But somebody'll have to convince me that the person who had a fight with Dr. Spatz, knocked him back against a workbench, is not the one who killed him. It would have taken only a few minutes. You saw tonight how headstrong Milano is. I'm surprised Raymond Aiello even came here with him. I'm sure Milano insisted. I think he's more worried about his reputation than anything else. But time will tell."

"I want to get a warrant tonight," Webb said, "to search the Spatz's garage, the workbench, the floor, the inside and outside of Mrs. Spatz's car. I want blood samples, pubic hair, fingerprints, anything we can find."

"Draw up the affidavit and the warrant. Let me see it. I'll make sure the judge is available." The chief looked at Perci. "You go find Janet. Let's hope we're not too late."

"If there's anything there, Janet will find it," Webb said.

"When do you want to question Mrs. Spatz? I'll have to arrange it through her brother."

"Not until after we've gone over the garage. The minute I read the warrant to her, she'll phone him, I'm sure."

"And he'll get on the phone to me," the chief said. "But that's no problem. When do you want to talk to Eleanor Tezzetti?"

"When this part is finished."

The chief's gaze lingered on Perci for a moment, but there was no hint of reprimand in her expression. Perci wanted to believe she had made a few points. With the chief it was hard to tell.

As Webb and Perci were leaving the office, the chief said, "In your opinion, would Spatz have expelled Milano if he had survived—considering Milano's prominence?"

"The very next morning," Webb said. "No question about it."

"I thought so."

The chief walked them to the outside door. "My impression, and tell me if I'm wrong, the athletic program isn't as important at Cleeve as people think, is it? I mean with the administration."

"Until Milano came, it was just something to keep the students happy. No big alumni demand."

"And when he's gone?"

"It'll go back to that. It's only a Division II school. Getting a player like Milano was a fluke."

Out in the corridor, turning her face from the ammonia smell, the chief said, "Tell Janet I'll be as generous as necessary with overtime. Stay there until you get everything."

She seemed pleased with the evening's work. She even gave Perci a smile.

It took Webb only a short time to write up the affidavit and the search warrant. After they had been approved by the chief, he and Perci drove to Judge Kaplan's house and got his signature.

"I didn't mean to interrupt you," Perci said. "It just came out."

"Glad you did," Webb said. "It gave Agatha a chance to see what you've got. She was impressed."

"You think so?"

"She may ask you to stay."

All the way to the Cleeve campus, Perci wondered whether that was the truth. And if the opportunity were there, would she want to stay?

CHAPTER FIFTEEN

Outside City Hall on a quiet street Vinnie was standing on frozen slush two parking meters down from where Mr. Aiello was talking with Uncle Dom. Aiello had tossed his briefcase onto the passenger seat of his new Seville and was smoothing a scarf under the fur collar of his overcoat, white spurts of vapor coming off his mouth that smelled, Vinnie remembered, of something the lawyer had been eating, onions maybe.

"That's all very well and good," Vinnie could hear him saying, "but unless he tells the truth, I won't represent him. Unless he follows my advice, I won't represent him. He made me look like a fool in there. Think I'd've let him go in there if I'd known he was a liar? I don't need this, Dominick. I don't need it."

"He's nervous," Dom said. "That's all it is. He's telling the truth."

"He was fucking her, Dominick. Why didn't he tell me that? I asked him. He lied."

"His fiancé was right there!"

"Bullshit. Cops aren't stupid, and neither am I. This is a murder investigation!"

"I'll talk to him."

"Have him in my office ten o'clock tomorrow morning."

"He'll be there."

"And tell him no more lies."

"I'll tell him."

"You just find out whether he killed that guy. Get the truth out of him."

"He never killed him, for Christ sakes, Raymond! Don't even think that. Please!"

"You find out. Find out what he did do. I want no more surprises. Ten o'clock in my office."

Vinnie nervously watched his uncle come up the sidewalk, madder than Vinnie had ever seen him.

Toni wouldn't talk to him. She had locked herself in the front seat of Dom's Cougar. When he had come out of the office, her face was frozen. She didn't look at him, didn't say anything all the way outside. He tried to open the car door for her and she knocked his hand away.

"You idiot!" Dom said, coming up to the car, standing with the door open, barely able to see over the roof, little curly hairs on his bald head glinting from the streetlight. "You be at the lawyer's office ten o'clock tomorrow morning I don't give a shit how you get there. You tell the truth tomorrow or I'm through with you. The truth! Everything! You hear me? You killed that guy?"

"No!"

"That the truth?"

"Come on. I wouldn't kill anybody."

"I don't understand you. What's the matter with you? You got the whole world out there and you just throw it away!"

"The door's locked over here," Vinnie said.

There were tears in Dom's eyes. He was looking at Vinnie like he didn't know him. Without another word Dom got into his car, started the motor and drove off, leaving Vinnie at the curb yelling.

"Hey! My car's at your house!"

The Cougar didn't stop. Vinnie went to the middle of the road and watched taillights grow smaller, watched brake lights flare, watched the Cougar turn onto Main Street and disappear.

He walked slowly to the corner and stood with his hands in his pockets near a light pole that was wrapped in spirals of green and red ribbon. There was a big Santa Claus face on top of the pole. He watched a dog down the street lift his leg and piss on a Santa Claus's tripod. A red and black boot kicked the dog into the street where it trotted off in that kitty-corner fading kind of way, going down along the parked cars, its tail lowered almost to the ground.

All the way to Dom's house on the cold back seat of a yellow cab, he thought about Boyd Crozier, how he couldn't tell them what Boyd did. After Boyd helped him like that, how could he rat on him? But I hold back anything, they know I'm lying.

Toni's car was still in Dom's driveway up near the garage. She was probably inside with Dom and Aunt Ginny at the kitchen table drinking coffee. He wished he could go in, wished he could talk to Toni. But there'd just be a big argument. What he really wished was he hadn't gone into that garage with Mrs. Spatz. Why'd he do it? He didn't even like her.

The vinyl seat covers crackled as he got into his car. Fucking seat was freezing. Steering wheel freezing. Battery almost dead. Engine groaned as it slowly turned over. When he backed onto the street, he leaned into the windshield, looked up to see beyond the electric candles in the darkened dining room windows, his breath frosting the icy glass. Nobody came to look out at him.

On the long ride to the college, he turned on the radio, but there was nothing he wanted to listen to. For the first time in his life he wished he was dead.

The minute Vinnie walked into his apartment, Boyd jumped off the sofa and said, reaching for his jacket, "Where you been?" He was in his black leather army boots. They looked dry, like they'd just come out of the closet.

"I was down at Toni's," Vinnie said. "What's that gasoline smell?"

"What took you so long?"

Why was Boyd so scared? "Things I had to do," Vinnie said, going into the bathroom. He couldn't say he'd been at the police station, not yet.

The bathroom had been cleaned, but Vinnie still smelled the vomit. When he came out, Boyd said,

"Don't take your jacket off. We gotta go over to Elwell."

"What for?"

"Ditch my car. Jesus, you told them about me."

"Who? I never told nobody."

"They look in the trunk of my car, I'm dead! Jesus, I never should've done it. I never should've gone over there."

"Nobody knows it was you."

"It was her killed him, Vinnie! Who else? You ran. He was on the floor. He was dead when I found him. Who else? Why you think she brought that lawyer?"

"I never told them about you. What you mean she killed him?"

"Did you? You smother him?"

"No!"

"Then who else? But they won't blame her. They find out I was there, who they gonna blame? They already asked about me. They search my car, they'll know I stuck him in there. Come on. All fucking day I been waiting for you. What took you so long?"

Vinnie went into the bedroom and got gloves out of his dresser. She killed him? Her husband? Why'd she do that? But who else was there? Jeez, I never thought of that.

And tomorrow. What'll I tell Aiello? That Florida cop'll make me look foolish again if I lie. But I can't tell them about Boyd. I'll just say I don't know what happened after I left. And I don't. That's the truth. I don't. I wasn't there.

"Come on, Vinnie. Let's go!"

"I'm coming."

It took them an hour to get to Elwell, which wasn't much more than two saw mills, a piggery, and a half dozen greenhouses where Boyd worked one summer before coming to Cleeve. It was on a riverbank under steep rocky hills. There were high banks of snow along the road, snow in the trees, a few lighted windows, nothing else in the darkness but occasional streetlights.

Boyd turned off the main road and drove more than a mile up a crooked road past big pine trees. He pulled over near a rotted barn with the roof caved in, got out of the car, white breath puffing out his mouth as he came back to Vinnie's window.

"Just in front of me," he said, smelling of some kind of booze he must have had in his car, "a road goes in the woods. Follow me in just a little ways, leave your car there, parking lights on so we can see coming back. I thought I had a flashlight, but it don't work."

"I'll wait here in the car."

"No. Walk in where I am. It's a big pit, a quarry. Nobody uses it."

Freezing air hurt Vinnie's eyes. "How come it's plowed out?"

"Fire department. They get water in there."

"You gonna ditch it in a quarry? It'll be frozen."

"Water's in another part."

"They'll find it."

"I'll say somebody stole it. Come on."

Vinnie wanted to drive away. Ditching evidence is a crime. They find out I'm up here, what'll I tell Dom? What the hell am I doing?

Vinnie put the Trans Am in gear and followed Boyd's car into the narrow roadway, snowy pine boughs brushing his fenders. He drove only a little way, then stopped and got out of the car.

Whoever plowed it had kept the blade up and the snow underfoot crunched like dry popcorn as Vinnie walked out of the meager illumination of his parking lights and followed the taillights of Boyd's car, watching the outline of Boyd's head in the rectangle of his rear window, Boyd's headlights shining on big mounds of snow-covered granite boulders.

The air around him was like a block of ice, his face pressed into it—a stinging pain in his nose, cheeks burning raw, ears freezing, every breath a sword in the chest. Something fell off a tree in the darkness of the woods, startled him.

Okay, I owe him. He stuck his neck out for me. I'll do this, and he can't say I never tried to help him. But this is it. I ain't sticking my neck out anymore. If they find out, they find out. I can't help it. I'll say I don't know anything because I don't. How do I know what he did?

The red taillights went out of sight a hundred yards into the quarry, but Vinnie could see the flare of headlights behind a screen of trees. Then the lights went out and Vinnie could see nothing. He was surrounded by silence, could hear only his feet crunching on the snow. He lost his footing, fell, banged his hand on a rock. He took the glove off and sucked his knuckles.

"Put a light on!" he yelled, angry at Boyd, angry at himself, goddamn fool coming into a place like this!

Jamming the gloved hand back into his jacket pocket, he looked back. Couldn't see his parking lights. He could barely make out white spaces ahead of him. Then he saw Boyd in a little bulge of light behind his car with the trunk open. He watched him take out a red gallon can of gasoline, set the can in the snow, then drop to his knees and fit a screw driver into one of the slotted screws holding the license plate.

"What you got the gas for?" Vinnie said, even though he knew.

"Burn out the trunk. The gas tank will go up. The whole fucking car will go. They'll find it, but they won't be able to prove anything. I'll say it was stolen."

"So why take off the plates?"

"Jesus, I forgot!" Boyd said. It took him a while to get the plate off. He handed it to Vinnie. "Forgot the front one. And I'm right up near the edge."

He went around Vinnie to the driver's door, reached in and snapped on the headlights. He was breathing hard, sheets of vapor coming off his mouth, big dark spaces beyond him, outline of trees and snowy boulders in the distance.

"Stand here," he said. "Keep the car from sliding."

Vinnie wedged the heel of his hand against the rear window frame. He couldn't get a firm footing. Snow was like ice under his boots. If the car started sliding, he wouldn't be able to hold it.

But it didn't slide. Boyd got the front plate off, crawled around the fender and handed the plate to Vinnie.

They both walked to the back of the car. When Boyd raised the lid of the trunk, the car started sliding.

"Hold it!" Boyd yelled. He reached for the bumper, slipped, fell against the car and it slid forward, jounced as the underside banging the edge.

"I can't hold it!"

Vinnie got his hands under the bumper; but, like Boyd, his feet slipped and the car kept moving. Vinnie fell down. The rear end flew into the air. A stream of sparks burned under the car as it slid into the pit. They heard it crash. There was a flare of light, then everything went black and they could see nothing.

"Son of a bitch!" Boyd yelled. "How can I get down there?"

"You can't," Vinnie said. "Come on, let's get out of here."

"I gotta burn it!"

It was then they heard voices, a male and a female out on the road.

"What the hell was that?"

The female voice said, "Come on, Duane, let's get out of here."

Vinnie heard car doors slam, a car engine turn over, wheels spin, then car sounds moving off in the distance.

"They saw my car!" he said.

"I gotta climb down there!"

"They saw my car! They'll go to the cops! Come on!"

Vinnie was already moving along the wheel track, hands in front of him like a blind man.

Boyd yelled, "I gotta burn my car, Vinnie!"

Vinnie kept groping along the track until he could see his parking lights. Then he ran. He got to his car, started the engine, put on his headlights, drove in to where his headlights shined on Boyd crouched at the edge of the pit.

Vinnie pushed his door open and yelled, "Come on, for Christ sakes, Boyd!"

Boyd got up, looked down at the gasoline can, then at Vinnie's headlights, then down into the pit.

"Come on!" Vinnie yelled, revving the engine. He suddenly realized he had Boyd's license plates on his lap. He threw them on the back seat. Boyd slowly walked to Vinnie's car and got in, putting the can of gasoline on the floor between his feet.

"First thing tomorrow morning, we come back. I can't just leave it there."

"Not in the morning," Vinnie said.

"You got to! They'll find out it's my car. They'll examine it, find out I put him in it. Jesus, Vinnie. I helped you."

"I gotta go someplace," Vinnie said.

"Then let me take your car."

"I can't. I need it."

Vinnie said nothing more until they were back on the main road heading toward the college. Then he told Boyd he had an appointment in the morning with his lawyer. He told him what had happened at the police station.

"You went to the cops? You talked to the cops?"

"I had to! My uncle . . . Jesus, Boyd, what could I do?"

"You talked to the cops?"

"I didn't say anything about you."

All the way back to the apartment Boyd sat next to him like a statue.

Upstairs, as he was unlocking the door, Vinnie said, "I never told them about you, Boyd."

"Fuck you."

"I never said anything about you!"

Boyd walked across the room into the bathroom and slammed the door.

CHAPTER SIXTEEN

As Webb pulled into the Spatz's driveway he surprised Perci by asking her to stick the flasher on the roof and tap the siren. Although there were cars blocking the driveway, Perci didn't think the situation called for fanfare.

"A little cheering up for the grieving widow?"

"Just plain democratic hostility," Webb said. "If I announce myself in Swill Village, I announce myself here."

Getting out of the car, Perci glanced down the drive at the police van where Janet Lucia was waiting, unhappy because she had had to break a date to come out here. The campus security jeep was with the van. Evidently the man in the guard booth had sent out an alert.

A tall woman came to the door. She glanced disparagingly at Perci, smiled at Webb.

"I remember you," Perci said.

"And you," the woman said. "You're Persis something. I believe it's Greek."

Laughing because she couldn't come up with a rejoinder, Perci walked past the woman into the hallway. This is the woman who, a few weeks ago, told Edison about Perci's involvement in the Umber investigation, prompting Edison to talk the chief into dragging her off the investigation.

It seemed odd to Perci that this woman—the television reporter, Lorraine Lord—had come to the back door, greeting them the way a member of the family would.

"Guess I'm at the right place at the right time," Lorraine said, grinning at Webb, ignoring Perci. She was holding a pink drink in pale red-tipped fingers. There were more lines in her face than Perci had noticed before and a faint look of gray near the roots of her hair, a tall woman with dark eyes and strong Mediterranean features.

It was possible, Perci thought, that she had been alerted, but more likely she was just out snooping for a story.

About ten people stood in small clusters in the great room. There was no sign of Senator Edison or Haskell Paine. Claire Spatz, this time in a skirt and blouse, was standing near a window holding a glass. She appeared to be sober.

Webb said a few words to her and followed her into another room where Perci imagined he read the warrant and told her he'd list all items seized and leave her a copy of the list. Perci had never done it, but she believed that was how it worked. When they came back, Claire went to a decanter and reloaded her drink while Webb, in a loud voice, asked whoever had cars blocking the driveway to please move them.

He touched Perci's arm, and they went together out the back door, followed by Lorraine Lord. They couldn't prevent her getting a story, but they could keep her out of the garage. At least she hadn't brought a camera crew.

"Mind telling me what's going on?"

"Police work," Webb told her.

"Why clear the driveway?"

Webb walked away from the question, leading Perci around the house to the main entrance. In brutal cold, vapor puffing from their mouths, they waited more than ten minutes for someone to come out and move a car.

"Screw this," Webb said. He strode down the driveway to the van. Perci could see him in the jump seat when Janet pushed the 4WD through a snowbank, crossed the snow-covered lawn, and parked in front of the garage door, completely blocking it.

"I thought Dr. Spatz didn't use his car," Lorraine Lord said.

Perci pretended not to hear her. She crawled over the seat into the garage behind Webb. Lorraine started to follow her. Perci turned.

"Off limits," she said, not sure she'd be obeyed, wondering how she'd handle it if she wasn't. Damned if she'd call Webb.

But Lorraine made the face of the humiliated, then backed out and closed the door. And now she's really my enemy, Perci thought.

Webb waited until Janet got her gear out of the van, then rolled the garage door down.

"How about that window?" Perci said, pointing across the roof of Claire's Cadillac.

"She's in high heels and no boots. I doubt she'd walk in there."

"She wants the big story," Perci said. "Wet feet won't stop her."

"Then go stand in front of it."

Janet's portable lights threw big shadows across the garage as Perci went around front of Claire's Cadillac and stood on an upturned bucket and wedged her rump against the cold windowsill just as Lorraine Lord came up outside and rapped on the glass. When Perci didn't budge, she went away yelling something Perci couldn't make out. Perci sat there hugging herself against the cold, fingers gripping the rough fabric of her jacket, shivering for a half hour before Janet said she had something.

"That Cadillac's been detailed," Janet said.

"Detailed?" Perci asked.

"That means thoroughly cleaned," Janet said. "And I don't expect to find much on it, but I'll look."

From her perch at the window, Perci saw Janet point at the

corner of the workbench, then at the floor. "And there are five spots of blood leading to the door, probably off footsteps." She led Webb toward the door, squirting luminol on the cement. "Here, here, here, here, and here."

"Sure that's blood?" The spots were very small and could easily have been overlooked by anyone coming into the garage not looking for them.

"Presumptively. And back here," she said, returning to the bench, "is what caused the bleeding," pointing to a smudge on the workbench. "I'd guess that's the source of the iron filings Charlie talked about. Maybe Spatz fell against the bench, maybe hit his head."

"Someone with blood on his shoes went out that door?"

"Or went as far as those marks near the door. I'd say that's where the oil and grime we found on Spatz's suit came from. I'd guess he fell—maybe staggered up there and collapsed. Have to take a closer look in daytime. And that last print up there is so faint, there's no point looking outside."

"They're not drips?"

"Wrong pattern. And it repeats. It was printed," Janet said.

"Maybe if we keep quiet about this we can check some shoes."

"Probably won't help unless the perp took them off outside and hasn't worn them since."

Perci reached down to try the door of the Cadillac, then remembered she shouldn't touch it. She asked Webb,

"If you open the back door of one of these, does an inside light come on?"

"A Cadillac? Yes."

"But that wouldn't give much light, would it."

"Let's find out."

He got Claire's keys out of his pocket, unlocked the Cadillac, and opened the back door. Janet shut off her lights. After giving their eyes time to adjust, they all agreed they'd be able to see a man lying where Spatz presumably had fallen.

"While we're at it, let's take a look in the trunk," Webb said.

They found only a few sheets of a newspaper dated July 7, a plastic bottle of sun blocker, and a yellow beach sandal with a broken strap. Janet lifted the paper, found nothing under it.

"Looks like it's been there a while," Janet said. "I don't think the body was lugged away in this. But don't touch anything. I'll see what I can find."

"Want me to do the sketches?" Webb asked.

Janet told him where to find the tape and the sketch pads.

"Photographs?"

"I'll do those," Janet said.

Perci asked Janet, "Did Charlie say how long Spatz would have been knocked out?"

"Said there's no way of telling. Could've been a few minutes, could've been longer."

"A half hour?"

"You'd have to ask Charlie."

After Janet had placed evidence in paper bags and plastic bags and stored them in the van, she took some pictures. Perci left the window to help Webb with the tape measure and watch him make sketches.

"Every inch of this car has been scrubbed clean except maybe the undercarriage. Unless you want me to. . . ."

"Might be worth it," Webb said. "Get everything you can."

"I'll look in the vac bag back at the hall, but I don't expect to find much. Somebody really tried hard to make this factory-fresh."

They were there more than two hours, Perci most of the time just standing around freezing. When Janet was finished and Webb had closed the garage door, Perci crawled through the van wondering what had become of Lorraine Lord. Probably gone home, like everyone else: all the guest cars were gone from the driveway.

When Webb went to the back door to leave some papers with Claire Spatz, Perci thought she heard Lorraine Lord's voice coming from inside the house. Did she enjoy some special kind of relationship with the Spatz family? With Claire? Maybe with Claire's brother, the senator?

Something to think about.

Standing in the driveway outside the main entrance, Perci satisfied herself that a plume of exhaust could easily be seen coming out of the garage on Claire's side.

"Was Lorraine Lord in there?" she asked Webb, walking down the driveway with him. "Thought I heard her voice."

"She let me in," Webb said.

"What member of the family is she a friend of?"

"Beats me."

"What'd Claire say?"

"Not a damn thing."

"Is that natural? Wouldn't she wonder why we were in the garage?"

"Maybe she doesn't have to."

As they drove down country roads back toward the city, Webb said, "I suppose we know that someone hovered near the body long enough to get blood on a shoe. And those blood spots weren't from someone running. A long-legged athlete like Milano would have sprinted out of that garage in far fewer steps than ten."

"It was only on one shoe?"

"Right."

"Mrs. Spatz?"

"Maybe. Or maybe Milano was just backing away."

"You believe he panicked and ran?"

"I'm trying not to believe anything. We don't know enough."

They were on city streets when Perci said, "There's another car I want to look at."

"Crozier's?"

"You thought of that?"

"I checked his tag number against that list the gateman gave you."

"So did I," Perci said. "And I guess you know he keeps his car near the gym. He could have left the campus unnoticed and come back to the apartment."

"You say he's muscular?"

"Enough to hang a body on a tree, I'm sure."

"So are a lot of people. Don't lock anything like that in your head. We've got a long road ahead of us. Make a note to check when the senator got home. He lives in one of those security buildings with a parking garage in the basement. Maybe he was logged in."

When Webb turned onto her street and pulled up along a snowbank across from her building, she said,

"Wanna come up for coffee?"

"No thanks. It's getting late."

She was feeling a little disheartened as she walked across the street and down the shoveled path to the back door of her building. She didn't glance back. She believed he was waiting before driving off, playing the protector, making sure she didn't get waylaid up there on the dark walk. It was like in her childhood when Mr. Piperopoulos would tarry behind her, looking after her.

Upstairs making coffee she remembered the woman taking her aside in the nurse's office at school and telling her that Mr. Piperopoulos had committed suicide and that she'd have to go live with a family of strangers. She went into the other room and turned a lot of lights on and pushed the thermostat up and glanced around the apartment. Everything seemed so uninspiring—the half empty box of Grape Nuts she had left on top of the refrigerator, an empty shopping bag hanging from the worn knob of the bathroom door. Nothing whatever in this place meant anything to her.

She was thinking about going into the bedroom and getting out a photo album when the doorbell rang.

She couldn't imagine who would be calling on her. She doubted it was Webb. But who else even knew where she lived?

Without putting shoes on, she went hesitantly down the cold stairway, waited a few seconds, then pulled the door open.

Chapter Seventeen

The man on the icy steps looking up at her was Tennyson Smith, editor of the student newspaper. He had a pale, thin face. Tufts of blond hair stuck out from under the yellow toque he had pulled over his ears. Worried blue eyes stared at her through tinted glasses.

"I surprised you?"

"What are you doing here?"

"Freezing."

"Oh, I'm sorry. Come in."

Even in that cold air she got a heavy whiff of cologne as he moved past her. She closed the door and urged him up the stairs ahead of her.

She had to wait at the small landing outside her door while he unbuckled his overshoes and set them neatly at the edge of the landing.

"Ah, heat," he said, pulling off his hat as he came into her living room, wiping condensation off his glasses as he stared at the picture of the egret. "I swear, Perci, it's not always this cold up here. I think the gods of the north are showing off for you." He looked around as though for a mirror, running a gloved hand over his blond hair.

"Well, I'll forgive them if they stop," she said, watching him pull off his gloves, one finger at a time, and tuck them into the pocket of his gray gabardine.

"Just drape it over the chair," she told him.

She watched him hold the coat by the shoulders, give it a snap, then fold it and lay it carefully over the back of a chair she had bought at a Salvation Army store, neatly folding the scarf before setting it on the coat.

While watching this ritual, Perci felt grateful to him. Whatever reason he had for coming here, he had succeeded in lifting her out of the doldrums she had allowed herself to fall into. He had never been here before. He had had to go out of his way to find her. This wasn't a casual visit.

"Coffee?"

"I'd love it," he said. "Black, if you don't mind."

There was just enough effeminacy in his voice to make a signal, not enough to provoke ridicule. Weeks ago, during her first interview with him, he had said he was gay—not to apologize but to help explain his attitude toward the question of sex on campus.

"So what brings you here?" she said, setting a cup and saucer in front of him, going around the table to sit opposite him.

His hand trembled as he held the cup to his mouth, his palm under it like a small tray. His upper lip retreated from the hot liquid. Maybe stalling for time, he set the cup down, took off his glasses, wiped them on his shirt. He was very nervous.

"You want a tissue?"

"No, I'm fine." He put his glasses back on. "It's just, well, I know you were on campus today asking about Alicia."

"Please! Don't put that in a story. It would cause me a problem."

"Oh, I know," he said, holding both hands up in denial. "I remember last time. But this is not for a story. You asked me why I stopped writing about Alicia." He paused over the name, stared worriedly at something across the room. It was unusual for him to be this nervous.

"I noticed," Perci said, "after that editorial about me, you

147

didn't mention her again. In the next two issues there were only those letters from students and that one article by Wanda what's-her-name."

"Because I'm a coward," he said, and let the word hang out there to gather scorn.

"In what way?"

He took a deep breath, took a sip of coffee. "My parents are retired. They don't have much money. Every discretionary cent pays my way here. I would never do anything to hurt them. What happened. . . . Well, I learned something I couldn't print. It would have got me expelled. But because my head was exploding with it, I couldn't write anything except some unctuous drivel, and I refused to do that. As you know, Alicia was a very dear friend. I've known her practically my whole life. I think I'm the only person she ever really talked to. So when that damned fanatic went to that clinic and . . ."

Tears came into his eyes. He again took his glasses off. Perci got a box of tissues from her bedroom. She handed it to him and watched him dab at his eyes.

He said, "It was Senator Edison who made you stop investigating Alicia's death, wasn't it."

"If you won't quote me," Perci said.

"He pretended he was protecting the college, but that's not the reason. He was afraid you'd find out about him and Alicia."

That was a jolt. "Him and Alicia?"

"Yes. Do you know the Mayfair Lodge out off I-95?"

"I've heard of it."

"The night manager, more or less, is . . . Well, one of us, sort of. None of us likes him. In the company of gays he's an obvious queen, but when he's with straights he ridicules us. He's always confiding things in me like we're friends. But I find him disgusting. Anyway, I was there with some friends the day after Alicia died. He came running up to me, practically pushing into my face a copy of the Herald that had Alicia's picture in it. He said she was the girl he had seen with Edison struggling out in the back parking lot."

"Struggling?"

"Well, maybe you don't know what the back lot is out there. People who want the lounge or the restaurant park their cars in the front lot, which is floodlit. People who just want bedrooms use the back lot, unmarked, more or less an empty field, very dimly lit. Some of those rooms rent on an hourly basis."

"I've heard," Perci said. "But what do you mean 'struggling?' "

"He wanted her to come inside, but she chickened out. Albert was standing right there inside the door. He saw and heard everything."

"And he's sure it was Alicia?"

"He said he'd swear to it."

"In court?"

"Oh, no. No, no. They'd fire him. If he ever gave out names . . . No, he'd never do that."

"And he's sure it was Edison?"

"He knows Edison very well."

"And this was when?"

"About a month ago. A week or so before Alicia died. Albert didn't really think much about it until he saw that story in the paper."

Is this why Spatz was so concerned about Alicia's pregnancy? She asked, "Did she ever talk to you about Edison?"

"A lot. He made her nervous, looking at her all the time in his office, but I never knew she went out with him. She was very naïve. She wanted to please everyone. She'd let just about anyone push her around. She was one of those people raised in such a strict way she had no guidelines for living a normal life. When she crossed the narrow boundaries she was raised by, she was like in outer space."

"Did Vinnie Milano push her around?"

"I don't think so. She liked him. But his friend might . . . Crozier. I think you know him. She was just the kind a man like him would want."

"What do you mean? He's supposed to be an aggressive stud."

"That's what he wants people to think," Tennyson said. "But he's anything but. He's as immature as she was. Alicia made no demands on him."

"But they went together?"

"Nothing sexual, from what she said. She thought he was strange, but I guess their friendship gave her some sense of protection. I don't know. It was complicated. She was complicated. I think the people she called her parents were really her grandparents. There was another daughter, supposedly Alicia's sister, who died in her early teens. My parents said they had heard gossip . . . I don't know."

"You think the senator played father to her?"

"I think she wanted him to. On the surface he played that role, I guess. But his real aim was to seduce her."

Perci remembered a girl in Gainesville who had come under the wing of a sociology professor. She had wanted affection from an older man. He had wanted sex. "I know the situation," she said. "This Albert. He's the manager?"

"Night manager. Also a pimp. He says Edison goes there a lot. You won't ask me to say this in court, will you?"

"It wouldn't have any value in court. It's hearsay. But why didn't you tell me this before?"

"I suppose I didn't want to get involved."

"And now you do?"

"It's all going to come out, isn't it? I mean eventually? If I didn't come forward with this, I'd hate myself more than I do now. Alicia was my friend."

"Why do you think this will come out?"

The question scared him, but he said, "Everybody seems to think there's a connection between Alicia's death and what happened to Spatz. I think there has to be."

"Why?"

"I don't know. It's just that Spatz went out of his way to hurt Alicia. He was more involved than he should have been. There has to be a reason."

He had become so nervous she decided to pull back. "Can you tell me Albert's last name?"

"He calls himself Albert Stewart, but he's really Albert Steinmetz, and he may have a police record. But, God, don't let anyone know you got this from me."

"I won't. But you did want me to know about it. Who is it you want punished? Edison?"

"I just want . . . I don't know. If he made Alicia pregnant, I want the whole world to know it."

After pondering the table a few seconds, he got up, his hands trembling as he pushed back his glasses. She believed he had more to say, but she didn't want to press him. He had obviously gone through a lot of anguish just to come here.

"I understand that Spatz visited Alicia's parents," Perci said. "Did you know that?"

He was near the door, putting his coat on. "She told me."

"Did she tell anyone else?"

"I don't know. She might have."

"Boyd Crozier or Vinnie Milano?"

"Maybe."

A few minutes after Tennyson was gone, Perci went to her phone and punched in Webb's number.

"I need a favor."

"Shoot."

"Albert Stewart, night manager at the Mayfair Lodge? We

have anything on him?"

"Why?"

She told him everything Tennyson had told her.

"And he has a couple of other aliases," Webb said. "We've never been able to put him away. What you got in mind? You want to go out there?"

"Is it okay?"

"Just don't do anything foolish."

"Right, dad."

Foolish or not, she put some clothes on, went down to her car, and headed west toward the interstate. She had never been to the Mayfair. She had no idea why she was going there. Maybe just to look at the place, look at Albert Steinmetz. Maybe just to get out of her apartment.

CHAPTER EIGHTEEN

A doorman named Freeman, in a black hat and bright red coat, took Haskell Paine's keys and handed them to a kid who would take the Lincoln to the reserved spaces at the end of the parking lot, hopefully without breaking a fender. Freeman then took four long strides under the tasseled canopy and opened the glass door, smiling at Haskell who coughed into his gloved fist and walked past him into the faintly whiskeyed air of the Mayfair Lodge.

At the coatroom, working gloves off long fingers, pretending not to notice the chubby bosom of the girl who wanted to take his coat, he said, as though to the room, not looking at the girl, that he wanted to see Albert Stewart.

"I'll be at that small table behind the Boston ferns over there," he said, pointing.

"I can't leave the booth, sir."

"Just get him to my table, honey."

He wandered into the lounge. Moving through fragrances of whiskey and cologne past bald heads and naked shoulders to a table from which, without being conspicuous, he could watch what everyone was doing.

He had hardly fitted a cigarette to his lips when he saw Albert Stewart striding across the dance floor toward him, smiling at every face that happened to be turned his way—a tall, thin man with wavy blond hair and nearly colorless blue eyes. Haskell watched Stewart slide into a chair opposite him showing yellowed teeth in a simpering smile.

"Because you come here only to see me, I darted right over," he said, as though expecting a reward.

Haskell picked something off his tongue. Dragging on his cigarette, he studied the pale eyes a few seconds, wondering whether he would ever pull the string on this pimp and have him jailed.

Not while he can hurt the senator.

Savoring the smell and taste of his cigarette, he glanced up at the clarinetist on the platform who had just finished a solo of "Do You Know What It Means To Miss New Orleans?" and was bowing to a strong applause.

"Busy, busy, busy," Albert Stewart said. "An endless night of whimpering bitches. But I love it."

Haskell wasn't interested. "A few weeks ago, on a Tuesday night around this time, you were standing inside the back door watching a friend of mine having a discussion with a young woman."

"I was?" smiling as though amused at being caught in an indiscretion.

"And when my friend came into the lounge, you were sitting at the bar with a college student named Boyd Crozier."

"And which friend is that. You have so many."

"Don't get cute. You know who I mean. After we saw the girl's picture in the newspaper, you and I sat here discussing the word silence. We had a long talk about the word silence."

"Ah, that friend. Yes, I remember."

"This Crozier," Haskell went on. "A friend of yours?"

"Describe him. I'm not sure . . ."

"Save the crap, Steinmetz."

The smile vanished. The ivory holder almost fell to the table. "All right. I know the guy."

"What were you talking about?"

"That was a long time ago."

"You were breathing into his face. It was business. You weren't just sucking up to a customer."

Albert Stewart spent a few thoughtful moments removing the cigarette from the holder, mashing the butt into an ashtray, running a stained forefinger down the lean end of the yellowed ivory. "He sometimes provides for me."

"Girls?"

"Entertainers is a nicer word."

"And that's what you were talking about, these 'entertainers?' "

"That's all we ever talk about. I don't socialize with him."

That drew a smirk. "He would know my friend by sight. He would also know the girl. I want to know whether he saw the girl."

"Didn't we talk about this last time? Didn't I say he never saw the girl—at least, he didn't mention her?"

"How long had he been here?"

"That evening? Probably not long. He comes in for a beer. I spot him. We make our arrangements. He doesn't hang around."

"You've seen the publicity about the murder at the college? You know they're trying to link it to what happened to that girl. So far this place hasn't been dragged into the scandal. But it could be."

"Look, I don't know anything. I'm not going to say anything. Why would I?"

"I don't know why you do things. But there's speculation that Crozier may have had something to do with the murder. He may be questioned. He may throw names around."

"He'll never get a name out of me. I promise you that."

"The girls he sends over here. Where's he get them?"

"I suppose at the college. I don't ask."

"Who pays them?"

"He does."

"And the johns pay you?"

"Look, they won't say anything. Nobody can say anything without incriminating himself. Including Crozier."

"How many people know that Crozier does this?"

"I don't know. Why would he tell anyone? I certainly haven't. Why would I risk losing a supplier who's not a professional? You have any idea the trouble I could have from real pimps? This is business. Why would I do anything to hurt it?"

"How'd you get connected with Crozier?"

"Kids at the college. I don't know. He came to see me."

Haskell dragged on his cigarette, looked around. "That night, before you sat with him at the bar, when you were out back watching my friend, where was Crozier?"

"I don't know. He was at the bar when I came back in. I didn't see him before that."

"How long had you been out back?"

"Just a few minutes."

"What made you go out there?"

"I don't know. Sometimes I walk out there just to get away from the noise."

"And you just happened to see my friend and the girl? Crozier didn't tell you they were there? Crozier didn't follow them here?"

"I don't know whether he followed them. But I didn't go out there for him. I'm the manager here! What the hell would I—"

"He didn't tell you the girl was out there?"

"He didn't tell me anything!"

"Keep your voice down."

"Was she his girlfriend? I always figured he was gay. He isn't gay?"

"I have no idea." Haskell busied himself crushing out his cigarette, making sure every burning speck was extinguished. "Until now, the police have not bothered to shut you down, but don't think you're immune to prosecution. If there's a scandal, you'll go to jail. I'll see to it."

"Why are you scaring me? I haven't talked. I never talk!"

Haskell stood up. "We haven't had this conversation."

"Yeah, right," Albert Stewart said, looking up. "I don't even know who you are."

Without a nod or a flick of the hand, Haskell left the table. He got his coat and put nothing in the little dish on the counter.

"Good night, sir," the girl said, serenading his departure.

Outside, gloved hands deep in his pockets, coughing against the pain of breathing freezing air, he waited for the boy to bring his car, wondering whether Stewart had told the truth. Impossible to tell. The reason he gave for Crozier's being here was plausible enough. But was it the truth?

Crozier, whatever his dealings with Stewart, could still have followed his girlfriend out here. And Stewart could have gone to the back entrance because Crozier had asked him to see for himself who Edison was with. But would Stewart do that? Why would he care?

So Boyd Crozier's a pimp as well as a parasite. Can I use it?

When the kid brought his car up, Haskell walked around it checking the fenders, then dropped a single into the outstretched hand. It wasn't a tip. It was protection in case he ever came back.

He had put on his seat belt and was adjusting the heater when he noticed a face in the windshield of an incoming MG.

Perci Piper! What the hell is she doing here?

She recognized him! Stared right into his eyes! In the mirror he saw her car go to the end of the lot and pull into a parking space. He banged his fist on the steering wheel, pain invading the bone. Damn, damn, damn!

He wanted to wait, wanted to follow her inside, but maybe she hadn't recognized him. Can't give her a second chance.

Before she could get out of her car, he drove to the opposite end of the lot and burned rubber getting onto the highway.

She has to know something! Why would she come to the Mayfair unless she knows something!

Before Perci could get out of her car, she knew that the damage had been done. No question it was Haskell Paine. No question he had recognized her. No question he would run to Senator Edison. And, if Tennyson Smith's story was true, Edison would be scared she was checking on him. Not in a million years would he think she had come here just to get a drink.

She stood behind her car on a slippery ridge of ice watching the rear lights of the Lincoln move down the highway. If she had arrived five minutes later, he would never have known she was here. If wishes were horses. . . .

Maybe she shouldn't go in. But the damage was done. At least she could get a look at Albert Steinmetz. He wouldn't know her, would have no idea why she was here.

She'd love to flash the badge, sit him down, drive questions into him, scare hell out of him. But she didn't have enough leverage to get anything from him but a sneer. He wouldn't talk. And, if he knew people in high places. . . .

So be wise. Take Webb's advice. Don't do anything foolish.

She waited for the doorman to open the door, waited a few seconds inside, welcoming the heat, wondering whether she could put a drink on Webb's expense sheet. She smiled, thinking what his reaction would be.

She was surprised to hear Dixieland coming from the lounge. She'd never heard it outside the South. Most places up here, maybe not this upscale, had nothing but a man or woman on a piano. Or the usual amplified longhairs banging guitars.

She took off her jacket and laid it across the counter, telling herself she had no reason to apologize. Okay, so it isn't mink.

"Could you point out Albert Stewart?" she said when the girl handed her a numbered disk.

The girl gave her a funny look. "I can't leave the booth, but I'm sure he's in there. Tall and blond, a white suit, walks around the tables, sits at the bar. He's really not hard to spot."

"Thanks."

She found an empty stool half way down the bar. Dark green padding felt good under her forearms.

"Ice water," she told the bartender, a dark girl with shiny black eyes and curly bangs and a stain on her shirt. "And squirt some grenadine into it."

"That's it?"

"I'm a recovering alcoholic. I'm just here for the atmosphere. Which one's Albert Stewart?"

"Don't do it, honey," the girl said, giving her a serious, big-sister look.

"Don't do what?"

The girl studied her a few seconds, shrugged, went down to get the ice water.

When she came back, dropping grenadine onto the little blocks of ice, she glanced out across the lounge. "The tall one there by the bandstand."

"Don't do what?" Perci said.

"Just talking to myself," the girl said, sadness in her eyes as she walked away.

It was a long twenty minutes before Perci decided there was no point staying here. She could learn nothing. She shouldn't have come. She had probably accomplished nothing more than to further irritate Senator Edison.

At an all-night filling station a few blocks from her apartment, she picked up a novel that had a half-naked Tarzan on the cover breathing into the cleavage of a fainting girl. After shower-

CHAPTER NINETEEN

Freezing air sliced in from the crack at the bottom of the bedroom window as Boyd Crozier lay in the darkness sucking spit off the polyester border of the woolen blanket he had put on top of his other blanket but still hadn't been able to sleep it was so fucking cold.

Vinnie over there in the shadows snoring, worried about nothing, the son of a bitch running to a lawyer, throws it all into their hands like he does everything else, let them do it, tell them everything, worry about nothing. And every one of them hates me. If Vinnie didn't do it and I was over there, I must've done it, right? It's what they want, chance they been looking for. Get rid of me finally, forever.

Well, up yours, Milano. I burn the car they can't prove a thing no matter what you tell them. Maybe I never went over there. Maybe it was you took my car.

He sat up and swung his legs over the side of the bed. He had to grope across the darkened room to the door. He put the bathroom light on and left both doors open and went back to the bedroom and got his jeans and sweatshirt off the chair. After rummaging through a pile of laundry to find an old pair of Nikes and four dirty socks, he took his clothes into the bathroom, closed the door and got dressed.

Last night's footprints would still be out there in the snow. He'd tromp all over them with his sneakers. Tonight he'd burn the army boots and the sneakers in the furnace at the greenhouse down back of the campus, job he had the winter before he got Mr. Armstead to pay his way here, goddamn queen everybody praised at the funeral like he was some kind of saint, rich old bastard leaving me two years I gotta hustle for every penny just to stay alive.

With the bedroom barely lighted by the open doorway he lifted Vinnie's pants off the closet doorknob. Took a ten, took a five, put the wallet back. Couple of times a month he got money like that, and Vinnie never knew it, just ran to his uncle for more. He lifted Vinnie's keys off the dresser and walked out of the apartment.

Air stung his nostrils as he stepped on frozen boards that crackled when he went down the wooden stairs. A high moon in misty clouds illuminated the snowy field across the parking lot, dark naked trees beyond it like a wall. Nothing moving on the empty road down to the streetlight on the corner. Everything around him quiet as he crunched over dry snow toward Vinnie's car, streams of vapor puffing off his mouth.

He couldn't unlock the door. Had to hold the flame of a cigarette lighter against the lock, stick the key in, then heat the key. Damned lighter almost out of fuel. Should've bought a new one. Never trace it back to him: he didn't smoke, why would he have a lighter?

He finally got the door open. Seat was frozen stiff. He pumped the gas pedal, turned the ignition. Only a groan, engine barely turning over. He put the headlights on, waited a few seconds, tried again . . . nothing . . . nothing. On the fourth try it caught. It died, caught again like on two cylinders. He cautiously fed gas and gradually the engine picked up.

Sun would be up by the time he reached Elwell. There'd be nobody around. He'd torch the car and get out of there before anyone saw him. Then all the cops in the state couldn't prove anything.

What you talking about? Me? I wasn't there! Milano said I did that? You crazy? I came straight home from the Highwayman and went to bed. No, I didn't see him. He wasn't there. How the hell do I know where he was? I don't know what you're talking about.

What they gonna prove?

He was humming this to himself as he drove down the highway, ears hanging on new country, hands banging the steering wheel, heater throwing warm air at him, gasoline can tucked under his legs.

Get it done, get back, be asleep when he wakes up, tell the bonehead nothing. Probably wonder how come the car starts so good. If there's a station on the way back, replace the gas. What's he gonna know?

And it went just like he wanted until he turned onto the road that led up the hill to the quarry. He saw the headlights flash in his mirror. Figured it was some guy probably going to work.

Then rooftop rollers started flashing.

Damn!

Had to pull over.

"Some problem, officer?" he said, rolling the window down, cold air bruising his face.

"Your license and registration," the cop said, flashlight shining into Boyd's eyes.

When he squirmed around to get his wallet, his foot knocked over the gasoline can. The cop shined the light down, had to see it. Boyd reached for the glove compartment and his foot hit the can, making a dull, tinny sound. Cop had to know what it was. The way he held the flashlight, Boyd couldn't see his face, just the shiny badge on black leather. He could smell the leather.

"Was I speeding or something?"

"This Vincent Milano," the cop said, reading the registration, "He's a friend of yours?" sour breath puffing into Boyd's face.

"Yeah, he let me borrow it."

"Any reason you're here in Elwell this early in the morning?"

"Just riding around. I sometimes do that when I can't sleep."

"In somebody else's car? You don't have a car?"

The cop was shining the light on the back seat, looking hard at something back there. He put the light in his left hand, holding it with thumb and forefinger so that it shined on his palm. Then he got out a pen and wrote something under it on his skin.

"Wait right here," he said, and went back to the cruiser.

Boyd turned on the dome light and squirmed around to see what the cop had been looking at. In plain sight on the seat were the two license plates he had taken off his car last night.

Aw, shit!

He snapped off the light and straightened up the gasoline can, pressing it against the underside of the seat with his legs. In the mirror he could see the cop on the driver's seat of the cruiser, the door open, holding something at his mouth.

A phone! He's running the plates!

For a minute Boyd had to fight an impulse to bolt. How the hell could he explain anything? But running would be stupid. The plates are to my car. Nothing's been reported. Okay, so I got my own plates on the back seat. So what? No law against that. See what happens. The worst thing is they know my car's in the quarry.

When the cop came back, he said, "I want you to turn your vehicle around. Wait for me to come around, then follow me."

"Something wrong?"

"Be careful when you make the turn. This road is narrow and slippery."

Okay, I do what he says, find out what's going on. Can't be anything. Okay, so they know my car's in the quarry. They saw the tire tracks. Maybe those kids reported it. But it's my car.

I'm not asking for insurance. What am I guilty of, trespassing?

The police station was down by the river near a funeral parlor, a one-story brick building with small recessed windows you'd have trouble sneaking up on. Four years ago Boyd was in there when a girl who worked for Mr. Armstead said he'd "molested" her. All he did was rub against her in the high-school parking lot, get a hand on her chest, nothing they could prove.

"Just sit over here," the cop said, in a waiting room you couldn't get out of until the guy behind the big windows pushed a buzzer. Smelled like somebody'd been farting.

When the cop went into the office, Boyd grabbed a torn copy of Popular Mechanics off a table, sat down and was looking at the classifieds when a white-haired guy in a gray shirt with a badge opened the office door and told him to come inside—the same cop who'd brought him in four years ago—stale smell leaking off him, needed a bath. Boyd followed him inside and sat at a desk near a bank of gray filing cabinets, old newspapers piled on one of them.

"Boyd Crozier," the cop said, reading from a paper in a manila folder. He lowered the folder, leaned back, wrinkles near his eyes like he was smiling, but he wasn't. "Yes, I remember you—Randolf Armstead's protege."

Boyd stiffened. How the hell'd they know about that?

"Sent you to college, didn't he?"

Boyd nodded. They knew Armstead was queer? They call it a protojay?

"I guess he saw more merit in you than the rest of us did."

"Look," Boyd said, getting nervous. "What'd I do? I mean, what am I here for? I was just driving around."

"At five in the morning on Granite Hill? Why?"

"I couldn't sleep."

"So you drove all the way out here from Cleeve. You don't live here. You've got no people here."

They know! Son of a bitch's playing with me.

"Me and a friend of mine . . . Okay, last night we were up in the quarry."

The cop opened the folder, head tilted back, reading through the bottoms of his glasses. "This guy Milano. He with you?"

"Yeah, we had a couple of girls."

"Girls? And?"

"When we started to leave, my car wouldn't start. I had to leave it there. I was taking the plates off so no one would steal it and it started sliding. It crashed down into the pit."

"And you came out here at five in the morning to see if it's still there?"

"I was gonna find a garage, maybe a wrecker to pull it out. I came early because I got classes."

"You really expected to find a garage open this time of morning?"

"Like I said, I've got classes. I gotta get back."

"And the can of gasoline. What's that for?"

"I don't know. It was in the car."

The cop from the cruiser stuck his head in the door. The two of them went outside and talked. The old cop came back to his desk and said it would be necessary for Boyd to hang around for a while.

"I'm under arrest or something?"

"Just a few things we have to clear up."

"You found my car up there?"

"It was reported," the cop said. But that wasn't what he was thinking about. There was this look on his face. "Would you explain exactly how this happened? I have to make a report."

He's lying. They picked me up because the cop knew Vinnie's car was here last night. What else'd they find out? "Like I said, me and my friend were in there with a couple of girls."

"Local girls?"

"We met them in a bar. I think they lived out this way somewhere."

"You didn't bring them home?"

"No, we took them back to the bar. They had their own car there."

"And . . ."

"Well, I remembered the quarry from when I worked here, so we went up there."

"In the two cars. You in front?"

"Yeah. I drove all the way and he came . . . Well, I thought he was coming all the way in, but he stayed down near the road."

"And then . . ."

"Well, like I said, we were in there a while, and when it was time to leave, I couldn't get my car started."

"It was ten degrees above zero last night. Why'd you shut the engine off? You didn't need the heater?"

For an awkward few seconds Boyd couldn't find an answer. "I don't know. Maybe it ran out of gas. Yeah, I remember the girl saying it was getting cold. I remember. I tried starting it. The starter motor worked all right. The car just wouldn't start. That must be it. It must've been out of gas."

"And that's why you brought the five gallons this morning?"

Boyd leaped on that. "That's right. I forgot. That's why I had the can."

The cop lowered his head and laughed. "So you and this girl got out of the car?"

"Yeah, that's when I took the plates off?"

"She was standing outside the car?"

"Yeah." Why's he asking that?

"And your friend. Where was he and his girl during all of this?"

"They were out by the road in his car." Goddamned mouth getting dry.

"He didn't come up to help you?"

"He came up when the car was sliding. We both tried to hold it."

"And his girl came up, too?"

"I guess so. I didn't notice. The car was sliding."

The cop wasn't writing anything down, just sitting there with his hands in his lap. He got a pencil off his desk and started stroking his mustache with the eraser.

"One big problem," he said. "We had two men out there last night. Kids reported hearing noises. Our men didn't see any footprints could've been made by girls. Only two sets of big men's boot prints. Why you suppose that was?"

Boyd had to fight an impulse to grab the pencil and ram it up the cop's nose. The impulse scared him. He wanted to bolt but knew that would be stupid.

"Maybe it was just you and your friend up in that front car," the cop said. "Maybe he left his car down front so nobody'd come in and see what you were doing."

Son of a bitch knows about me and Armstead! "What kind of thing is that to say?" He pushed his chair back, started to get up.

"I think you better sit right where you are," the cop said, like he'd lock him up if he didn't. "You just stay right here."

He left the office, taking the manila folder with him. Boyd could tell he went into the next office where the other cop was. He could hear them talking.

I can walk out of here. They got nothing on me. But he knows about me and Armstead. They gonna dump it all on me. They probably called Vinnie, see if the car was stolen. Probably a BOLO on it. Why the cop stopped me. What am I gonna say?

There was sweat running off his armpits, a sour taste in his mouth. He got up and stuck his head in the next office.

"I gotta get back," he said. "What I want to know is can I

send somebody up there and get my car out?"

"That has to be cleared," the old cop said. "That's private property in there."

"All I want is get my car out."

"That whole area will have to be checked for hazardous waste. And that has to be done by specially licensed people. I'm afraid you won't be able to get your car for at least a week. But we'll keep an eye on it for you."

"From what I could see," the uniformed cop said, "the front end's been badly smashed. The frame's probably ruined. The car's probably totaled. You got insurance?"

"I'm not trying to collect any insurance," Boyd said, knowing there wasn't a thing he could do. Run up there and burn it? Worth a try. His own car. If there's no insurance claim, what's the crime? "I gotta get back to the college," he said.

The old cop handed him a business card. "Give us a ring Monday morning. We'll know more by then."

The cop in the leather jacket followed him out of the station, followed him down the road, a hundred yards behind him all the way to the town line. No way Boyd could get up there and burn his car.

He was coated with sweat. They know something. Why would they care what I do with my own car? They know something. While he was in with the old guy, the other cop was making phone calls. They know there were no girls up there with me and Vinnie.

Man, I'm in trouble.

Nobody to go to. Not a person in the world gonna help me. Vinnie's got a lawyer. What have I got?

They'll hold the car. They'll pull it out and find things that'll bury me.

Gotta think.

Okay. Spatz was in the trunk. But who says it was me drove

it? Who says I went over there? Who says I wasn't asleep when Vinnie came in and never knew what happened until I saw it on TV?

They won't put a guy like Vinnie in prison. He'll have the best lawyers in the country, like OJ, for Christ sakes! They'll say it was an accident. A lawyer already told him that.

I came home from the Highwayman and went to bed. Even Vinnie told them I was asleep when he got back. I had his keys. He had to come up. He grabbed my keys, went up to the gym and got my car and went over to Spatzie's garage. Why not? Why would he wake me up and tell me? He'd do it himself. Who'd see him?

He stuck the body in my trunk and brought it to the woods. If she says she saw me in her yard, I'll say she's a liar. Vinnie says he told them everything except what I did. Okay, I didn't do anything!

I didn't do it! I was in bed. I didn't know anything until I saw it on TV!

Why'd you come out with him to dump the car?

Because he asked me. He's my friend.

But it's your car. If you're so innocent. . . .

I am innocent! But I knew you wouldn't believe me. Look at you. How many of you believe me?

About three miles outside of Cleeve, he turned onto a country road. He emptied the gasoline can into Vinnie's tank, wiped his gloves all over the can and threw it into some bushes.

To hell with Vinnie Milano. He was never going to take me along with him anyway.

CHAPTER TWENTY

The paperback fell to the floor as Perci leaned across the bed and grabbed her phone. It was Webb.

"Eat something substantial," he said. "We're going for a little ride."

"Where?"

"Tell you when we get there."

She sat on the edge of the bed a few seconds rubbing her eyes. She noticed the book on the floor, picked it up, studied the cover, tossed it aside. Couldn't remember a word she had read. After showering and fixing her face and hair, she was in the kitchen making coffee when the downstairs doorbell rang. She hurried into her bedroom, grabbed a blouse, was buttoning the front of it when she opened the downstairs door and stepped back from a rush of cold air and a strong odor of witch hazel.

Webb came briskly into the hallway, clean-shaven, mustache trimmed, bright-eyed. He shut the door behind him. "Better put something more than that on," he said—a criticism for her not being ready, she suspected.

She led him upstairs and into the kitchen. "Have I got time for a bowl of cereal?" she said, getting nervous and maybe peeved. He was just standing in the doorway watching her, probably not intentionally putting pressure on her, but it was there. She turned heat off under the coffee pot; then, to hell with him, poured cereal into a bowl, got milk from the fridge, went over to the table and sat down.

"Enough coffee for two?" he said.

"I don't have any sugar." She knew he used it. "But you're welcome to anything you want . . . if I've got it."

He started laughing, coaxing a smile out of her.

"You didn't give me much time," she said, surprised by the apology in her voice. "You couldn't've been home when you called."

"I was downtown," he said. "I had an idea you might go out to the Mayfair Lodge and thought we could talk about it."

"Well, that's where I did go. I saw Haskell Paine out there."

"Talked to him?"

"No. I'm not sure whether he saw me. But he might have."

"Did you talk with Albert Stewart?"

She shook her head. "He was pointed out to me. I knew he wouldn't tell me anything. I just wanted to get a look at the place. Is that where we're going?"

"No, we're paying a little call on your friend Milano. Looks like he and Crozier were out in Elwell last night dumping Crozier's car into an abandoned granite quarry."

"Last night?"

"Late at night. Kind of confirms a theory, doesn't it? And Crozier went back this morning with a can of gasoline. In Milano's car. Police out there tried calling him. I guess you were right. His phone is disconnected."

"So they called you?"

"Called downtown. Wanted to check whether the car'd been stolen. Apparently they've got a file on Crozier. Juvenile stuff."

"They holding him?"

"Holding the car. I asked them not to scare him."

Perci hurried through her meal, left the bowl and spoon in the sink. She put on a sweater and a leather jacket, turned down her thermostat and followed Webb down to the street.

In Webb's warm car, she asked,

"Last night. You said they both drove out to a quarry?"

"In two cars," Webb said. "Which'll make it hard to deny intentional dumping."

"Then I guess we were right about Crozier's car."

"Kind of takes the shine off Milano's halo, doesn't it?"

"And I was beginning to feel sorry for him," Perci said.

It took them twenty minutes to get to the raised deck outside of Milano's apartment. A cold wind was coming off the hardwood trees beyond the white field. Webb had just knocked on the door.

"Why do colleges have bell towers?" she said, looking at the Cleeve tower above the trees. "Tradition?"

"Could be," hitting the door with the beefy edge of his hand, saving his knuckles.

"Maybe it's a substitute for a church and belfry?"

"Could be," Webb said, again hitting the door.

This time it was opened. Vinnie Milano stood in the doorway obviously surprised to see them. He didn't invite them in. He was dressed in woolen slacks, a white shirt and tie, dress shoes.

"We come in?" Webb said.

"I guess so." Vinnie stepped back. His face looked drawn the way people look who've recently lost weight.

"Your roommate in?" Webb asked.

"No. He took off somewhere. I haven't seen him."

"Is your car here?"

"Around the corner down there, just outside."

"Want to show me?"

The request puzzled Vinnie, but he didn't seem to be lying. They watched him put a coat on—an expensive woolen topcoat, Perci noticed. They followed him down the wooden steps to the corner of the building. He stared at an empty space against the snowbank across the parking lot. He seemed genuinely puzzled and a little scared.

"It's gone."

Perci couldn't read Webb's reaction, but she believed Vinnie had truly expected to find his car over there against the snow-bank.

"Well, let's go upstairs and talk about it," Webb said.

In the apartment Vinnie took his coat off, expecting apparently to be there a while. He invited them to take their jackets off. He went into his bedroom. They were on the sofa when he came back. He said his keys were missing.

"I guess Boyd took my car." He looked at them with a kind of helpless confusion. It shouldn't have been a surprise since he knew that Boyd's car was in a pit in Elwell, but he didn't seem to be dissembling. He was dressed to go out but possibly hadn't yet looked for his car keys. Webb seemed skeptical.

"He had your permission?"

The question worried Vinnie, and he didn't answer it.

"You say you didn't see him this morning?"

"No. He was gone when I woke up. Maybe he just went to the store."

"No," Webb said in a tone that froze the look on Vinnie's face.

Webb raised an ankle to his knee, toyed with his sock, stared across the room at a poster of a naked woman, looked at Vinnie. "Tell us about last night. We know you were in Elwell."

"Aw, shit," Vinnie said, head down, fingers groping through his hair, probably wishing he was anywhere but in this room with two cops.

"Just tell us what happened."

"He asked me to follow him out there. I didn't know why. He said he'd need a ride back. I just thought he was going to leave his car. He knows people out there. Used to work there. He was raised only ten miles west of there on a farm."

"There was a can of gasoline in your car."

"Not mine. I didn't bring gasoline out there."

"It was in your car this morning."

"All I did was go out there with him last night. He asked me to. I didn't have any gasoline."

"Why did he have it? What'd he plan to do with it?"

"Ask him. I didn't even know he had it."

"You followed him into the quarry."

"No! I got my car off the road. I didn't follow him."

"Your tracks are out there, Vinnie. You walked in to where he was, and you drove in there. You helped him push the car into the pit."

"I didn't go there to help him do nothing. He said he needed a ride back. That's all I went for."

Perci touched Webb's knee, wanting to ask a question. He nodded.

"We want to believe you, Vinnie," she said. "But you must have had some idea."

"Look, I don't know why he did what he did. I just know I had nothing to do with it. I was there to give him a ride back. That's all."

He got up and walked to the door, evidently hoping they'd get up. They didn't.

"I'm supposed to go in town," Vinnie said. "I can't stay here."

"You got a ride?"

"I'll make a phone call down at the corner."

"We can give you a ride," Webb said.

"No, look, I don't want this in the paper. I'm seen with you . . ."

Perci said, "Publicity isn't your biggest problem, Vinnie. Believe me."

"I told you what happened! I didn't do anything. What'd I do? I gave him a shove, that's all. You keep coming here. I didn't do anything." Like an aggrieved child.

"You've told us what you did," Webb said. "You haven't told us what Boyd did."

"I don't know!"

"When you came here Tuesday night, after your problem with Dr. Spatz, did Boyd leave the apartment?"

"I don't know. I was in taking a shower. I was tired. I went to bed. Look, I gotta get out of here. Ask him. All I know is I didn't do anything. It was an accident. Her lawyer even said . . ."

"Her lawyer? Whose lawyer?"

It stopped him. He shot a nervous glance at Perci.

She said, "Mrs. Spatz's?"

He looked away, muttered something about seeing his own lawyer. "I'm supposed to talk with him this morning. He told me not to say anything to you."

Perci leaned toward him. "Vinnie, have you talked about this with Mrs. Spatz?"

It didn't get an answer. He got out of the chair and was heading for the bathroom when they heard a key slide into the lock on the front door. They all watched the knob turn, the door open, and Boyd Crozier come inside. All motion stopped when he saw them.

Webb got up, extended his hand. "I guess you're Boyd Crozier. I'm Lieutenant Harrington, Cleeve police. I think you know my partner, Detective Piper."

Boyd ignored the hand. He glanced at Perci, then looked over at Milano. "What's going on?"

"Why don't you close the door," Webb said. To make his presence less menacing, he sat down. "We got a call from the Elwell police, thought you might want to tell us what happened out there."

Boyd looked accusingly at Vinnie, clearly worried about what Vinnie might have told them. He closed the door, started to take off his jacket. As he walked past Vinnie he tried to catch his eye, get him to leave the room with him. Vinnie had sat down and was staring at the floor.

For the next five minutes there wasn't a sound in the apartment except for Boyd's footsteps in the bathroom, coming out, going into the bedroom. He stayed in the bedroom about three minutes, came out in a sweatshirt, pants and stained white socks. He went over and stood near the poster, cocky smile, hands in his pockets—typical arrogant delinquent.

"They called you from Elwell?" he asked, like there was something funny about it. "I guess they thought I tried to ditch my car." To Vinnie he said, "What'd they ask you? Think I stole yours?" like it was a joke.

"I didn't tell them anything," Vinnie mumbled, head down, fingers roving through his hair.

"Why not? We got nothing to hide. Not our fault the car ran out of gas."

Vinnie kept his head down. There would be lies flying around the room, and Vinnie didn't want, or wasn't able, to come up with expressions to match them is how Perci read it.

"Your car ran out of gas?"

"Yeah, I couldn't get it started so I took the plates off. Lot of ice under the snow in there. Goddamn thing slid into the pit, probably totaled, whole front end smashed. And I don't have collision. I mean it's like five thousand bucks down the drain."

And who would deliberately destroy five thousand bucks, right? Perci's instinct was to challenge him, trap him in a contradiction, but Webb, her mentor, evidently intended to let him think his story had been accepted.

Webb got up. "You told all that to the police out there?"

"That's right. They said they'd have to hold the car. Something about hazardous waste." He looked at Vinnie. "We never should've gone in there."

177

"It wasn't my idea," Vinnie said.

Boyd smiled, not a friendly smile, a smile pregnant with malice.

"Why did you go in there?" Perci asked.

"Just wanted to show the place to him. Great place to take a girl."

"But it's kind of ironic, isn't it?"

"What?"

"You ran out of gas, but you had five gallons of it in Vinnie's car."

The question stopped him only for an instant. "I had a can. There wasn't any gas in it."

"I didn't know anything about the gasoline," Vinnie said.

Webb put a hand on Perci's knee, pressing a finger into her kneecap, a signal—no more questions, let the gasoline thing go.

They both got up.

"Sorry you guys had to come way out there," Boyd said, big friendly smile, leading them to the door.

"Just doing our job," Webb said, like a big Maine farmer who's been completely taken in by Boyd's cleverness.

Perci was outside on the deck zipping her jacket when she saw Webb turn and say to Vinnie. "Oh, by the way, whose idea was it to talk with Mrs. Spatz and her lawyer? Yours or hers?"

Denial crawled over Vinnie's face. "I never said I talked to anyone," looking guiltily at Boyd.

"That was mean," Perci said, going down the stairs.

On the way to Webb's car, she asked, "Why would Claire Spatz bring her lawyer to a meeting with Milano?"

"If it was Haskell Paine's idea, I'd guess he wanted to get Milano's story before we did."

"Why?"

"To coach him. Also to size him up, maybe set a trap for him if he needs it."

"You think he's dishonest?"

"He's a lawyer. And he's not looking out for the interests of Vinnie Milano."

On their way into the city, Webb said, "I have a sneaking suspicion those two boys'll be turning against each other before long. Right now they're probably arguing about the discrepancy in their gasoline story. That was good work getting that out of them."

"Why'd you stop me?"

"Didn't know how far you were going with it. I want Crozier to think he's getting away with everything. There's still too much about this we don't know."

"I could have handled that lie about the can being empty."

"I'm sure," he said. "But be patient. By the way, did I tell you the meeting with Claire Spatz has been changed to Edison's office? And did I also say you can't attend?"

"Why not?"

"Chief says Edison doesn't want you there."

"Damn him, I want to be there. What reason did he give?"

"Don't know."

"Why's he afraid of me?"

"Why don't you spend the afternoon finding out? We need to know what time he got home Tuesday night . . . if he went home."

"Is he supposed to know we're checking on him?"

"Won't hurt anything if he finds out."

Chapter Twenty-One

Lorraine Lord in a bright red dress leaned over Senator George Edison's shoulder and ran a cold hand under the lapels of his robe, down his chest to his navel, causing him to lower the newspaper and look up at the red mouth descending upon him.

"Have a good day," he said, wiping lipstick off his mouth, hating the taste, the pasty feel of it.

"I adore your enthusiasm," she said. "I can just imagine what it would be like if we were married."

He gave a slight shudder against the fingernail dragged across the back of his neck.

"I save my enthusiasm for evening hours," he said. He picked up the newspaper, then lowered it. "Before you leave, call Haskell and ask him to come over, will you?"

"And call Winona and tell her you'll be in the office around one?"

"Just odds and ends," he said, knowing she wouldn't buy the stall but wouldn't give him any grief over it: she wouldn't want to jeopardize an important source of news. If he had wanted the media to know about the meeting with Claire and the police, he'd've held it at City Hall.

He again raised the newspaper. This morning nothing appeared on the front page about the murder. He found an op-ed article about morality on college campuses with a brief reference to Cleeve, and a reader's letter hoping the Spatz case would be resolved before Christmas so that people could turn their attention to a different tree from the one Samuel Spatz had been "displayed" on.

"When do I find out what they were looking for in your sister's garage?"

"As soon as I do," he said.

"We're on a two-way street, George. Remember?"

"Gee, I thought it was love."

He raised a hand in response to her goodbye called out from the front door. Alone, he gazed absently out the side window at distant snowy hills where he could see black specks moving down the cleared skiing slopes cut out of the pine forest. Four years ago he had introduced legislation to prohibit the creation of publicly owned Crestwood Slopes. It was the first of many defeats. He had wanted the hills to remain as they were when he had hunted deer there with his father. So long ago.

Thoughts of his father sneaked out of his mind when Haskell came in, dropping his briefcase on the floor beside the chair at the table, the smell of cigarettes leaking off his brown suit. Instead of asking for coffee, he touched his fingertips to the side of the cold coffee pot and gave the senator a questioning stare.

"There's instant in the cupboard," George said, watching Haskell push from in front of him the lipstick-smeared cup Lorraine had left there, probably noticing the crushed cigarette butts in the saucer. Lorraine wasn't one of Haskell's favorites. For reasons she had never explained, she was indifferent to him almost to a point of contempt. Perhaps she had once tried to seduce him.

"You can make more if you want," George said.

Apparently Haskell wasn't that interested. "Any change of plan?"

"What do we think they know, Haskell?"

As though reluctant to start the day's work, Haskell leaned back in the chair and took a deep breath, which triggered a fit of coughing which caused him to get up and go to the bathroom. George could hear him gagging in there. When he came back to the dining alcove he was still coughing. He settled into the chair, coughed into his raised fist and said, clearing his throat,

"I hate mornings."

"Lay off the cigarettes."

"Right." He again coughed into his hand, again cleared his throat. "We know they know that Sam was smothered while unconscious, that he was taken to the woods before the storm, that Claire picked up Milano at the roadhouse. We know they brought Milano in for questioning. We don't know what they got from him except enough, apparently, to get a warrant to search Claire's garage. We know they brought blood samples back to the lab. They must know that Claire had her car scrubbed clean, but possibly they don't know yet that she had scheduled the cleaning before Sam was killed. Thank God for that."

"How sure are we of that?"

Haskell took a deep breath, which seemed almost to cause him pain. "It's what she said, whatever that's worth. Anyway, I think we can safely assume that Milano denied smothering Sam. I doubt that he can testify convincingly about what Claire did or did not do. I'm sure he'll insist that he pushed Sam away and ran from the garage."

"So what do we know that they don't know?"

"Well, if we believe Claire's story, Milano was more or less pulled out of the car, probably had his pants off or down around his knees. She saw Sam go back against the workbench while she was leaning across the seat to get her keys out of the ignition. She then gathered up her pants and boots, got out of the car on the wall side, wrapped herself in the blanket and went barefoot from behind the car, across the driveway and into the house."

"While they were still fighting?"

"She was vague about that, trying to protect the boyfriend, I suppose. How long would it take a giant like Milano to knock down a runt like Sam? Thirty seconds?"

"So you think she was still in the garage when Milano ran off, and she must have seen what happened."

"At the very least. What they're going to be looking at is the five hundred thousand dollars she gets from his insurance. That's a lot of motive. I could put together a very convincing scenario, and I'm sure they can. For example, everyone knows she did that thing on television at the Red Cross."

"The CPR thing?"

"Right. Well, imagine her leaning over Sam. She intends to help him, gets her hand on his nose, her mouth about to close over his. She's angry at the indignity he's just put her through. She looks at the face she's hated for ten years. There's nobody around. Why not put her hand over his mouth? Take only a minute. She comes into a half million dollars and gets rid of a tyrant. You'd have to be blind not to know she's happy that Sam's dead."

"That doesn't mean she killed him."

"But she easily could have."

"What can they prove? I don't care what they think," George said. "What can they prove?"

"Milano's story will fit very well with the facts. If they believe his story, hers had better be reasonably consistent with it. But even I find her story thin. Barefoot? She ran across that frozen pavement barefoot? What the hell was her hurry? How long would it take to put boots on? And look, George, if she says she dropped Milano off at the store, how does the rest of it make sense? Why was Milano in the garage? Why was Sam there? Why did Milano incriminate himself? How did the blood get in there?"

"So you want her to tell the truth?"

"Not necessarily," Haskell said. "But I do want her to tell me the truth."

George got up and carried the coffee maker into the kitchen, rinsed it out, went back and cleared dishes off the table, put them in the dishwasher, fed detergent to it, turned it on. Coming back into the dining alcove, he asked, "What's she want to do?"

"She wants to say she dropped him off at the store," Haskell said.

"All right, let's say she tells it her way. What would it imply except that she doesn't want to admit having had sex with a student. The truth would be a backup."

"Or the truth could send her to prison. If I'm going to represent her, George, I'd like to know the truth. I don't give a damn one way or the other. But I'd like to get a story from her that fits."

"Well, I want you to represent her," George said. "I don't want a stranger coming in on this."

"If she's indicted, you'll have to get a criminal attorney. I wouldn't be any good in front of a jury."

"I'm sure it won't come to that."

"Then you must know something I don't know. From where I sit she looks very good for it. Don't forget, Milano's a big hero around here. Nobody's going to want him indicted."

"So we change that. We stop coddling him. Sam's the hero. Sam was out there protecting his wife. When that comes into the open, we'll get Milano suspended from school. Maybe that'll take a little glitter off him."

"Want me to look into the procedure for that? Tongues will wag. It could hit the press."

"I want it to. And if the coach objects or any of those other assholes . . . Well, never mind that. Just impress everyone over there that it's the president of the college and the reputation of the college we're protecting, not some womanizing jockstrap. I don't care how much so-called star power he has. Just keep my name out of it."

Haskell would enjoy the assignment, George believed. Right now his mind was tangled with other things. Flaws in Claire's story undoubtedly troubled him. But what was really giving Haskell the shakes had nothing to do with Claire. Old ghosts were haunting him. The eye twitch was back, and the trembling fingers. He was beginning to look like the drunk who staggered into the office ten years ago begging for a job after his own practice had collapsed.

There was, of course, an off chance the police could charge Claire with at least accessory to murder. But unless Claire was actually charged, there would be no outside attorneys coming in and searching the closets.

"Let's just find out what those bastards come up with," he said. "Let's see if they even mention the Umber girl. Maybe it was a mistake to get Piper excluded from this meeting."

"Well, we can't change that without putting spotlights on her," Haskell said.

He had walked to the window and was looking out at the distant hills. When George came back from showering, shaving, and getting dressed, Haskell was still at the window.

"Call Claire," George said. "Tell her to come into the back entrance on Cross Street. I have an idea Lorraine will be checking the main entrance." He watched Haskell lift the receiver, stand with one hand on the desk to steady himself.

"Says she'll be there in a half hour," he said, lowering the receiver.

"Which, knowing her, means about an hour. So tell me about

last night. You think Piper saw you?"

Haskell nodded. "I'm pretty sure she did."

"You think it means anything?"

"We can't underestimate her, George. I'm sure she resents the pressure you put on her last time, and she wants to blame somebody for what happened to the Umber kid. I'm sure you're a target."

"You think it's a personal vendetta? You called me paranoid when I said that."

"That was before I saw her at the Mayfair. She's up to something. That's for sure."

"You don't think she was out there checking on Crozier?"

"There are only two links between Crozier and the Mayfair. One we just learned about, and that has nothing to do with us. But she probably wouldn't be investigating that unless she's just backgrounding the guy."

"And the other is me and Alicia Umber."

"She did call your office, George. And she asked about interns. There's no doubt in my mind that she knows something. I wish you'd tell me how Sam found out the Umber girl was pregnant. Did Lorraine tell him?"

"How many times I have to say it? I don't know! She could have."

"Wasn't she in the bedroom when Alicia came here? She could have overheard something. Maybe she saw you give the kid the money."

"You're like an old woman. Give your nose a rest. You don't have to know everything."

"What I'd really like to know is why you keep Lorraine around. She can't be trusted."

"She's prime time on the mattress, Haskell."

"That's not a good reason."

"How the hell would you know?"

Haskell was hurt by the insult. But he absorbed it. George had no reason to belittle his sex life. George knew nothing about it. Besides, who was he to talk?

"Go after Agatha," George said. "Get that Piper woman off my back."

"It won't be easy. We can't push Agatha around. She's very solid with the city council right now, and you're not."

"How about the bribe?"

"We can try it."

In disgust George said, "How about a bullet?"

Nothing close to a smile touched Haskell's face as he watched George and quietly dragged on his cigarette. The son of a bitch probably took the suggestion seriously.

So why don't I tell him not to? Not that I'd consider asking anyone to commit a murder for me.

But he did wonder, as he was driving into the city, whether anyone in the police would look into the Umber situation if the Piper woman were eliminated. Except for her, there had never been any investigative interest in the matter. As far as the police were concerned, Alicia Umber had died of self-inflicted injuries. Without Piper the Umber story would fade into the past. And so would any chance of his being implicated in it.

George and Haskell arrived at the office a good hour ahead of Claire, which provided time to discreetly handle two urgent messages left on his answering machine. The first was from Lorraine Lord, who said she was at the TV station waiting for his return call. The other was from a male voice demanding that he call a phone number at exactly five-thirty that evening. It took Haskell less than a minute to locate the phone.

"It's on a wall near the storage lockers at the bus station," he told George. "Will a Polaroid be enough?"

"According to who it is," George said. "If it's someone we

know, find out what he wants." He leaned off his chair and punched numbers into the phone, made a face. "I'll hold," he said. While waiting for Lorraine to get off another line, he checked the papers on his desk—nothing interesting. "Yeah, what's up?"

It took Lorraine ten minutes to unload a story about Boyd Crozier and the Elwell police. She wanted to know why Webb Harrington had been called in on it.

"Beats me, Lorraine. If you find out, let me know."

When he hung up, he gave Haskell a big smile, told him what had happened.

"And Milano was right there helping Crozier dump the car. We've got witnesses. And it happened without any nudges from us." He leaned back in his chair and triumphantly clapped his hands. "Find out what it takes to get these two suspended from school. I want it as soon as possible. Lorraine will have his face on TV tonight, and tomorrow every newspaper in the country will know what a slimeball he is."

"It could be dangerous, George."

"How?"

"If Claire thinks it came from us, she'll . . . I've tried to tell you. She doesn't just have sex with these young men. She falls in love."

"Handle it so she doesn't find out."

George was all smiles when Claire came into the office and dropped into the chair across from his desk. She looked tired and in a bad mood, but she was sober.

"Who's coming?" she said, getting a cigarette out of her handbag.

"I wish you wouldn't smoke," George said. "It smells up the office."

"So do most of your clients," she said, tilting her head back, letting smoke stream gently from her nostrils.

CHAPTER TWENTY-TWO

As Webb watched Claire Spatz light her fifth cigarette since he had arrived at the senator's office, he wondered why a celebrated young guy like Vinnie Milano would risk his career for a few minutes in the back seat of a car with a pampered, self-indulgent retread like Claire Spatz. She was a good-looking woman, but the Cleeve campus was afloat with good-looking young women. Why the risk? A guy from a working-class family gloating to dominate a college president's wife? What were his feelings when he knocked the president down? Was there malice when he pushed the little man away? He expects soon to be a multi-millionaire, and the man unconscious at his feet could take it all away. Isn't that a pretty good motive for not letting the man get up?

And this woman, sitting here for the past hour denying ever having been in her garage with Vinnie Milano, ever having had sex with any student—what motivates her? Contempt for her husband? Did she want him to find her with Milano in the garage? Why didn't she take him somewhere else? Why use her own back yard?

"Why did you take the blanket out of the car?" he asked. "Hadn't it been there since summer?"

"As I told you, Lieutenant, I had an appointment to get my car cleaned. I took the blanket to the laundry because it was smelling up my closet."

"Why'd you put it in the closet?"

"Because I didn't want it smelling up my car."

"Let's go back a little," elbows on his knees, leaning almost out of the hard chair Edison had provided for him. "That little store. You say you stopped there."

"I didn't *say* I stopped there. I did stop there. I let him off there, as I've said a dozen times."

"Isn't it possible that, maybe without your knowing it, he got back into the car under the blanket?"

"I'm sure it's possible, but it didn't happen," she said.

"Maybe you didn't know it had happened."

"Lieutenant, I'm getting tired of this. Let me say it once more. And please listen. I let him off at the store. I drove onto the campus. Into my garage. I went into my house. I went to bed. I can't imagine anyone saying anything different because that's what happened."

"And you didn't hear your husband come home or anything happening outside."

"That's right."

"And you suspected nothing was wrong, even when your husband didn't show up on Wednesday."

"That's right."

"Didn't someone from the college call you on Wednesday?"

"I believe there were two calls. My housekeeper took them both. At my instructions she said she had no idea where my husband was. She also said I wasn't home."

"But you were?"

"Not to my husband's secretary. She's paid to take messages. I'm not."

"And by Wednesday evening when you still hadn't heard from your husband, you weren't worried?"

"I had no reason to be. He often stayed overnight somewhere. I'm not a watchdog."

Webb sat back, looked at Haskell, at the senator, again at

Claire. "Then why, if nothing seemed wrong, if you were never in the garage with Vinnie Milano, why, after your husband's body was discovered, did you and your attorney hold a meeting with Milano?"

Claire's face froze. The cigarette tumbled out of her fingers. She had to stand up and brush it off her dress. In her nervousness she stomped the butt into the carpet.

"What meeting is this?" Haskell said, perfectly composed, as though merely curious.

When Claire sat down, Haskell leaned past her legs and picked up the cigarette butt, rubbed his thumb over the blackened end, tossed the butt into a padded wastebasket next to Edison's desk.

Webb waited for Claire's answer.

"I don't recall any meeting," she said, taking a cue from Haskell. "When did it take place?"

"After the body was discovered," Webb said.

Haskell, lazily dragging on a cigarette, said, "Well, let's see now . . . since that was Thursday . . ."

"All I want to know is why you met with him," Webb said. He didn't want to spar with the lawyer since he wasn't even sure a meeting had taken place, nor the where nor the when of it. Without having the whole answer he shouldn't have asked the question. But it was out and he couldn't get it back.

"Don't even bother answering that," Haskell said to Claire. "And please, Lieutenant, we came here to help your investigation. There's no call for insulting us with trick questions. There never was such a meeting and you know it."

"It wasn't a trick question," Webb said.

Edison, behind the desk, stood up with a big friendly smile. "Well, I guess that's it. Wish we had more answers."

Webb wasn't ready to be dismissed. "I believe, Senator, you said you brought Sam home sometime around midnight

Tuesday evening. Did you go straight home from there?"

Edison gave it a brief pause, made a little wave with his hand. "Probably, I don't remember doing anything else."

"And you heard nothing, saw nothing unusual, didn't notice the garage door was open?"

"Not a thing."

"I don't think the garage door would have been open," Haskell said, apparently to strengthen Claire's statement that she had been in the garage alone and had left it in a normal way, locking the door.

"Then how," Webb said, "would Milano have got in there? He must have been in there. If he'd been let out of the car at the store and had not come within a mile of Dr. Spatz that night, why would he say he'd been in that garage struggling with a man who had been murdered?"

Haskell didn't budge a muscle except to say, "I don't know the kid, Lieutenant. I don't know why he does things. Or why he dreams up lies."

"And if the garage door was locked, as you have implied, how did Dr. Spatz get in there if he left his keys in the closet where we found them?"

"I don't know that he was in the garage," Haskell said, with as bland an expression as Webb had ever seen. But Haskell hadn't foreseen the contradiction. Neither had the senator. Claire was sitting with frozen face scratching at the burnt mark on her lap, pretending not to have heard anything.

"I'm sure you realize," Webb said, "that we can easily prove that the blood we found on the floor of the garage came from the wound on Dr. Spatz's head. We can also prove that Dr. Spatz arrived on campus only a short time after Mrs. Spatz got there. There's no question he was in the garage. No question at all." He turned to Claire. "I think you'd better give some more thought to your story."

He let himself out of the office, realizing he had revealed a few things he shouldn't have, but the lapse was worth it if Claire now knew she had to change her story.

As Perci drove along the country road, sunlight glaring off the snowy fields, she came upon a house and a barn with the word "EDGEWORTH" in large painted letters over the door. There was a man in the driveway, watching her.

"I'm looking for Nonny LaChance," she told him.

"That's me."

He was an average-size man with a weathered face and thin gray hair, maybe in his early sixties, wore glasses. Had a slight cast in his left eye.

"My name is Persis Piper," she said, surprised to catch herself using her formal name. Why'd she do that?

He took her extended hand.

"You work nights at the Eldorado in Cleeve?" she asked.

"I do."

"The day man, Ben something, told me where you live. I need some information."

"Is that a fact," he said. From the look on his face she thought she might not get any, but she hadn't yet learned to read Maine people. Unlike Southerners they didn't advertise their feelings.

"It's about one of the tenants—Senator Edison. You know him?"

"I know who he is."

"Would you happen to know . . . I suppose it's not something anyone would remember, but it's important for me to know what time he came in last Tuesday night."

"That's when the college president was hung up on that tree." Evidently he had recognized her. He smiled at something in her expression. "His spot was empty."

"All night?"

"From midnight to eight in the morning is when I'm there. And his car wasn't."

"Why would you remember that?"

"Do you know why Eskimos give so many names to different kinds of snow? Forty-nine, I've heard."

"Because winter up there is so interesting."

"Try spending all night in a parking garage," he said.

She laughed. "You wouldn't happen to know where he might have spent Tuesday night?"

"Probably with his TV girlfriend."

"TV . . . ?"

"Newswoman. I heard he sometimes stays over her place. Just gossip."

"Lorraine Lord?"

"I guess that's her name."

She was surprised he was so willing to talk. Maybe the senator had slighted him. Maybe the senator was a little short with the Christmas presents. Wouldn't surprise her.

She thanked him and drove back to the city.

At the reception desk of the TV station she ran into a man who recognized her and invited her into his office because he wanted information about what he called "the Elwell thing."

"Is that what Lorraine Lord is working on?" Perci asked.

"Could be."

"And if she is, would she be in Elwell? Or maybe on her way there?"

"I doubt it."

"On the Cleeve campus?"

"Could be," he said, smiling. "That's a hot story. Is it linked to the crucifixion?"

"I don't know." Perci thanked him and headed for the college.

She found the TV panel truck outside the gym. Lorraine

Lord, a cameraman and a girl in jacket and jeans were inside looking up the stairs toward the coaches' offices. A security guard was blocking the stairway. Lorraine Lord was saying, "Can you at least tell me whether Mr. Milano is here?"

"All I know, lady, is you can't come up."

"I have an appointment to interview him," Lorraine said. "He told me he'd be here at the gym. Can you at least say whether you've seen him?"

"Afraid not."

With a look of disgust she turned to say something to the cameraman and noticed Perci. She quickly held a microphone to Perci's face. "Detective Piper, are you here to see Vinnie Milano?"

"Please," Perci said, holding both hands up, trying to put on a pose that wouldn't look idiotic on the evening news, remembering last time.

"Can you tell our viewers why the Elwell police contacted you about what happened in Elwell?"

"Nobody contacted me," wedging her way between Lord and the cameraman. Fortunately the security guard knew who Perci was and allowed her to pass. There was some kind of argument behind her on the stairs, but she kept moving, hoping the camera wasn't following her.

She found a student coming out of an exercise room and asked her to go downstairs and ask Lorraine Lord to turn off her cameras. "I want to talk to her, but I don't want to be on camera. Will you do that for me?"

"No problem," the girl said.

Perci watched her go down the stairs. She came back within a minute. "Said she'll meet you outside."

"No cameras?"

The girl smiled. "That's what she said."

Perci waited about three minutes, then walked to the stairs.

The security man said the entire TV crew had gone outside.

The best news Perci had had all day was that Lorraine Lord was sleeping with Senator Edison. It didn't surprise her. It did answer a lot of questions. The knowledge by itself wasn't enough to pump information out of Lorraine Lord, but it gave credence to a hunch that would.

And Perci couldn't wait to play the hunch.

They had left the cameraman and his assistant in the truck and were walking on a path at the edge of the parking lot. Perci hadn't invited Lorraine into her MG, which was only a few feet away, because Lorraine was smoking.

"Well, I'm afraid I don't believe you," Lorraine said, breath misting in the cold air. "I'd have to have rocks in my head to believe the Elwell police would call Webb Harrington just to report a car falling into a granite quarry."

"They didn't call Lieutenant Harrington. They might have called the station, probably to determine whether the car was stolen. It's routine."

"Oh, right, right. And I suppose it's routine to get your chief homicide detective out of bed every time there's an auto accident within fifty miles."

"They got him out of bed?"

"That's my information."

"And where'd you get that?"

"It's what I do."

Perci had noticed weeks ago that Lorraine got offended when her credentials were questioned. She had once been an anchor at a major station in Massachusetts and was fired by the owner's wife, for unstated reasons. She considered this job beneath her, Webb had been told. She considered the people of Cleeve beneath her.

They had stopped at the end of the path. Beyond them were

a hundred acres of snow-covered playing fields which they both stared at for a few seconds, bleachers out there behind a barrier of trees.

Perci said, "You know, I came out here to see you."

"Let's be truthful. You came out here to find Milano, but I got in your way."

"No," Perci said, smiling. "Honestly, I came to find out what time Senator Edison arrived at your apartment Tuesday night after he dropped off Dr. Spatz."

It jolted her, maybe even scared her. "And who gave you that idea?"

"You have a lot of neighbors."

"Who don't know a damn thing about my private life."

"You'd be surprised. You're a celebrity. People are curious."

Lorraine, apparently unaffected by the flattery, took two quick drags off her cigarette, tossed it into the snow, got a tissue from her pocket, blew her nose, crumpled the tissue and threw that into the snow. "So, you've been prowling around my apartment building?"

"We have the senator dropping off Dr. Spatz at midnight on Tuesday, making him one of the last people to see Dr. Spatz alive."

"And making him a suspect?"

"Not necessarily."

"But he needs an alibi?"

"He could use one," Perci said.

"He told you I was it?"

She seemed to be running the idea through her mind, maybe wondering how she could use it. Daylight, Perci noticed, wasn't kind to her. It emphasized too many sags that weren't notice-able on the evening news.

"It would be a lot easier on both of us if you'd confirm this," Perci said.

"I'm sure it would. But let's hold it in our cheek for a minute and chew on something else. Why are you protecting Vinnie Milano?"

"I'm not."

"Oh, come on," Lorraine said. "He went with a friend to Elwell, thirty-some miles from here. He went in his car, the friend in his own car—two separate cars. By 'accident' the friend's car fell into a granite quarry. Doesn't that sound a little phoney?"

Perci shrugged. "College kids, probably been drinking."

"But why would they go out there in separate cars?"

"I have no idea."

"Well, I've got a great idea. It's called quid pro quo. You tell me how this car-ditching event is connected to your murder investigation, and I'll tell you whether Senator Edison was in my bed last Tuesday. I suppose that's what you're getting at."

It wasn't, but Perci let it ride. She was staring across the parking lot at a plow working among the snow-covered students' cars, making a lot of noise and a lot of wear and tear on the asphalt.

"Cultivating friendships with important people is necessary to your work, isn't it?" Perci said.

"And you think that's why I go to bed with George Edison?"

Perci wondered why this forty-year-old woman persisted in advertising her sex life. "I was thinking about where he went, not after he brought Dr. Spatz home, but before."

She gave that a few seconds to penetrate, then added—emboldened by the fear she saw, or thought she saw—"As we've pieced this together, Dr. Spatz had been invited to give a talk at a meeting of the Champions of the Unborn in New Hampshire. Not many people knew about the meeting or the invitation. Only members of the Champions had been told about it. Even Dr. Spatz's secretary didn't know. But somehow Senator Edison found out and talked Dr. Spatz into canceling his appearance.

Did you know about that?"

Something like death came into the cold gaze fixed on Perci's eyes. Lorraine got a cigarette out of a pack of Virginia Slims. She turned her back to a slight breeze while she lighted it. Perci noticed how red and rough her knuckles were as she cupped her hands around the small flame.

"After they had dinner at the Heritage Club," Perci went on, "the senator took Dr. Spatz to the West End to see Mrs. Eleanor Tezzetti. You know her, don't you? I think she owns your TV station."

Lorraine nodded, visibly subdued.

"One of the things I'll be asking about," Perci said, "is who in the local chapter of the Champions could have told the senator about the New Hampshire meeting. It's my understanding that Mrs. Tezzetti is anxious to find out. She had her heart set on Dr. Spatz going to New Hampshire. She was very disappointed."

Lorraine seemed to have aged while she stood there unable to respond. In meek tones, she asked, "Will you let me think about this for a while? You don't have to talk to Mrs. Tezzetti right away, do you?"

Strike while the iron's hot, Perci told herself. "He was at your apartment, wasn't he," she said.

"Yes."

"And what time did he get there?"

"I'm not sure. I really don't remember. It was late."

"How late?"

"I'd tell you if I knew. Look, I know you can hurt me, and you probably want to, but—"

"I don't want to hurt you," Perci said. "Just tell me. Was he nervous, agitated, something like that?"

"I don't think so."

If she was lying, it was hidden in the frailty that had come over her. The resistance and arrogance of a few minutes ago had disappeared. Staying within the good graces of Eleanor Tezzetti was obviously crucial to her.

As though speaking from her knees, Lorraine said, "Could I call you . . . maybe tomorrow? I must sort things out."

At another time Perci would suspect duplicity, but Lorraine looked too scared to be trying anything except to gather her thoughts. Perci had forced her into a trap and she didn't know how to handle it. Maybe Perci had stumbled onto something more important than when Edison had arrived at Lorraine's apartment.

Perci tore a page from her notebook, scribbled her phone number and address on it. "If I'm not there, leave a message."

Avoiding Perci's eyes, Lorraine took the note, folded it, and slipped it into her pocket.

"I appreciate this," she said.

Perci thought: if the rumors are true and Edison is losing his clout and probably on his way to losing an election, Lorraine might be weighing the relative advantage of sucking up to the police at the expense of her relationship with Edison. Maybe she's tired of him.

And maybe I'm an idiot. But I'll keep the pressure on and see what happens.

CHAPTER TWENTY-THREE

They were in this big office with hundreds of law books on a long wall. Uncle Dom was sitting across from Vinnie in a big chair next to Mr. Aiello's desk. He looked sad.

This time I really hurt him, Vinnie thought. Wish he'd yell at me. But Dom just stared at the floor with this sad look on his face. A few minutes earlier Vinnie had told him and Mr. Aiello about last night in Elwell and the cops coming over this morning. Uncle Dom exploded. "You fucking idiot!"

"I didn't know why he wanted me to go out there," Vinnie said.

"You knew," Aiello said. "You're not that dumb, Vinnie. You knew he was getting rid of evidence, and you knew it was wrong to help him. Didn't Boyd tell you when he came back to your apartment Tuesday night? Didn't he tell you what he did?"

"I was asleep."

"You fell asleep? You thought you had just killed a man, and you fell asleep?"

"I was tired."

Aiello gave Dom one of those do-you-believe-this looks. But Dom wasn't paying attention. He was studying the floor, like a man defeated.

Mr. Aiello sighed. "Let's get back to that meeting at the lake. Was it her idea or yours?"

"She called me. But I wanted to talk to her. How'd I know what she told the cops? Even Boyd said . . ."

"Boyd! Boyd!" Dom yelled. "Every time you take a fucking leak you gotta ask Boyd?"

"He helped me," Vinnie said, eyes pleading with Dom to understand. But Dom just shook his head, frustrated.

Aiello leaned across the desk. "This I want to hear about. That night. Let's get back to that night, okay? You run out of the garage. It's just beginning to snow. Boyd's in the apartment. He's like half-dressed watching television. That right?"

"I told them he was asleep. He said tell them that. But it was stupid. I never should've said it."

Aiello waved that off. "What I want is what you told Boyd, exactly what you told him."

"I said I pushed Dr. Spatz and he hit his head and was on the floor. I said I killed him. I thought I killed him."

"And then you ran. You pushed him and ran. You didn't say anything else? Like say you leaned over him, looked at him?"

"I didn't. I just ran."

"What'd you tell him about Mrs. Spatz, what she was doing?"

"Nothing. I didn't see her."

"You mean when you were struggling with Spatz?"

"I wasn't struggling. All I did was push him," Vinnie said.

"But did you tell Boyd that Mrs. Spatz had left the garage?"

"I didn't tell him nothing about her."

"Okay. So what did Boyd do?"

"He put his boots on and a jacket and went out."

"What did he say? He say where he was going, what he planned to do?"

"He said, 'I gotta see,'" Vinnie said, "like he wanted to see Spatz lying there."

"Nothing else? 'I gotta see.' That's all he said?"

"That's all I remember."

"Okay, so when you talked to him again, what did he tell you he did?"

"All he said was it was taken care of. He said they'd never know anything about being in the garage with Mrs. Spatz."

"If he's your friend," Dom said, "how come he didn't tell you call the police? A friend would've told you call the police, Vinnie. It was an accident."

Aiello said, "You didn't ask him to go over there?"

"I just told him what happened."

"You didn't ask him to take care of things for you?"

"No. It was his idea. I didn't know what to do."

Aiello sat back in his chair studying Vinnie's face. "How long did it take you to get back to your apartment?"

"I don't know . . . fifteen minutes."

"And it took you a few minutes to unload this bad news on Boyd. It took him how long to get to his car?"

"He got dressed and, I don't know, fifteen, maybe twenty minutes. It was up by the gym."

"Even if he ran?"

"Yeah, there was a lot of snow."

"And it would take him another ten minutes or so to get to the president's house?"

"Yeah."

"Which adds up to let's say almost an hour."

"What you getting at?" Dom wanted to know, like this was suddenly interesting.

"I was just wondering how long Spatz would've been unconscious."

Dom looked hopeful. "You think Boyd killed him?"

"A whole hour went by before Boyd got there," Mr. Aiello said.

"They say he was unconscious when he got smothered."

"Well, they're a little hazy about that. All they know is, at least from what I understand, it didn't look like Spatz had fought off an assailant. So we'll have to wait on that one. I'll look into it." He glanced at his Rolex, put his hands flat on the desk like the meeting was over.

"Jeez, Raymond, I really appreciate you giving it all this time," Dom said.

"Oh, we haven't even begun, Dominick. We have to know every little detail." He got out of his chair and came around front of the desk, standing over Vinnie, looking down. "I don't want you giving any more information to the police. I don't want you talking to them. You call me if they bother you, which they'll surely do. And I want you to move out of that apartment today. I understand the coach will find a place for you on campus. I want you to stay completely away from Boyd Crozier. He's not your friend, Vinnie. Believe me, he's not your friend."

Vinnie knew that was coming. He knew he'd have to do it.

"I mean it, Vinnie. He's not your friend. You've got to look out for yourself. You're in big trouble. Don't underestimate this. You're a prime suspect."

"Why? I didn't do nothing."

"Think about it from their point of view," Mr. Aiello said, "If Spatz was unconscious, or they think he was, when he was smothered, who would have done it? Somebody who got there an hour later? Or someone who was there just after he got knocked down? I'm not saying you did it. I'm saying it's reasonable to think you did. I'm saying you've got to protect yourself, not go shooting off your mouth to Boyd or the cops or anyone. From now on, if you have to talk, you come to me."

"But I never did anything!"

"We know that. But they don't. They don't know who did it. All I'm saying is you're a prime suspect."

"That lawyer said it was just an accident."

"He's her lawyer, Vinnie. He's protecting her. I'm your

lawyer. You do what I tell you. Agreed?"

"Yeah. Okay." What else could he say?

Going down the stairs after leaving the office, Vinnie said to Uncle Dom, "I'm sorry about this. I really fucking hate myself."

"We'll see you through it," Dom said. "You just do what Mr. Aiello told you. Don't talk to nobody, and get out of that apartment. We'll go right over the garage now, get the pickup. I'll call the coach."

"What did Toni say?"

"Nothing. You broke her heart. What's she gonna say?"

All the time at the garage and out on the highway following Dom's truck Vinnie could think only about Toni. He was always hurting her. Her whole life everybody hurt her. Her father. Her second year in high school he said he needed her full time at the store. If it wasn't for Mrs. Costa telling him off, Toni wouldn't've never finished high school.

Vinnie told her get a student loan and come with him, or take nursing at the hospital, do something more with her life than wrap sandwiches. But her mother got sick during Vinnie's first year at Cleeve, and after that Toni couldn't go anywhere.

She came to some parties. She thought his friends didn't like her. She wasn't comfortable. She thought college kids looked down at her. And that's crazy, he told her. She was better than any of them.

It was the girls. They said things that hurt her feelings and she stopped coming. A whole year he saw her only on the Christmas break. She didn't come to games, said it was too far. They fought all the time and he got sore and stopped going down to see her.

Then his mother died and he didn't know it until Toni came to the college. She stood in the doorway and from the look on her face he knew something bad had happened. They sat on the sofa and she took his hand and told him—like a nun in the first grade telling a little kid.

Every day until after the funeral she was with him, cooked meals for him, stood with him at Correlli's Funeral Home thanking people for coming. After that he drove down to see her every weekend. For a couple of months he never looked at another girl. They talked about getting married. She said she'd leave home. She was excited about the football draft, even got a book to read about it.

Then she read in the paper he was one of Alicia Umber's boyfriends. They had a big fight. She stopped taking his phone calls. When he came in the store she wouldn't talk to him. He told her he never touched Alicia Umber, but she didn't believe him. She knew other times he had lied.

And now this.

He couldn't believe he wouldn't get her back. Since grade school he had loved her. He'd crawl on his knees to get her back.

"If Boyd's up there," Dom said, getting out of the pickup truck near the stairs, "just tell him the coach said you gotta live on campus. He don't want the publicity."

"Boyd knows I was at the lawyer's," Vinnie said. "I gotta tell him. I can't just walk out and say nothing."

"You gotta look out for yourself. You gotta learn something from this."

"I gotta tell him," Vinnie said.

Boyd was in front of the sofa on the floor with two girls from the next apartment building. He was laughing. He looked half drunk, waving a can of beer.

"Hey, Uncle Dominick! How you doing?"

"Hi, Vinnie," one of the girls said. "Been waiting for you."

"Tell them to clear out," Dom said. "We got things to do."

Boyd didn't move, didn't argue. All the time the girls were

getting up, complaining, putting shoes on, getting jackets, he just sat on the floor watching Vinnie like never in their lives had they been best friends.

Vinnie stood in the doorway watching the girls go down the outside stairs when Uncle Dom said,

"Come on, Vinnie. I gotta get back."

Vinnie closed the door, noticed Boyd had got up on the sofa and was watching him. Dom was looking at the poster of the naked girl. He'd seen it before.

"So what's happening?" Boyd said, legs out, beer can at his mouth in a lazy half smile, like his mind was riding over a hurt he knew you knew about.

"I gotta move back on campus," Vinnie said.

"Oh, that's a big surprise."

"It ain't my fault."

"Of course not. The lawyers made you do it, right? Who's paying them? The college? How many lawyers they give you?"

"Fuck you, Boyd. It ain't my fault."

"When do I get my lawyer? They got one for me?"

Dom was bent over the TV, unplugging it. "Come on," he said to Vinnie, "give me a hand."

Boyd said, "They told you just walk out, to hell with Boyd Crozier, right?"

"They didn't talk about you."

Dom unhooked the cable. "I can get this," he said. "Go hold the door for me."

Boyd tilted his head back, sucking on the can. "That TV's half mine," he told Dom.

Dom was across the room hugging the set, waiting for Vinnie to open the door.

"I bought this TV for Vinnie. I pay for the cable," Dom said.

"Ten dollars of it's mine. A bet. Super Bowl last year."

Dom pushed the set into Vinnie's arms, got a roll out of his pocket, peeled off a ten, went over and shoved it at Boyd, who wouldn't take it, sat there laughing.

Dom dropped the bill on the sofa, went over and lifted the TV out of Vinnie's arms. "Get the door."

Vinnie held the door for him, closed it behind him and walked past Boyd into the bedroom. Boyd came in with another beer, stood in the doorway.

"Look, I'm sorry," Vinnie said. "I know you helped me. But they told me to move back on campus, and I gotta do it." He was walking toward the closet. "You got a jacket of mine."

Vinnie found his jacket and two of his shirts on Boyd's side of the closet. He threw them on the bed. He put folded sheets and pillow cases into a laundry bag, emptied the top drawer of the bureau into the bag and pulled the draw strings. He got three plastic garbage bags from the kitchen and filled them with shirts and sweaters and underwear. He was getting stuff off the wall when Dom came back, looked around, picked up the bags.

"Box spring and mattress," Vinnie said. "Whyn't I leave it here?"

"Take it," Dom said. "That chest of drawers? That yours?"

"It was here."

"How about in the kitchen?"

"Nothing I want," Vinnie said.

"Leave nothing that's yours. What's in the bathroom?"

"I'll get it," Vinnie said.

When Dom left the room, Boyd said, "Those lawyers of yours, what'd they say about my car?"

"Nothing. Look, I'm not doing this because I want to."

"Right," Boyd said. "You do what you have to do. I do what I have to do."

To show he had no hard feelings, Boyd held the door open when Vinnie and Dom carried the box spring and mattress onto the deck. All the time he had this wise-ass smile on his face.

Driving around the big loop onto the campus, glancing in the mirror at Dom's face in the windshield behind him, Vinnie told himself, I'm never gonna screw up like this again. From now on I do nothing stupid. I'll go down and find Toni and tell her on my knees I'll never do anything again to hurt her.

When he got out of the car at Dorm Six and walked back to where his uncle was waiting, Dom said, "You been crying? You crazy? That son of a bitch was never your friend. Never!"

"I wasn't crying about him," Vinnie said, wiping his eyes. "Leave me alone."

CHAPTER TWENTY-FOUR

Around four o'clock that Saturday afternoon Webb and Perci left the office and walked down Main Street to Kathy's Kitchen where they grabbed a corner booth near the windows and each ordered a swordfish steak, a baked potato, and coffee.

"For some reason I wasn't surprised," Perci said.

"At what, that's she's sleeping with Edison, or that she fell apart when you mentioned Eleanor Tezzetti?"

"That Lorraine and Edison are bunk mates."

"Doesn't surprise me," Webb said. "When's she supposed to call you?"

"Maybe tomorrow. She was kind of vague about it."

"Be careful how you handle it," Webb said. "Remember what she does for a living. Do you think Spatz might have known about George Edison and the Umber girl?"

"If you'll let me talk with the Umbers, I might find out. There's got to be a reason he went to them. I'd like to go there right now."

He shook his head. "Agatha—"

"I can justify it. Edison's a suspect. He's one of only four people as far as we know who had opportunity to kill President Spatz. I'd be checking on some very bizarre recent behavior of our murder victim, and besides . . ."

"Yeah, I know," Webb said. "Edison isn't going to complain."

"Not this time. He's got to be worried sick that we'll find out. I can handle it without giving the Umbers any reason to complain. What do you say?"

"I'll think about it."

"Think about how much ammunition it could give us. Lorraine Lord knows something important. I want to scare it out of her."

He gazed out the window, ran a finger over his mustache, finally looked at her.

"I'll probably get my ass in a sling for this."

She let out a sigh, sat back and smiled. "Thanks."

He gazed long and hard at her. "I've got a feeling you're cooking up a lot of things I'd like to know about."

All she could think to do was smile. "I'm not holding back information. You know everything I know. And you told me not to work a puzzle till all the pieces are out of the box."

"I did say that, didn't I."

When the waitress brought their meal, they nibbled at it for a while in silence. Perci said, "I wish Claire would tell us what she saw."

"Well, she knows she can't get away with what she's been telling us so far."

"I guess you can't blame people for lying to protect themselves. I've been thinking about Vinnie, the part about when he ran back to his apartment. If Boyd was asleep, as Vinnie says, why would Vinnie wake him up? Why create a witness? Why not take Boyd's keys, take his car, carry off the body and say nothing?"

"Well, I guess he said something—that night or later. Why else would Boyd dump his car?"

"That's another thing. Would he throw a car away just to protect Milano?"

"He could be protecting himself or protecting his investment," Webb said. "What's an old car compared to what Milano can buy him in just a few months—if he's not indicted for manslaughter."

"But Milano doesn't seem the kind to hang Spatz on a tree like that," Perci said. "That has to take a certain kind of motive beyond just covering up a crime. I don't see him as vindictive. He doesn't seem to have any great passions other than sex and football. And he's sure as hell not an intellectual."

"Avert suspicion. Why not? The 'crucifixion' idea wasn't original. He could have seen the cartoon."

"Just seems out of character."

" 'Out of character' only means it's outside your perception of him. There's a Mr. Hyde in every one of us."

Perci rolled her eyes. Thank you, Dr. Freud. "At least we can assume," she said, "that Crozier's car was what Spatz was carried off in, can't we?"

"Don't have to. Janet's going to Elwell tomorrow. They've agreed to hold off hoisting the car up until she can capture what footprints they haven't trampled on. Then she'll examine the inside carpeting for blood and fibers and prints and whatnot."

"How do they preserve footprints in snow?"

"Around here they spray wax on it, the kind you use on skis, then spoon in some kind of dental material. The FBI uses melted sulfur for the initial casting. Either way could ruin the imprint."

"Sounds complicated."

The waitress brought Webb a piece of apple pie and Perci sat there watching him eat it. "When I check out these car washes," she said, "How do I know Claire didn't pay those people to lie?"

"Don't think she'd do that. Might give them a little extra to do an extra good job, but attempting bribery just after her husband's murder would be stupid. She's not stupid."

★ ★ ★ ★ ★

There were only five shops in Cleeve that advertised detailing. Men at three of them said they'd never heard of Claire Spatz. A bald-headed guy at the fourth said Claire Spatz had driven in without an appointment on Wednesday and had asked for instant service. "And I wasn't sure what kind she meant, if you know what I mean. You ever seen her?" grinning.

"She had no appointment?"

"That's right. But business ain't so busy I turn people away, if you know what I mean."

"You detailed her Cadillac?"

"If my wife wasn't sitting there at the cash register, I might've detailed a lot more, you know what I mean? Yeah, I did her car."

"She give you any special instructions?"

"What for? She's been here before. Knows I don't just run a hose over it. That car of yours could use some help," glancing through a dirty window into the parking lot.

"Some other time," Perci said. "And say hello to your wife. She's a lucky woman."

The edge of a drawn curtain was pulled aside and two sad eyes peered out through steel-rimmed glasses, eyes in a round face devoid of curiosity. Perci held up her ID folder and badge. The curtain closed.

She stared at old cracks in a wooden door, at years of dirt around a worn doorknob. She glanced up the street at bare sidewalks and banks of shoveled snow. A yellow stain of urine on the banking. A street without trees. She hoped she wouldn't be here long.

The door opened and the man from the window now blocked the doorway. He needed a shave. When he spoke, his lips drew back tightly against inexpensive false teeth.

"Mr. Umber. Mr. Harold Umber?"

"What do you want?"

"I'm Detective Piper. I'd like to talk to you."

"What about?"

"May I come inside?"

A door opened just behind him and a woman in an old-fashioned dress and floral apron peered out. The instant she saw Perci she closed the door.

"Just tell me what you want."

"It's about your daughter," Perci said.

The flinch was instant and painful, and he stepped back into the hallway. Perci leaned her hand into the door to prevent his closing it.

"Mr. Umber, we can talk here in your home where it's private, or you can come down to the police station where there'll be reporters and TV cameras. It's up to you."

"My daughter is gone. Why do you . . . ?"

Tears came into his eyes making a mockery of the stories she had heard about his insensitivity. No question he grieved over the loss of his daughter. Sadness disfigured his face as he beckoned her inside and opened the door into a sunless room that smelled of melted tallow, a fragrance she remembered from a minister's home she had boarded in years ago in Cape Coral.

The woman in the apron was sitting on an old-fashioned divan, knees and feet together, hands in her lap, swollen ankles bulging over tightly laced black shoes. Perci held out her hand and introduced herself.

"You're Mrs. Umber?"

The woman nodded, mumbled something, reached up and allowed Perci to hold her dry fingers.

There was no TV in the room, nothing but old furniture and faded wallpaper. No pictures or ornaments. The drapes that framed the windows looked old and dusty. The air in the room was heavy with stale odors.

The man dropped into a cushion next to his wife. Perci sat across from them in a small overstuffed chair. Just sitting with this man and this woman told her more about Alicia Umber than she had learned in all the hours of her investigation.

"I know this is painful to you, and I'm sorry that it's necessary for me to be here. Our investigation of Dr. Spatz's death forces us to examine the last few weeks of his life. We know he came here and told you that Alicia had attempted to get an abortion."

"She had nothing to do with his death!"

They were too frightened not to have suspected there might be a connection. But she didn't go into that.

"I'm just trying to chart his movements of the past few weeks. I'm not trying to make any connection. Did he come alone?"

"Yes."

"And can you remember what he said?"

"He said he had saved her from murdering her baby."

"Meaning he prevented her from having an abortion?"

"Abortion is murder," he said, flashing defiance. She had learned in Florida that people who try to live by the Bible are often protectively defiant. They try to isolate themselves, protect their children from a world they consider sinful. No question Alicia had been strictly raised.

"Did he ask you to withdraw her from school? I know you came out there the next morning."

"He wanted her to come home so we could protect her. He was afraid she'd try again."

"Did she say she would?"

"When she lived here, she was a good Christian girl. That college corrupted her. We never wanted her to go there."

Perci gave that a few seconds. "It's very unusual for a college president to involve himself so intimately in a student's private life. It's almost unheard of. Was there some special reason he took this kind of personal interest in Alicia? I'm surprised he even knew who she was."

"I can't explain that. I don't know."

"Did Alicia tell you what he said to her?"

"She didn't tell us anything. She was turned against us. We didn't know anything about her life out there."

"Did you know she was working as an intern in Senator Edison's office?"

"We read about that in the paper."

"But Dr. Spatz never mentioned it?"

"He did say . . ." The woman looked at her husband to catch an objection. He didn't offer one. "He kept saying the college had done a lot for her. I thought he meant the scholarship, but she got that from the mill where Mr. Umber worked. Maybe he meant that job. I guess it was special to work for a man like the senator."

"Why would he know that? Why would he mention it?"

"Because she disgraced the college, and the college had been good to her." Tears filled the woman's eyes and she looked away, stared across the room, then raised the skirt of her apron and dabbed at the tears.

Perci had no more questions and saw no reason to further distress them. Maybe these people hadn't prepared Alicia for the world she had to live in, but they weren't bad parents. In a different society, they would probably be thought very good parents.

She didn't learn much from them about what had happened, but talking with them had given her an idea she was eager to follow up on.

There were long shadows on the snow when she arrived in front of Townhouse 17 on the Cleeve campus. Wanda Chernovsky was just getting into the driver's seat of a two-year-old Porsche.

"I'm in a rush," she said, turning on the ignition, one foot on the snow, one foot pumping the accelerator.

"Just be a second. Something I forgot to ask," Perci said, holding the door open, noticing two pizza cartons on the passenger seat under a six-pack of Miller Lite. "Did Dr. Spatz commonly go with your group to those protest sessions?"

"That was the only time."

"The only time?"

"We were surprised to see him. We didn't think—you know, all that heavy publicity he was getting. But he was very into it, you know."

"Were you near him when he spotted Alicia? Did one of you point her out to him?"

"Didn't have to. The minute she got out of the car, he went right over there. I didn't know her. I don't think any of us did."

"So you weren't there because of Alicia Umber?"

"No. We had no idea any Cleeve student would be there."

"Do you think he was there just to stop Alicia?"

"We all thought that. He stayed back of us, out of sight, kind of, maybe like he was waiting. The minute she got there, he crossed the street."

"Did you hear what he said to her?"

"Just, you know, how terrible it was what she was doing."

"Why did she go off with him? Did she struggle?"

"A little, at first . . . Tried to pull away. I guess she was ashamed. She was crying."

"You say she got out of a car. Whose car was it?"

"I don't know. I was watching Dr. Spatz. Then I was watching those TV people crowding around him."

"Like they knew this was going to happen?"

"I guess so. They were crowded around him. Look, I gotta go."

Perci stepped back, watched Wanda close the door, watched the Porsche fishtail as it hustled down the icy street.

So someone told Spatzie that Alicia would be at the clinic. Had to be someone close to Alicia or close to someone who knew she was pregnant, knew she was going for an abortion. They don't take walk-ins. Would a social worker or a psych counselor have blabbed? A doctor? Very doubtful. In anger, as a threat, Alicia may have told the man who had made her pregnant. But how would Spatz have found out about it?

Why would a girl raised as Alicia had been raised tell anyone she was pregnant? Maine law didn't require parental or any other kind of permission for an eighteen-year-old to get an abortion. And why would anyone have told Spatz?

It was dark by the time Perci returned to the city. Webb wasn't in the office. She talked to her IBM for about a half hour, printed out what she had said, filed the report, wrote for a while in her notebook, mostly about Alicia, speculations about family background. She stood at the window for a while watching Christmas shoppers hurrying along Main Street.

Maybe she'd walk through the stores, buy a few cards for friends back home. She could buy a present for Webb, but it might hurt his feelings if he hadn't bought anything for her. And why would he?

CHAPTER TWENTY-FIVE

Haskell Paine mingled with the people getting off the bus and followed the driver up an icy path into the station through an entrance marked "Employees Only." The driver gave him a quick glance, maybe wondered who he was but said nothing. While the driver ducked into the men's room, Haskell opened a door marked "Private" and went into the office behind the service counter. He was leaning on a wall when the ticket agent came in and asked what he was doing there.

"Surveillance," Haskell said, taking a wallet from his breast pocket as though to show a badge.

"You a cop?"

"I need your help," Haskell said, taking two twenties out of the wallet.

The agent looked at the money, studied Haskell, then went over and closed the door.

"What kind of help?"

"I'm expecting the phone over there near the storage lockers to ring at about five-thirty." They both glanced at the wall clock. It was twenty-one after five. "I expect someone out there to answer the phone. I don't want to be seen watching for him."

"Is he out there now?"

"I don't know. I don't know who it is. But he may know me. I'd like you to stand at the counter doing what you usually do and just let me know when he answers the phone."

"This on the up and up?"

"Nothing's going to happen. I just want to know who answers the phone."

Haskell held out the two twenties. The man looked at them, looked at Haskell, shrugged, gave a short laugh, took the money. "I won't get into trouble over this, will I?"

"There'll be no trouble."

"You gonna grab him or something?"

"No. I just want to see who it is."

"What the hell," the agent said, pocketing the bills as he walked back to the counter.

Haskell imagined whoever had made the call to Senator Edison was already out there watching everyone who came in, maybe expecting to see a guy in a felt hat smoking a cigarette behind a raised newspaper.

When the bus driver came into the office, Haskell smiled. "How you doing?"

"Tired." The driver dropped into a chair behind the desk. He spread some papers over the desk blotter. "Eyes get tired."

"This the end of the run?"

"Wish it was."

Haskell didn't hear the phone ring. The agent stuck his head into the doorway, glanced hesitantly at the driver. "He's over at the phone."

From the counter Haskell saw a blond man in a black leather jacket and jeans standing at the wall phone with his back turned. Although able to see only the side of his face, Haskell recognized him. It was the guy who used to come to the office to pick up Alicia Umber, the guy at the bar with Albert Steinmetz the night Senator Edison brought Alicia to the back lot.

Haskell brushed past three nuns and almost fell over their luggage before he could put a hand on Boyd's shoulder.

"Mr. Crozier," he said.

Boyd turned, stared into Haskell's face more surprised than

alarmed. He dropped the handset on the hook. Although he was shorter than Haskell, he gave off an aura of physical strength that was intimidating. Like standing in the presence of a well-trained German shepherd whose owner said was harmless.

"Let's go outside," Haskell said.

Boyd looked him over, little smile at his mouth. "Why not?"

"Where's your car?" Haskell asked. He knew exactly where Boyd's car was but didn't want Boyd to know it. It was a way of asking how Boyd had got here.

"Where're we going?"

"Just up the street, get some coffee."

"Let's go in your car," Boyd said. He knew who Haskell was.

They drove in Haskell's Lincoln to a nearby Burger King, got coffee, went to a corner booth and sat facing each other, Boyd like a cocky prize fighter measuring an opponent.

"I wanted to talk with Edison," he said, as though he was too important to deal with an underling.

"We don't always get what we want," Haskell told him. "What did you want to talk about?"

Boyd leaned back, toying with a salt shaker, dumped salt on the table, flicking it around with his finger. "They're gonna call me as a witness about what happened Tuesday night in the Spatz's garage."

Maybe he expected the announcement to cause alarm. It didn't raise an eyebrow.

"Who's going to call you? And what garage are we talking about?"

"Spatz's. What you talked about with Vinnie Milano Thursday night in that A-frame at the lake. You and Mrs. Spatz. I know what happened there."

"I see."

"I can tell you how Milano got my car and went back to the

garage and took the body away. I could wrap the case up."

"Could you. You sure that's what happened?"

"Maybe it did. I could say it did."

"And why tell this to the senator?"

"Protection. Who the cops gonna blame? The big football star? The president's wife? Why blame them when they got somebody like me to pin it on, right? I gotta protect myself."

"Did he tell the police you went to the garage?"

"And maybe you told him to."

Big shoulders jammed into the corner of the booth, one leg drawn up, sucking air through the slit between two front teeth. He was not only cocksure of himself, he was loaded with pain and anger. Haskell could imagine him dragging out a gun and blasting away.

"We didn't tell him to say anything. Did he go to the police?"

"I was never in that garage."

"And you didn't kill Dr. Spatz?"

"No. Why would I?"

"Then, if you're innocent, why do you need help?"

"Who'll believe me? Sitting right here staring in my eyes, you don't believe me."

To slow things down, maybe to slow himself down, Haskell got a cigarette out of a pack, offered one to Boyd who waved it off.

"What makes you think Milano told the police you were in the garage?"

"He said so."

"And what else did he say?"

"He said he killed him."

"He told you that?"

"He said Spatzie was dead. Vinnie pushed him or something."

"But you think the police will think you did it?"

"If I was over there, they could say I did. Who knows who

did it? Mrs. Spatz? Maybe she did it. Vinnie said he was dead, that's all I know."

"And you want the senator to call him a liar."

"All I want is for him not to let them blame me. They sure as hell won't blame the president's wife."

"But if Vinnie said he killed him . . ."

"He didn't tell them that. He told me that," Boyd said.

"The police aren't stupid. If Milano lies, they'll know it. If you had nothing to do with the crime, they'll find that out. If you're innocent, you have nothing to worry about."

"Yeah, right," Boyd said. "Well, maybe somebody else does." And cold accusation crawled into his face. He brushed salt off the table with the edge of his hand, wiped his hand on his leg. "I'm not here begging for anything."

"Then why are you here?"

"Because I know something you don't want the police to know."

"Ah . . ." Finally. Haskell watched ash fall off the end of his cigarette onto the floor. "And what is that?"

"You remember Alicia Umber?"

Haskell nodded. "Oh, yes."

"She told me who got her pregnant."

"Did she."

"And you know who I mean."

"I have no idea who you mean. Just what is it you think I know?"

Boyd made a quick glance across the room, leaned toward Haskell. "Don't kid yourself I won't take it to the cops."

Annoyed by a faint odor of sweat and oily leather that drifted across the table, Haskell pondered the face that threatened him. Boyd was handling himself pretty well. Not too bright, but he had guts. He was capable of violence.

"Any allegation you might make would be of no value to

you," Haskell said. "And if you're thinking of blackmailing anyone, I'd advise you to be careful. You're out of your league."

"I don't think so."

"Believe me, son, you are. Threats from a known procurer don't carry much weight."

"A what? What'd you call me?"

"A fellow who provides young women for shall we say illicit entertainment at a local motel."

Boyd's face went blank in stunned shock. He tried to invent a casual reaction, but his face wouldn't cooperate.

"I don't know what you're talking about," he said.

"Oh, I'm sure you know exactly what I'm talking about." Haskell smiled, drew on his cigarette, eyes narrowed against the rising smoke. "But let's not try to scare each other. Let's just say it would be very unwise for you to attempt blackmail."

"I wasn't."

"All right. No cause for alarm. Nobody wants to hurt you. But tell me, now that our cards are on the table, have you been in contact with that young police detective from Florida, Perci Piper?"

"What do you mean 'been in contact'?"

"Has she talked with you?"

"Maybe she has."

"And she talked with you a month ago when that poor Umber girl killed herself?"

"So . . ."

"Why didn't you give her your information then?"

"Why should I? There was nothing in it for me."

"You didn't give her a list of Miss Umber's boyfriends?"

"No. There's a lot of things I know I don't tell."

"I imagine. But you understand what a nuisance Detective Piper could be if she had such a list."

"Yeah, I understand. That's why I'm here. I don't want to

hurt anyone either. I could've ruined Spatzie if I'd wanted to, things I know about him. But I keep my mouth shut if I don't need to say anything. If you guys don't hurt me, I won't hurt you."

"Commendable," Haskell mumbled, poking out his cigarette. "And just what is it you know about Dr. Spatz. The man's dead now. It can't hurt to tell me."

"Oh, it'll hurt. You people think he was a saint. One word, believe me, and I could knock the roof right off that college of yours. He was a hypocrite!" The last words accompanied by a blaze of anger.

Maybe he really knew something. There were a lot of unpleasant rumors floating around about Sam Spatz. "And what word is that?" he said.

Boyd shook his head, little smile in his eyes.

Haskell said, "It have anything to do with why you 'crucified' him?"

"Who said it was me?"

"Wild accusations aren't going to help you," Haskell said. "Rumors are worthless."

"They aren't rumors."

"I see."

"Let's just say I don't think you want to tell anybody about those young women you mentioned a few minutes ago."

That gave Haskell pause, and Boyd knew it. He laughed. "I got nothing to lose you accuse me of murder."

Haskell raised both palms. "Calm down. What I'm trying to say is that threats from either side would benefit nobody. If you didn't murder Dr. Spatz, you have no reason to expect the police to think you did. If Milano did it, they'll get him. Being a football star won't protect him, believe me."

"Why should I trust cops?"

"All right, you don't trust them. But threats aren't the answer.

Look, let's turn this around. Let's talk about something else for a minute. I'm curious."

"All I want is protection," Boyd said. "You give me protection I won't say a word. But don't think I can't prove Edison was screwing Alicia Umber."

"All right." Haskell waved that off. "What I'm curious about is what Detective Piper wanted. When did you talk with her?"

"Today. Both her and that guy with the mustache—Harrington, something like that."

"And what did they want?"

"I don't know. They were talking to Vinnie most of the time. I just got there."

"He didn't tell you?"

"He got a lawyer. The lawyer told him not to talk to me. They're setting me up. I'm not stupid. That's why I'm here. I don't have a lawyer. All I got is myself."

"This Piper. She didn't ask about Alicia?"

"I don't know."

"She made an awful nuisance of herself when all that was going on. Except for her, no one wanted to investigate an attempted self-abortion. It wasn't a police matter. And she could be even more of a nuisance if she keeps sticking her nose in where it doesn't belong. She could open a lot of wounds. She could give us all a problem." He smiled. "Think she's ever been raped? I wonder how tough she is. I wonder if she was raped or beaten up if she'd go back to Florida. She's not a bad-looking woman. Might be fun to rip her clothes off. I wonder why someone hasn't taken her down."

"Because she carries a gun, for one thing."

"Make it all the more challenging. I understand she lives alone."

Boyd shrugged.

Haskell believed he had said enough. He put his cigarettes

and his lighter into his jacket pocket. He started to get up. "You need a ride back to your car?"

"I'm okay," Boyd said.

Haskell leaned across the table. "Believe me, we're not interested in causing you trouble. We don't want this thing to get out of hand any more than you do. If we can keep your name out of it, we'll be happy to. But as long as Detective Piper is around, she's dangerous to all of us. No telling what kind of unpleasant things she'll bring to the surface. You know what I mean?"

He stood up and smiled. "You sure you don't need a ride?"

"I told you what I need," Boyd said.

Haskell could feel the cold gaze following him all the way to the door. That's a very dangerous man, he told himself.

Chapter Twenty-Six

Perci leaned back in the passenger seat of Webb's car and watched the blades of his windshield wiper scrub rain off the glass.

"You slept until noon?"

"Rain on the windows reminded me of home," Perci said.

He had come to her apartment around twelve-thirty, just as she had finished showering and had made coffee in her kitchen while she was getting dressed. The chief had phoned him that Eleanor Tezzetti was leaving for Costa Rica Monday morning and would grant an interview if he could get to her house before three when she takes her nap.

"Don't feel right doing this," Perci said.

"We've got to confirm that Edison and Spatz were there, what time they got there, what time they left."

"But I more or less made Lorraine a promise," Perci said.

"And we'll keep it. No reason to compromise her. We'll treat her like any other source. I also want to check out whether Spatz stayed out of New Hampshire because he'd been threatened. I know Edison took credit for discouraging the trip, but he'd take credit for a weather change."

It was one-forty-five when they turned into the broad driveway at the Tezzetti house, a big white mansion on a hill, apple trees on a slope behind it and huge rhododendrons banked against downstairs windows. Webb drove to the sheltered front entrance and told Perci not to ring the bell till he joined her.

"You think I'll melt? Just park and we'll walk back together." *Great God, if I was a guy he'd never do that!*

He drove into the rain and stopped on the left side of a wide circular drive twenty feet from the entrance. He had to step through a soft snowbank to get onto the wet asphalt. At the door they both scrubbed their feet on a nubbled doormat.

They were let into the house by an old man with watery blue eyes and a limp who glanced disapprovingly at their wet feet, then led them down a corridor to a large, high-ceilinged room where an elderly woman in a robe and slippers sat by a window in a wheelchair. The room smelled faintly of lavender. The woman raised a small pale hand that Webb held for a moment, thanking her for agreeing to see him.

"And you are Detective Piper." She gave Perci a smile. "I watch the news on television and I read the newspaper," explaining her use of Perci's name. "Please sit down. May I offer you tea? Coffee? Sherry?"

"Not me," Webb said, easing himself into a ladderback chair that looked like it might collapse under him. The seat was hard and uncomfortable.

"Miss Piper?"

"No, thank you," Perci said. She went to a window seat and sat back against small cushions, something she had wanted to do since childhood seeing drawings of girls reading like this, rain sliding down the outside of the glass, yellow curls dangling on their shoulders.

After more than five minutes of amenities, Webb asked Mrs. Tezzetti what time Dr. Spatz and Senator Edison had arrived at her house Tuesday evening.

"Late," she said. "Just before the news. I remember having to tell Edison to shut up so that I could listen to it."

A little squeak of laughter slipped from Perci's mouth. To cover it up, just to say something, she asked, "Was it Lorraine Lord?"

"No. Lorraine was here with me. It was our new weekend girl. Perhaps you've seen her? Rebecca Pugh? A very bright young lady, young and vibrant, just what our station needs."

With "young and vibrant" in the wings, no wonder Lorraine is scared.

It took Webb a few minutes to get to the questions he wanted answered. Mrs. Tezzetti showed no signs of impatience. Behind the little-old-lady gentility was a quiet confidence probably from a lifetime of handling situations more threatening than anything Webb could provide.

"I'm very curious about what led you to me," she said.

Webb smiled. "Voices trickling down from upstairs."

"Ah . . . Along that old plumbing in City Hall. Any particular room?"

"It came up in a conference," Webb said, "in reference to a complaint, I believe." His face was totally absent of guile. Perci was impressed.

The answer didn't please Mrs. Tezzetti, but she didn't complain. All she said was, "I see," with eyes searching Webb's face.

"There was a meeting here, I believe," Webb said.

"And where did you hear that?"

"We know there was a small gathering here. We know that Dr. Spatz had cancelled an appointment to deliver a speech in New Hampshire."

"You seem to be well informed."

"It was called in."

"By . . ."

Webb smiled. "I'm sure that person would not have given us the information under ordinary circumstances. But this is a murder investigation."

"I realize that, Lieutenant. But I can't imagine how Dr. Spatz's brief visit here had anything to do with his death."

"Let's hope it didn't. Can you tell me why he came here?"

"He wanted to talk about an endowment I had promised the college."

"Is that why he cancelled his appearance in New Hampshire?"

"I think he said there was some sort of urgency at the college he had to attend to. You know, of course, that George Edison is chairman of the board of the college. He knew I was heading south. I suppose they wanted to assure themselves that the money was forthcoming. They also wanted to know what strings I might attach to it."

"Did they say what the emergency was at the college?"

"Just something apparently that required their attention. I didn't ask for particulars."

"And it had nothing to do with the New Hampshire meeting?"

"You seem to be very concerned about that."

"It's just that it was a meeting of the Champions of the Unborn. I believe you have some connection with that."

She seemed offended by the suggestion. "May I ask where you're getting all this information?"

"Little scraps here and there. You know how the body was disposed of on that tree."

"You think pro-choice people did it?"

"It's a possibility," Webb said, "Do you know of any threats?"

"No."

"This emergency you spoke of. Can you tell me anything about it?"

"Well, I didn't mean to mislead you, Lieutenant. Perhaps it wasn't an emergency." She frowned, looked away for a moment, made a little sigh of resignation. "It was a difference between

231

George Edison and Dr. Spatz. I really don't want to go into this, but I suppose . . ." She looked pleadingly at him. "This is important to your investigation?"

"The man was murdered, Mrs. Tezzetti."

"Yes, of course. Well, I'm not sure of the details, but George Edison somehow found out that Dr. Spatz was going to New Hampshire to do something the college board had prohibited. They came here to talk to me about it."

"Why you?"

"To avoid publicity, I imagine. The senator thinks my newspaper pays too much attention to Dr. Spatz's campaign against abortion. He didn't want this little incident to blossom into a story."

"How did Edison find out about the New Hampshire meeting?"

Perci's heart took a jolt, but nothing changed in the old woman's expression.

"I wish I knew," she said.

"Did he know you had a group here?"

"It wasn't a 'group,' Lieutenant. It was an informal gathering of friends saying goodbye to me."

"But while these friends were here, you made a phone call to New Hampshire."

"I wanted to be sure they understood what had happened. It was through my office they had contacted Dr. Spatz."

"Did your meeting break up when Dr. Spatz left?"

"It wasn't a meeting. But I think they did all go home."

"At what time?"

"I'm not sure. I had gone upstairs. It was past my bedtime. I didn't actually see anyone leave."

"Your butler?"

"Oh, he had gone to bed hours before that."

From what Perci could see, Mrs. Tezzetti didn't suspect Lorraine of betrayal and possibly knew nothing of her relationship with Edison. Maybe hanging out with the senator had been worth the risk before any of this had happened. But would Lorraine keep taking the risk? She's vulnerable. No question about that, if she wants to keep her job. She must at least be considering breaking up with the senator. Sooner or later Mrs. Tezzetti is going to put two and two. . . .

It's what she asked Webb while they were driving back to the city.

"Sounds good," he said, typically committing himself to nothing more. "After we do the report, let's take a ride to the hospital."

"What for?"

"That's where Charlie does his autopsies. He may have something for us."

"Sunday?"

"He's there."

"Tissue breaks down very quickly after it's thawed," Charlie explained. "Can't keep a body waiting," little grin on his face, celebrating the witticism.

He had been reading a Louis L'Amour novel, sitting at his desk in the basement of the Veterans Hospital west of the city. Perci noticed strange chemical odors seeping through the batwing doors of an adjacent room. It was her first visit to the pathology lab.

"Nice of you to wait for us," Webb said.

"Nice and quiet here. Got a kids' party at the house."

"So, anything startling and new?"

"What's new isn't startling, and what's startling isn't . . ."

"Same cause of death?"

". . . new. He was smothered, but not where he first fell. I'd say he got up and walked to the front of the garage, then collapsed. That's where he lay the longest. This time in a supine position—that's face up in case you didn't know."

"Why the front of the garage?"

"The footsteps and particles of cement on his head."

"How long was he down?"

"After death, I'd say forty minutes, at least. And that bruise on his mouth? That was postmortem."

"How would he get that?"

"Banged against something when he was lifted. Maybe out there in the woods. Maybe putting the body in a car. Janet might have something to tell us when she gets back. She called, said she's sure Spatz's body was in the trunk of Crozier's car. Also found some rope she thinks will match the ligature."

"That's good. You got anything else?"

"Corroborating stuff, like blood distribution, engorgement. A lot of it'll come back to us from Portland."

"How about fingerprints?"

"On the face or neck? Not after two days of freezing."

"You're convinced he was smothered."

"I'd say it's the most likely cause of death. You have to remember there was a lot of postmortem damage to the throat and neck. And freezing out there didn't help. But the cause of the asphyxia did not come from internal blockages. And it wasn't pressure on the carotid sinus that killed him. I'll break this all down in my report, which I'll get out probably by tomorrow. Right now I'm resting in the West." And he reached for the paperback novel and leaned back in his chair, virtually dismissing them.

Back in Webb's car, Perci said, "If Spatz was dead at least forty minutes at the front of the garage, it couldn't be Boyd Crozier who killed him, wouldn't you say?"

"We don't know a damned thing about what Crozier did. We

know only that his car was used. It looks to me right now more likely that Milano killed Spatz, ran home, got the keys to Crozier's car, came back and got the body."

"Not to me," Perci said.

"Because you think he's not bright enough for that 'crucifixion' decoy?"

"Not just that. Those blood prints on the garage floor were perfect matches. I agree with Charlie that Spatz staggered to the front of the garage where maybe he fell. I can't picture any assailant just standing there watching him do it. And I can't believe those prints wouldn't be smudged or stepped on or something if there had been a struggle."

"Did Janet find blood on the shoes?" Webb said.

"No, but the last print was very faint. In fact, she thinks Spatz might have taken a step where she couldn't find any blood. You know, Claire Spatz could have watched what was happening while she was getting dressed. She'd've had to practically stumble over her husband getting out of there. How much space we dealing with? About eight feet between the cars, six feet inside the big door? How could she get dressed and get back to the house without knowing what was happening?"

"Before we talk to her again, I want to go after Crozier. I think we've got enough on him now to squeeze a little truth out of him."

"Then we don't tell him he's no longer a suspect?"

"Whatever it takes," Webb said.

"You notice there wasn't any buildup of snow inside the garage? Whoever removed the body must have closed the doors before the snow started."

"Or it was swept out."

"I looked for signs of that. Didn't see any."

"Probably closed the door to make things look normal," Webb said.

"But not before the body was removed, or else how would they have got in? Also, if Spatz had gone to the back door and tried to get in without keys, would his wife have opened the door for him?"

"Maybe not. Maybe she'd think he had only to walk down to the security booth. Give him time to cool off a little."

They drove back to City Hall and spent an hour entering a report into the IBM. Perci looked over the photographs and sketches they had made in the garage.

"You know what bothers me?" she said, as they were leaving the office.

"You're hungry."

"I mean about the evidence. It bothers me that Senator Edison did not come straight over to see his sister when he learned the body had been discovered."

"Probably more interested in the college than in his sister's feelings."

"Maybe. But a better reason could be that he already knew and had already talked to her about it. Maybe right after it happened."

It was dark when they went out to the parking lot behind the station. Streetlights were on. A few stores were open on Main Street. Not many people on the sidewalks. It had stopped raining but the air was cold and heavy. Felt like snow.

"This going to freeze?" she said, standing next to Webb at his car. Hers was back at her apartment.

"More than likely," he said.

She got out of the car and walked in near darkness toward her back door. There was ice under her feet and she had to step carefully. She was on the back stoop fitting her key into the lock when the first bullet hit her. She fell against the rail and grabbed

236

it for support when the second bullet knocked her against the door. She suddenly felt very tired, and then she felt nothing.

Chapter Twenty-Seven

Webb was at the doorway of the single-occupant hospital room looking at Perci who lay very still under a white sheet, apparently asleep. Her face was turned toward the windows. There were bloodstains on the bandage covering her right shoulder. She was under sedation and was not to be disturbed.

Webb didn't realize that the chief and Janet Lucia were standing behind him until the posted guard, a young cop named Nolan Carlyle, tugged at his sleeve. "You got company."

"How's she doing?" Janet asked.

"Okay, I guess." Webb stepped aside so that the two women could see into the room. "She was in pain earlier, and she lost a lot of blood."

"She say anything?"

"Not to me. She's been like this since I got here."

"You talked to that guy who found her?"

Webb took a card from his pocket on which he had written the man's name and phone number. He handed it to the chief.

"All he saw was Perci on the snow bank waving for him to stop. The shooter was long gone by then."

"And leaving no footprints that we could find," Janet said. "But we did get some evidence."

"I put Rudy out there with two men," the chief said. "Maybe some neighbors saw something."

Webb asked Janet, "Find the bullets? Doctor said they passed right through her."

"Barely passed through her," Janet said, taking two plastic bags out of her evidence kit. Each bag contained a slug. "A thirty-two from a low-velocity revolver. I'd guess an old Smith and Wesson."

"Why old?"

"Poor alignment of the chamber and the gun barrel." She pointed at one of the slugs. "That edge there. Same on the other one. I'll send them out, of course, but it looks to me like the bullet had some trouble getting into the barrel. Happens from years of flipping the cylinder instead of opening it properly."

"Close range?"

"More than fifty feet, I'd say. Both hits are on the right side. From what the surgeon said, and he knows gunshot wounds, the bullets hit her from the back. One broke a rib, the other bruised a bone in her shoulder. We found her keys right under the door. I'd guess she was trying to get in when she got hit."

"Thank God she had the presence of mind and the strength to get to the street," the chief said. "How long they plan to keep her here?"

"A couple of days," Webb said. "Doctor said that shoulder'll give her a lot of pain."

"I don't want her back in that apartment. Not for a while."

"She'll stay with me," Webb said with a finality that surprised him as well as the two women.

The chief looked worriedly at him. "Don't blame yourself. You had no way of knowing."

"I should've gone in there. It was dark. I should've walked in with her."

"Going in there after dark is something she's done every working day since she's been here. No reason to punish yourself."

Webb gazed sadly at the tumble of hair on the pillow and at

239

the blood-stained bandage. He should have walked her to the door. He knew she would have chafed at that, but he should have gone in with her.

The chief said to Nolan Carlyle, "You got to take a leak do it in the john in her room. Otherwise don't budge from this chair."

"Yes, ma'am."

"No one goes in except doctors or nurses or technicians you recognize. Just because someone's got a stethoscope doesn't mean they belong here. If you don't recognize them, get somebody you do recognize to identify them. She's got no family up here. Don't let anybody bamboozle you."

"I understand," he said. "The lieutenant explained all that."

She said to Webb, "You want to come downstairs, get some breakfast?"

"Might as well." He'd been standing there more than an hour, hadn't had anything to eat. Maybe a couple of eggs would cure his headache.

Downstairs while they were eating, Janet talked again about what she had learned at Elwell. "I'll have to get comparison prints from Crozier and Milano. Don't know what it'll tell us. The inside of that car was filthy."

"People out there tell you anything about Crozier?"

"Said he was wild, raised on a chicken farm. Parents died while he was in high school."

"I suppose you want to talk with him," the chief said to Webb.

"Both of them."

"Think they might be connected with this shooting?"

"I'll sure as hell find out," he said with steel in his eyes.

"Just don't do anything rash."

Webb got up from the table, in no mood to be sociable. He went back upstairs and stood outside Perci's door for a while. He was told she'd probably remain asleep until late afternoon. He sat next to her bed for a few minutes, resting fingers on her hand as he looked down at her. Her hand was warm.

After more than an hour searching around the campus of Cleeve College, Webb found Vinnie Milano in the Administration Building with his lawyer. He heard someone yelling down the corridor near the provost's office.

"All this kid's done for these people and they try to throw him out! What kind of a place is this?"

"Dominick, please! They're not going to throw him out."

"Only because you scared the shit out of that guy."

"The battle has been won, Dominick."

"All this kid's done for this place! What's the matter with these people?"

The voice faded into the distance of the corridor. A door slammed.

Webb hustled down the corridor, caught up with the three men as they were going down the back stairs.

"Raymond!"

The three men stopped, watched him come down the stairs.

"I heard what happened," Mr. Aiello said. "She all right?"

"No permanent damage," Webb told him. He was searching Vinnie's face. Is this the guy who shot her?

"Could I ask your client a few questions?"

"Let's go outside in my car," Mr. Aiello said.

They walked across the parking lot to the lawyer's Cadillac.

"In front with me," Mr. Aiello said, going around to the driver's side.

With Vinnie and the short man in the back seat, Webb, twisting around, said, "I'm not accusing you of anything, Vinnie. I just want to know where you were last night."

"What time?" the lawyer asked.

"Around midnight."

The lawyer was laughing. "Tell him where you were, Vinnie."

"I was at the police station. My car was stolen."

"It was Boyd Crozier," Mr. Aiello said. "A kid saw him."

"He must've had keys or something," Vinnie said. "I didn't tell him he could use the car."

"When'd he take it?"

"Around nine-thirty, something like that," the lawyer said. "It's on a state-wide bulletin."

Webb looked at Vinnie. "Does Boyd have a gun?"

"A gun? I never saw one. You think he shot the detective?"

"Somebody did."

"I don't think he'd shoot anybody."

"Did he take Dr. Spatz's body into the woods?"

Vinnie went blank. He shot a pleading glance at his lawyer.

"We don't know what Crozier did," Aiello said. "We do know that Vinnie did not go into those woods where you found the body."

"That's right," Vinnie said. "All I did was push him."

"Shut up," the lawyer said.

When they were out on the road heading into the city, Vinnie asked Mr. Aiello, "You think he believes me?"

"It doesn't matter. See how he sneaked that question in? Didn't expect it, did you?"

"No."

"You gotta watch them every minute, Vinnie. But you handled it okay. I do the talking for you. That's all you have to remember."

"You think Boyd could've shot that woman?"

"Who knows? Put it out of your mind. You didn't. That's all you worry about. That kid's on his own. Who knows what he does."

"I think he'd shoot his own mother," Dom said.

Vinnie told him. "She died a long time ago."

"He shoot her?"

Mr. Aiello let them off at Dom's garage.

"You'll have to gas up," Dom said, giving Vinnie keys to the pickup. "When you get back there, go over the library and study. What you got, two exams this week?"

"I'm gonna go find Toni."

"That provost, he a Polack?"

"I don't know," Vinnie said.

"Provost. I think it's a Polack name. Why'd he want to kick you out of the college? What was his reason? I never heard him say a reason."

"I'm on probation, that's all. It don't matter. I been on that since my first year. They never said nothing before."

"They can kick you out for that?"

"It's like a warning. Like if you don't get your grades up they can."

"So now the season's over they try to kick you out. Where was the coach? He know about it?"

"He couldn't do anything."

"He could tell them give you good grades."

"That's not how it works," Vinnie said. "Look, I gotta go. Thanks for sticking by me."

"Like you're not family. Get the hell out of here," punching his arm.

Vinnie pushed wheels into the soft snow across the street from Toni's father's store. A car went by as he was getting out of the truck and splashed slush on his leg. He looked at it, leaned down and knocked some of it off. Road grime all over his leg but he didn't care. Snow got down inside his shoe. He didn't care.

He crossed the street and stood on the sidewalk watching Toni inside at the refrigerator with her back turned. Two women in big overcoats and scarves were at the counter talking to her.

A kid went by bouncing a rubber ball on the wet sidewalk, a little black and white dog jumping at the ball. He watched them cut into a yard and he put his hands in his pockets and went over to the driveway. Toni's yellow Mazda was in back, fresh tracks of the panel truck in front of it. Her father was probably out making a delivery, maybe picking up something. Who cares?

He leaned on the clapboards at the edge of the driveway until the women came out of the store. He peered inside through the lighted tubes of the beer sign. Toni was wiping something off the counter. The little warning bell jingled when he opened the door. She looked up. Her hand stopped moving. She didn't seem surprised to see him.

"I'm sorry, Toni," he said. He felt like dropping to his knees, felt like crying. "I'm sorry I did all those things. Honest to God, I'll never do anything again to hurt you."

She finished wiping off the counter. She tossed the rag into the sink and took a paper towel off the roll and wiped her hands. "Do what you want," she said. "I don't care what you do."

There wasn't hatred in her face or anger or anything. Like she really didn't care.

"I don't want you to hate me," he said.

"I don't hate you, Vinnie. You are what you are. You can't help yourself." She picked up a metal tray and took it to the refrigerator, put something in it, brought it back, wiped her hands down her apron. "I don't want you coming here anymore."

"Aw, Toni, don't be mad."

"I'm not mad, Vinnie. I just don't care. It's over. I don't care anymore."

"But I love you. I fucking love you, Toni!"

"You're scared, Vinnie, that's all. You'll be all right. You'll get past this like you always do."

"I changed. Honest to God, Toni . . ."

"I don't care! I don't care if you changed or what you did. I just don't care. I don't want anything to do with you anymore."

"I love you! I never knew it till now."

"If you love me, go away. Leave me alone. Let me live my life."

Tears filled her eyes and she got angry at herself and walked into the back room and closed the door.

"Please, Toni, I love you!"

He shoved the door open, found her sitting on a bag of flour, her face in her hands. Made him feel rotten seeing her crying.

"I love you, Toni."

"Just go away," she said, not looking at him. "Just go away."

"I don't know what to do!"

"Vinnie, you'll be all right. Just do what your Uncle Dom tells you. You'll be all right. Just don't come to me anymore. I don't want you here anymore."

"Aw, Toni . . ."

She looked up at him, tears flooding her eyes. "Leave me alone, Vinnie! Leave me alone!" She lowered her face into her hands, sobbing. "Leave me alone! Just leave me alone!"

While he was standing there, helplessly watching her, the little bell over the outside door jingled. She raised the apron to her face and wiped her eyes, got up and pushed past him.

It was her father. He was standing just inside the door looking at her.

"You," he said, pointing at Vinnie. "Get out of my store!" He yanked the outside door open, almost knocking the bell off the spring. "Get out or I call the cops."

Vinnie felt like saying call anyone you want, felt like knocking him on his ass. Felt stupid standing there nobody wanting him.

He kept looking at Toni, leaning into her hands on the counter, staring at the floor, waiting for him to leave.

"I'll be outside," he told her, ignoring her father's angry eyes.

The door slammed behind him and he crossed the street and sat in his uncle's truck. He stayed there more than an hour. She didn't come out. He knew she wouldn't, not to go home for lunch, not for anything, not while he was there.

He finally drove away. He went up to the Eastern Promenade and sat in the truck by the old bandstand looking out at the Civil War fort in the harbor. It's where he used to hang out when he was little, used to run along the railroad tracks, steal waste out of the wheel boxes, cops chasing him down the ties, him and this kid called Rat-eye.

Around eight-thirty that evening he was in Uncle Dom's truck across the street from Toni's house trying to decide whether to go in, ring the front doorbell, ask to see her. He could see her yellow Mazda and her father's panel truck in the driveway. He knew she was up there. Maybe she knew it was him down here in the truck.

All day he'd been riding around thinking about her. Didn't want to go back to school. Study for exams? What for? They want to kick you out they'll do it, say you didn't get your grades up. You get their names plastered on the sports pages, sometimes even national, and they tell you what a great guy you are. Then when your senior year's finished, they say you're an embarrassment.

Aw, who cares.

He got out of the truck and crossed the street, went up on the front porch and rang the bell. Nothing happened. He rang it again and the hall light came on. He couldn't see through the curtain who it was, but the door opened and Mr. Costa was standing there.

"Get off my porch," he said.

"I want to see Toni."

"She don't wanna see you."

"I want to see her. Come on."

Vinnie started to push past him, but Mr. Costa shut the door and went upstairs and turned the light off. Vinnie stood there a while, then pushed the button. He tried the door, felt like smashing the window, letting himself in. He went out on the sidewalk and looked up at the lighted second-story windows.

He was standing there yelling for Toni to come look at him when flashing blue lights came up the hill and a police car pulled into the curb. Two cops got out, one standing back, the other coming up to Vinnie.

"Are you Vinnie Milano?"

"I'm not doing anything. Just trying to see my girl."

"You gotta move along. You can't stay here. There's been a complaint."

"I just want to see my girl!"

"Move along, Vinnie, or I have to take you in. You can't stay here."

"What am I doing?"

"Disturbing the peace, making a public nuisance. Now come on."

He took Vinnie's arm. Vinnie pulled away. He looked up at the windows. She was standing there, a dark silhouette in the living room window. He kept looking at her as he walked backward across the street and got into his truck.

"We'll be patrolling this area," the cop told him. "Don't come back."

"I love you, Toni!" he yelled at the figure in the window.

She didn't move. He kept looking at her as he drove away. He knew she'd come back to him. He wouldn't want to live if she didn't come back to him.

CHAPTER TWENTY-EIGHT

Rudy Zawada came into the office, grabbed the chair under Larry Bird's picture, turned it around and straddled the seat. Both arms resting on the chair back, a guy with big blue eyes and big wet mouth and spaces between his teeth. He grinned a lot.

"How's our girl?"

"She'll be fine," Webb said. He saved what he had in the PC and leaned back. "What you got for me?"

"Bill found something in the gun file—an old Smith and Wesson registered to one George Edison." He handed Webb a printout that listed names and gun numbers.

"Anything else?"

"No footprints. Did you see anyone around when you were there?"

"No."

"Would anyone know what time she was expected home?"

"No."

"Both apartments over that little grocery store are unoccupied. There was nobody in her building. Nobody heard shots. No dogs were barking. According to her neighbors that area's as quiet as the moon. We've come up with nothing."

"You're looking for the gun?"

"In back of every fence. In the sewers. We checked every curbstone drain, every trashcan. We're still looking."

"Let me check with Edison," Webb said.

"It's why I came here. Think there's a chance? I never liked that son of a bitch." Rudy got up to go—a high-energy guy, always moving. "Tell Perci we're all rooting for her."

A half hour later Webb's knees were rubbing the edge of Perci's mattress, and he was telling her what Rudy said. When he asked whether she had caught a glimpse of her attacker, she said,

"My back was turned. I didn't even hear the shots. Something hit me, then something else hit me. I don't even remember falling."

"Well, the doctor says there's no permanent damage."

She turned her head aside and gazed out the window. She lay like that in silence for more than a minute. When she again looked at him there were tears in her eyes.

"Nobody has a right to do that," she said. "Nobody has a right to violate another person."

Sadness brushed her eyes, then quickly vanished. He didn't have any answers for her. All he could say was how sorry he felt, and she didn't need that.

The roses came while he was with her, and he felt embarrassed when she read the card, but her face brightened. "What a thoughtful old guy you are," she said. "They're beautiful," grinning at him.

"Been a long time since I've bought any," he said. "Damn things are expensive."

She laughed until pain made her stop. For a long moment she smiled at him with affectionate indulgence. She handed him the box and he set it on the table.

"So what have you found out?" she said.

"For one thing, Janet says Boyd's car had half a tank of gasoline, which proves something, I guess. And she says you were shot by an old revolver, and we found out that Edison owns an old revolver."

Her eyes widened. "You checked it?"

"I'll call on him the minute I leave here."

"Wish I could go with you."

"That shoulder hurt?"

"I know it's there," she said.

He told her about his talk with Aiello and Vinnie Milano. "We've got a BOLO out for Crozier. Milano's finally turned against him, I guess, although he won't say Crozier put the body on the tree. Says he doesn't know who did it."

"Adolescent loyalty," Perci said. "He really doesn't realize how serious this is."

"Could be. But the big question still centers on the garage. Milano was there a lot earlier than Crozier, if Crozier was there at all. And Milano did fight with the man."

"I suppose you can't wait for me before you talk with Claire again."

"As soon as I leave here, I'm calling on Edison. Claire can wait."

"Do me a favor," she said. "Even if you can't find Edison's gun and test it, find out where he usually keeps it—at his house or at his office."

"Why?"

She laughed. "An idea I'm playing with. Gotta do something besides stare at the ceiling. You coming back here after you've talked with Edison?"

"I might be persuaded to do that," he said.

He couldn't imagine George Edison being fool enough to wait out in Perci's back lot and shoot her with his own gun, even though he wanted Perci to disappear. There was Haskell Paine, who commonly did Edison's dirty work. But even Haskell wouldn't do anything so obviously stupid. Crozier? If he stole Milano's car around nine-thirty, he had time to get into the city and do it. He could know where Perci lived. He seemed delinquent enough to be capable of it. But why would he want to?

It took him a little while to drive to Edison's office, stand there in a strange mix of odors—stale cigars and a cheap deodorizer—arguing with the secretary.

"Somebody's in there," he said, looking at the closed door marked "Private."

"It's not the senator, Lieutenant. Believe me, he's not here."

"If it's Haskell Paine, would you ask him to come out?"

She sighed, pushed the chair back, went over and opened the door. Before it was closed, he stared straight at Haskell Paine and Claire Spatz, both standing in the center of the office, both staring out at him.

He was kept waiting more than five minutes—angry voices coming from the room. Finally the door was opened and he was invited inside. Claire had propped her rump on the corner of Edison's desk in a pose designed to make her appear at ease. It didn't. Her left forearm was pressed tight into her belly and the hand holding the cigarette was trembling.

Although he had been invited in, neither Haskell nor Claire seemed eager to greet him. After a few seconds, Claire abandoned her pose and went around the desk and sat down, both arms in front of her on the desk.

Webb took a chair facing her.

"I do have questions for you," Webb said, "if you're in the mood to answer them."

"Did you know I'd be here?"

"No, I came to see the senator."

"Did he ask you to come?"

"Claire, for God's sake, we're not working behind your back!" Haskell said.

She waited for Webb's answer.

"No."

"But you have questions for me?"

Her symptoms of nervousness had diminished, but the room bristled with tension. He couldn't know what they had been arguing about, but she had Haskell over there biting his fingernails.

Webb said, "Just wondering why you said you had an appointment to get your car detailed."

And Haskell apparently hadn't known she had lied about that.

She ignored the question.

"I'm open to anything you want to tell me," Webb said.

"You think I killed Sam?"

"You were in a position to. You were there. You were in your car when your husband struggled with Milano."

She dragged on her cigarette, did not look at Haskell. "My husband was standing in the middle of the garage when I went into the house."

"And where was Milano?"

"Claire, please!" Haskell pleaded. "This is not in your best interest!"

"Haskell, why don't you leave if you don't like it?" Again looking at Webb, she said, "When I left the garage, Vinnie was running toward the woods."

"And your husband was alive? He was standing?"

"That's right. And I went into my house and locked the door."

She gave Haskell a drop-dead look, making sure he understood what she had said.

"You'll say that under oath?"

"I'll shout it from the gates of hell."

Her hand trembled as she poked out her cigarette on what seemed to be the handle of a letter opener—no ashtray in sight.

"There's more," she said. She got cigarettes out of a leather handbag, fitted one to her lips and lighted it. "Twenty minutes after I was in my room . . ."

"This is not necessary," Haskell said. "You've told him what you wanted to say. Now please!"

She ignored him. "Twenty minutes after I went to my room, the downstairs doorbell rang. Several times. Long persistent rings. I refused to answer it. My husband didn't have to come in. He could go to a hotel. I didn't give a damn. I tried to call my brother. I left messages on his machine asking him to call me. Then I took a Valium and two sleeping tablets and went to bed."

"Was it your husband rang the bell?"

She glanced at Haskell whose face was a stone. "I don't know," she said.

"Wednesday, when your husband didn't show up . . . ?"

"I called my brother."

"Why him?"

"I thought he might know where Sam was."

"You told him what had happened?"

"And I asked him to check with college security. I was sure my husband would have gone to the booth."

"You knew by then his keys were in the closet?"

"Yes."

"Why didn't you call Security?"

"It would just have started more rumors. I asked George to check with them."

"And did he?"

"No. For the same reason. He said we should wait."

"Why are you telling me this, Mrs. Spatz?"

Her eyes glinted angrily when she said, "You know what happened this morning at the Provost's office. You were there."

"I didn't get the whole story."

"Well, the whole story, Lieutenant, is that I will not help

anyone destroy the career of Vinnie Milano. I don't give a damn what you or anyone else thinks. He did not kill my husband."

"Do you know who did?"

"I know I didn't. I know Vinnie didn't. My husband was alive when Vinnie was running away. He was alive when I went into the house."

Webb had more questions but they could wait. He wanted what she had given him on record, under oath.

Haskell didn't accompany Claire to City Hall, and all the way across town Webb kept checking his mirror, making sure Claire was following him. They went into a small interrogation room where they were joined by one of Rudy's detectives. He set up the recorder. Webb made the preliminary statements, then turned the machine over to Claire. Without hesitation she told the machine what she had said in the senator's office, leaving out only the part about the Provost's efforts to suspend Vinnie Milano from school.

"And you're making this statement of your own free will?"

"Nobody has forced me to say anything," she said.

Almost before Claire had left the building, Webb was hurrying across town to get this news to Perci at the hospital.

CHAPTER TWENTY-NINE

When Webb came into Perci's room, she asked, "Did you find the gun?"

She was sitting in bed with the telephone in her lap, her right arm in a sling. When she turned, her upper body moved stiffly, the right elbow tight against her ribs. Despite feeling uncomfortable, she seemed in good spirits.

The roses, he noticed, had been put into a plastic vase on her bedside table, his card propped against the vase.

"Not that I know of," he said. "Rudy's people are looking."

"Have them look near St. Lawrence Street at Atlantic."

"Why there?"

She gave him a teasing look. "Just do it," she said.

When she tried to lift the telephone with her left hand, Webb reached across the bed, put the phone on the table next to the roses.

"That's about a quarter mile from your apartment. You remember something?"

"Not what you think, not something when I was shot. I'll tell you about it, but first tell me what you found out."

"You got an idea who shot you?"

"Come on," she said. "Let me do it my way."

"Who've you been calling?"

"Be nice. Tell me what you found out."

He told her about Claire's statement.

"Wow! How'd you get that out of her?"

"I didn't. She and her lawyer were arguing when I got there. She was madder than hell, blaming Haskell and her brother for trying to get Milano kicked out of college."

"She said that?"

"It's how I read what happened."

"She's that fond of Milano?"

"Looks that way."

"You believe her?"

"I like this story better than the other one. It doesn't necessarily clear Milano. He could have come back without her knowing it."

"And smothered Spatz? Then ran down to the front door and rang the bell?"

"Maybe Spatz rang the bell. Maybe nobody rang the bell. She could have thrown that in to confuse us."

"I think somebody rang the bell. But not Spatz or Milano."

"Who?"

"All the pieces aren't out of the box."

He laughed. "They probably never will be."

She put her left hand on her bandaged shoulder as though to steady it while she took a deep breath. Her face showed pain. It was in her eyes though she tried to hide it.

"Must hurt like hell."

She ignored that. "I think we're ready to eliminate a few suspects," she said, leaning back on the pillows. "We know the fight and the murder had to happen inside a little more than an hour."

"Because you think the garage door was closed before it began to snow."

"There was no snow anywhere inside that garage except a little that Claire's car tracked in. That didn't melt, so why would any other snow have melted?"

"Okay."

"And because the body had been in that same position for at least forty minutes before it was lifted into Crozier's car, the murder had to have taken place around quarter past or twenty past twelve, no later than twenty-five past, and that's really stretching it."

"Which means Claire could have done it while Vinnie was running away. Or Vinnie could have done it before he ran away. Or he could have come back after Claire had gone into the house. Or Crozier could have gone there before he went for his car."

"I've already told you why I don't think Vinnie did it," Perci said."

"And Crozier? Wouldn't he want to see for himself the guy was dead before he brought his car over?"

"Maybe he did. Spatz was probably dead by the time Crozier got there, even if he ran."

"And Claire?"

"I like her story," Perci said. "Why would she come out with it if she had murdered her husband? Why not stick to her original story and make us disprove it?"

"So who do you think did it?" Webb asked.

"The same person who shot me."

"If it's one of the three, I'll take Crozier."

"Couldn't have been," Perci said. "I'm so glad you told me about the doorbell. That is so important."

"Why?"

"For one thing, it's hard to imagine why either Crozier or Milano would have rung that bell. For another . . ."

Someone was shouting outside in the corridor. Something pressed on the door, then they heard the cop telling someone to stand back.

Webb went to the door.

It was Lorraine Lord and a camera crew. The lean uniformed

cop was holding them against the opposite wall, his arms outstretched.

Webb told Perci who it was.

"Let her in," she said. "But no pictures. I don't want any pictures."

When Lorraine came in she seemed shaken by the incident in the corridor. She went to the foot of Perci's bed. "I'm so glad to see you're all right," she said.

"I'm fine."

"Can't I have just one brief shot of you? People want to see how you're doing."

"I've had enough shots for a while. Just tell them I'm fine."

Lorraine went to a chair by the window, rested a big handbag in her lap as she sat down. Webb had closed the door after telling the cop to move the camera crew down the hall. He stayed at the door, both hands behind him leaning on the knob.

"I was so afraid for you," Lorraine said.

"It was just a couple of nicks. Nothing serious."

Lorraine got a yellow pad out of her bag, wrote something. "That's great news. We were just up there. Did you see anything? Have any idea . . . ?"

"You know everything I know," Perci said.

"Think it was connected with your investigation?"

"It's possible. But let's talk about the senator. You're supposed to tell me something."

Lorraine seemed startled. She gave Webb a glance, maybe wondering why he had to be in on it. "Have you talked with Mrs. Tezzetti? She's gone to Costa Rica. I suppose you know that."

"She's only a telephone call away," Perci said.

Lorraine reached into her bag, maybe for cigarettes, then withdrew her hand, settled for clutching the bag and staring out the window. She was nervous.

"I think it was quarter to one, something like that, when he got to my place," she finally said.

"Did he seem excited, nervous, anxious, anything like that?"

"He seemed tired. I guess it had been a long evening."

"He tell you what he had spent the evening doing?"

"No."

"But you were at Mrs. Tezzetti's when he and Dr. Spatz got there."

She looked down at her hands, maybe hadn't expected the question.

"We know you were there," Perci said.

"Yes, but he didn't say anything to me. We didn't want her to know we're seeing each other."

"Because you don't want her to know who told him about the meeting in New Hampshire? Nobody else would have told him. Who else knew about it?"

"All right, I told him," Lorraine said, as though relieved to get it out.

"And it was you who told Dr. Spatz that Alicia Umber was going to that clinic, wasn't it."

An admission of guilt crawled over Lorraine's face as she again reached into her handbag, probably dying for a smoke.

Perci couldn't let her go. "It was you, wasn't it. You wanted a big story."

"It's my job."

"Was it your job to tell Edison about my inquiries at the college?"

"I didn't have to. Nothing happens at that college he doesn't know about. He sees to that."

"How'd you find out Alicia Umber was pregnant? How'd you even know about her?"

"If I tell you . . . ? Look, I don't want to lose my job, and I will if you tell any of this to Mrs. Tezzetti."

"I don't want to tell her anything," Perci said.

Both she and Lorraine glanced inquiringly at Webb. He had nothing to say. It was Perci's show.

"Alicia came to George's apartment," Lorraine said. "It was about a week before she died. I didn't want to be seen there so I went into the bedroom but kept the door ajar. The kid was very upset. She had made an appointment for an abortion and wanted him to pay for it."

"So you ran to Spatz with the story."

"I got national coverage! What else of any interest happens in this little jerkwater! Think I want to stay here forever?"

"It doesn't bother you that you caused a young girl to die?"

"I didn't cause her to die. I didn't make her pregnant."

"You just told the world about it."

"That's right. That's my job. That's what I'm paid to do."

This time she reached into her bag, got cigarettes and jammed one between her lips.

"Don't smoke in here," Perci said.

"I don't intend to." Lorraine closed he bag and stood up. "I assume we have a deal?"

"I won't say anything to Mrs. Tezzetti."

"I'll tell my viewers how beautifully you're doing."

Webb opened the door for her and closed it behind her. He coaxed a smile out of Perci.

"That's not the end of it," she said. "Now I want Edison."

Webb laughed. "Somehow I think he's going to have trouble becoming the next president of Cleeve College."

"The doctor said I can go home tomorrow."

"I'm taking you home with me."

She didn't argue.

CHAPTER THIRTY

Late Tuesday morning Senator Edison was at his desk when Haskell Paine came into the office, out of breath and apprehensive. "I just heard it on the radio coming over." He dropped into a chair, put an ankle on a knee and fiddled nervously with a black sock. He looked exhausted. "They spotted the car in a filling station outside of Raleigh, North Carolina."

"And Crozier?"

"Apparently holding him pending some action from here."

"No gun on him, I suppose," Edison said.

"No mention of one. Probably threw it out the window crossing a bridge somewhere."

"How will bringing him back affect us?"

"Make it a lot easier to sell him as Sam's murderer. Why else would he have shot Piper?"

"Sure, but what happens if he says you put him up to it?"

"I don't need that, George," Haskell said, raising both hands to his face, squeezing his eyes shut and massaging his temples.

"Tell me you didn't at least put the idea in his head," George said.

"I told him she was a nuisance. I didn't tell him to shoot her."

"But you know damn well he'll say you did."

"Ravings of a desperate felon. Who'll listen to him?"

"There's a witness you picked him up at the bus station."

"The ticket clerk? He was bribed, George. He won't say anything. I'm not worried about Crozier. It's your sister who's the loose canon. I don't know what she said at City Hall, but what she told Harrington right here shines a light on you."

"How?"

"You brought Sam home."

"I left long before anything happened," Edison said.

"But they don't know that, and you can't prove it."

"And they can't prove otherwise."

"So who rang the bell?"

"How the hell do I know? Probably nobody. Look, don't be fooled by the illusion she's telling the truth."

Edison had just noticed cigarette ash on the handle of his letter opener. Holding the opener by the blade, he carried it across the desk and banged the handle on the rim of his wastebasket. "She sit here?"

"And Harrington over there," Haskell said, pointing at a chair.

"Did she know he'd be here?"

"She thought you sent for him."

"So she came here to try her story out on you. Why didn't she go straight to the police if she was so anxious to hurt me? I'll tell you why. She doesn't give a damn about Milano. She told that story to protect herself. She had to reinvent her alibi because that total denial didn't make any sense."

"And the bell ringing?"

"It's bullshit," Edison said. "She doesn't know what you and I know, what Charlie told you. She has to account for Sam being alive after she and Milano left the garage. So she invents a mysterious bell ringer. The cops can think it was Sam. It keeps Sam alive after Claire was in the house."

"You really think she did it?"

"She was there, Haskell. She could have. That's all I know. I just want to be sure the cops can't prove anything against her."

"I'm sure they're working hard," Haskell said. "And given the facts as we now see them, she's got to be at the top of their list."

"At the top of my list right now is that idiot you recommended to be our provost. It had to be him told Claire you wanted Milano expelled. And he'd do it to make an impression on her. The idiot's always had the hots for her. Who else knew?"

"He and I, and I certainly didn't tell her."

"Maybe the Milano crowd. Who knows who else they told. See what you can do to keep it off the news."

"How about Lorraine?"

"If she gets the story, she'll check with me," Edison said.

"You're sure? She's been awfully nervous lately."

"She's worried about her job. She'll be all right."

"I don't think you should trust her."

"I know," George said. "And she doesn't think I should trust you."

"I still think I ought to be here when Harrington comes over."

"Why? I can't handle him?"

Perci raised her head from the pillow and stared at a framed pencil sketch across the bedroom on the papered wall. It was a landscape—birch trees in a green field. In a very clear hand in the lower right corner was the name of the artist: Sarah Palsey Harrington.

Webb, standing in the open doorway, saw her looking at the picture. "She liked to sit outdoors and do those," he said, going to the window, closing it.

"I noticed others downstairs."

"She did a lot of them. By the way, I laundered those sheets yesterday and hung that comforter out on the line. Still smells a little musty in here. Room's been closed a while."

"You didn't have to go to all that trouble."

"No trouble. Feel like a ham sandwich?"

"And coffee."

When he left the room, she pulled on the jeans and shirt he had brought from her apartment, not the most suitable clothes for the meeting with Edison, but she was determined to be there. When she got downstairs, Webb was at the kitchen counter. She went to the table near the window.

"You intend to sell this house?" noticing sparkles of sunlight on patches of snow down the field. Junipers sticking up in little spaces of yellowed grass cleared by Sunday's rain.

"If I can find a buyer."

"Too much to take care of?"

"Too many memories," he said. "You like mustard on the ham or mayo?"

"Mustard. Mayo's got eggs in it."

"What's wrong with eggs?"

"Nothing if you want to die young."

He laughed. "Take any of those pain killers?"

"I'm fine," she said.

He had brought her home around nine-thirty, and she had taken a nap while he was getting her things. She asked, "Cops still there?"

"Didn't see any."

"I just wish they'd find the gun."

"What makes you think he'd get rid of it?"

"It wasn't Crozier," she said, deciding it was time to come out with it. She didn't have all the evidence she wanted, probably not enough to get a warrant, but she had solid inferences.

The sandwich paused half way to his mouth. "What makes you say that?"

"And he didn't kill Spatz."

He studied her a few seconds. "I see. This have anything to

do with those phone calls you made at the hospital?"

"I'm going with you to Edison's."

"You're up to it?"

"I am," she said.

"I don't suppose I have to warn you how delicately we have to handle him."

"I'll try not to mention Alicia Umber, if that's what you mean."

The senator was alone when his secretary brought them into his office. He nodded at Webb, then said to Perci, "Sorry to hear what happened to you," coming from behind the desk, curling warm fingers around her left hand, a politician's sympathy decorating his face.

Without preliminaries, Webb said he wanted to see the senator's revolver.

"It's at home," Edison said, surprised. He tried to make a joke of it. "You must be checking every gun in the city to go after mine."

"Just doing our job," Webb said.

"Let me send somebody for it."

"Let's go over there and see it," Webb said.

So that a third party doesn't have a chance to smudge prints or heave the gun into the river, Perci thought. Edison was trying hard to appear at ease, but Webb's manner was scaring him. The observation shored up Perci's confidence.

"It's important?"

"An old revolver of apparently low muzzle velocity was used to shoot Detective Piper."

"There's probably one in every other house."

"I'd like to see yours."

"You think my gun did it?"

Webb didn't say. The two men stared at each other. Finally

Edison gave in.

They went in separate cars. Perci noticed that Edison, in the car ahead of them, made several calls on his cellular.

"Besides the gun, what do you want to find out?" she asked Webb. "And the way you handled that . . . Your version of delicate?"

Webb was too into his thoughts to respond. "How long did he stay in the driveway Tuesday night? We know he was there long enough to watch Spatz unlocking the door. It's safe to think he might have noticed something happening at the garage. He could have noticed the door open, the exhaust spewing out. Maybe he took a stroll up there in the darkness."

Perci said, "You think it was Edison rang that bell?"

"Not sure it was anybody. Maybe Edison told his sister to say that."

"If this guy got a teenage girl pregnant, for my money he's not above any kind of crime, including murder. It would've been simple: no one around, the victim unconscious in a dark garage, a big temptation for anyone who wanted him dead. You know, if Crozier had found the man dead, he might have thought Milano did it."

"Any reason you know why Crozier could have hated Spatz?"

"I know he blamed him for what happened to Alicia Umber. He liked that girl a lot. Just his type. Immature girl who made no demands on him."

At his apartment with Webb and Perci standing behind him, Edison reached into the top left-hand drawer of his bureau and pushed a few socks and handkerchiefs aside.

"It's not here." A lot of blood drained out of his face. The surprise seemed genuine.

"Anywhere else it might be," Webb asked.

"No, I leave it here in an oilskin wrapper." He opened the

drawer next to it, moved a couple of bow ties, a small bundle of letters. "And the bullets are gone."

"Was the gun loaded?"

"No."

"Who comes in here?" Webb looked around at a very ordinary bedroom—furniture-store pictures on three walls, a double bed.

"A cleaning woman."

Perci asked, "Lorraine Lord?"

He had to know she knew about him and Lorraine. He nodded.

"How about Haskell Paine?" Webb asked.

"Yes. I had a party here ten days ago. A lot of people."

"Haskell come to your bedroom?" Webb asked.

"I can't believe he'd take it. He'd have no reason."

He made a token search through other drawers in the dresser, ran his hand across the high shelf in his closet. He gave Webb and Perci a look of helpless disbelief. "It's gone."

Webb suggested they go into the living room. "A few things I'd like to clear up."

"I just can't imagine . . ." He looked on the verge of throwing up.

"I guess you know your sister Claire changed her story," Webb said. They were sitting around a table in a windowed alcove. "Now she says Dr. Spatz was alive after she saw Milano running away."

"Yes, I heard that."

"She says someone rang her doorbell about twenty minutes after she went into the house. Know anything about that?"

"Not a thing."

"You were there."

"Not twenty . . ." He abruptly closed his mouth, but the mistake had been made. He tried to cover it by saying, "Sam had just gone into the house when I left."

"Why don't you tell us the whole thing," Webb said.

"I've told you everything I know. I'm not obliged to tell you anything that might have been told to me."

Perci shot a glance at Webb, seeking permission to butt in.

He nodded.

She said to Edison, "After you let Dr. Spatz off, you say you didn't notice anything happening in the garage."

"I noticed nothing unusual."

"Did Lorraine?"

The question stunned him. "Who?"

He shot a bewildered glance at Webb, who seemed as surprised as he was.

"Lorraine Lord," Perci said. "She was at Tezzetti's. She left there with you."

He stared at her a full ten seconds with his mouth open.

"We've had some very extensive talks with Lorraine," Perci said. "And I think you've got a serious problem if you don't tell us what went on in those few minutes after you dropped Dr. Spatz off."

"Lorraine told you I saw something?"

"What did you see, Senator?"

"Nothing."

"You didn't walk up to the garage?"

He wanted Webb to intervene, but Webb just stared at him.

"I'm not sure I should say anything more," Edison said.

Perci knew she was way out of line and could even get fired for what she was doing, but Webb didn't stop her, and he was her boss.

She said, "I don't think you killed your brother-in-law, Senator. There were only two people out there who could have rung the bell. And one of them wasn't Lorraine."

"Meaning me? Why would I want to?"

She gave that a few seconds to sink in.

With a rapidly beating heart she went on. "I think Lorraine went up to the garage and came back and told you Dr. Spatz was lying on the garage floor dead. I think you went to see for yourself, then tried to talk to your sister. You didn't report his death because you wanted to protect her."

"What kind of nonsense is this?" Edison asked Webb. He might as well have asked the wall.

Perci went on: "If you had killed him, Senator, why would anyone have rung the bell? You wouldn't want a witness. And if you had thought Lorraine had killed Dr. Spatz, you would have gone to the police. You believed what Lorraine told you.

"You must have sweated out all day Wednesday wondering where the body was. But Wednesday wasn't a torment to your sister because she didn't know her husband was dead until the body was found Thursday morning."

"This is nonsense," Edison said. "Yes, Lorraine was with me. I admit that. But the rest of it . . ."

"I don't think even you know the rest of it," she said. "Did you know, for example, that Lorraine was recognized by a cab driver who picked her up at the corner of Atlantic and St. Lawrence streets about a half hour after I was shot? He took her to the Eastland Hotel where she was recognized by a second cab driver who took her to your place. And what was she doing alone, on foot, in my neighborhood, when I had just been shot?"

"She doesn't drive."

"I know that. She had her license pulled in Massachusetts for twice 'operating under the influence,' as they say down there. It's why she took this low-end job in Maine."

"I didn't know that," he said.

"Did Dr. Spatz know it was she who told you about the New Hampshire meeting?"

For a long time he gazed out the window, maybe doing a

little soul searching, probably wondering how much he should say.

"Did he threaten to tell Mrs. Tezzetti?"

"Sam was upset," Edison admitted. "He told Lorraine he wanted her out of the Champions."

"And that would have required an explanation, and she would have been fired."

He gave that a lot of thought, looked guiltily at Webb. "I told her that."

"She told us how she found out Alicia Umber was pregnant, Senator."

He said nothing to that.

"I think she killed Dr. Spatz. I think she found him unconscious on the floor of the garage, came back to your car and said she had found him dead. Didn't you suspect her?"

Staring at hands folded in his lap like a submissive child, he shook his head.

Perci looked at Webb. There was nothing in his expression accusing her of misconduct. He seemed impressed but skeptical.

"I think it will go easier on you," Webb said, "if you'll make a statement."

"What do you think I'm guilty of? I warned her about what Sam might do, but I didn't expect her to kill him!"

"I'm just interested in knowing what happened that night. I'm not interested in hurting you. I'm interested in solving this homicide. I can bring someone over from the DA's office, if you want."

Edison got up, stood there a moment staring at the floor. "Are you putting me under arrest?"

"No."

Perci couldn't read the look Webb gave her as they left Edison's apartment. She hoped he was annoyed only because she hadn't discussed her ideas with him before making those accusations. He didn't know she had no proof. He didn't know she had only inferences that maybe made sense only to her.

As they rode together toward City Hall, she carefully went over her reasoning, knowing she would have to explain everything in detail to Webb and to the chief.

She wished her heart would stop pounding.

CHAPTER THIRTY-ONE

The first thing they heard in the chief's office was that a gun had been found in a drain about two blocks from Perci's house and that bullets fired from it matched the slugs found on Perci's back steps.

"Fingerprints?" Webb asked.

"One very clear print on a shell and a partial on the bottom of the cylinder where it locks into the frame," the chief said. "Neither print was Edison's."

Feeling a little rush of adrenalin, Perci said, "Lorraine Lord's prints are on file in Boston."

That got her a questioning stare which led into an hour-long recital that had the chief on the edge of her seat, eyes stern with interest.

"And that could possibly have led you to suspect Lorraine Lord?" she said.

Perci had hoped to give her reasoning to Webb before giving it to the chief, but she had to settle for a brief glance of apology, which he acknowledged with a smile.

"Thinking about everything while I was in the hospital, I remembered there was a glut of cars in the Spatz's driveway when we went there to inspect the garage. When we came out of the garage, all the cars were gone. But Lorraine Lord was still in the house."

"Where was her car?" the chief asked.

"That's what I wanted to know. So yesterday I called the office and found out she doesn't have a car registered in Maine or a Maine operator's license. I called Boston and found out she'd been twice convicted of operating under the influence—what they call it down there—the second time resulting in a homicide. That's why she came to Maine. She lost her license, lost her job."

She glanced at Webb. Apparently he hadn't thought of it, and the real significance of what she had learned apparently hadn't struck him. "Lorraine was at Tezzetti's house Tuesday evening when Edison and Dr. Spatz were there. Because she spent the night with Edison, it seemed plausible that she went home with him and was with him when he dropped off Dr. Spatz.

"Now he's admitted that, and now we have on tape his admission that Lorraine went to the garage in the dark to see what was going on up there."

The chief asked, "You believe that?"

"Yes," Perci said. "She would have wanted the headlights off. If it'd been him, he'd've driven up there with the headlights glaring."

"Why didn't he?"

"Maybe he thought what his sister did in her garage was none of his business."

"So you think Lorraine smothered him, then went back and told Edison she had found Spatz dead? And that's why he rang the bell, wanted to talk with Claire?"

"That's what I think."

"So why didn't he suspect that Lorraine had smothered him—later when he learned that Spatz had been smothered."

"At the time, of course," Perci said, "he had no reason to think Lorraine had found Spatz unconscious on the garage floor, no reason to think she'd murdered him. When he learned of the smothering, he thought Claire might have done it. All he could think about was protecting his sister."

"Well, let me get it straight. You think Dr. Spatz went into his house by the front door, went to the back entry, took his coat off, hung it in the closet, then maybe heard something in the garage and went out to investigate?"

"I think he had an idea what might be going on when he saw the garage doors open with the car engine running. It might not have been the first time."

"Why wouldn't he have gone straight to the garage instead of going . . . ?"

"He had a TV reporter watching him."

"And you think Lorraine Lord asked the senator to stick around because she sensed something was up?"

"I don't think she would've asked. She probably got out of the car. She saw the plume of exhaust. It wouldn't have taken Dr. Spatz very long to cross through his house. She could have seen him go into the garage."

"And by that time, Edison's headlights were out. All right, fine, but it won't get us an arrest warrant."

"You know," Webb said. "I thought it funny Lorraine didn't show much interest in what we found in that garage. I went into the house and she just stared at me. Must have been scared. Maybe she'll plead, especially if the prints on the revolver are hers. Think I'll check with Janet."

When he got up, the chief asked Perci to stay. She wanted to talk about things like insurance benefits and plans for the future.

"You look all tuckered out," she said.

"I'm okay."

"That was good work."

"Thanks."

"You're officially on sick leave, you know. You won't have to see a doctor again for at least a month. You have plans?"

"I'd like to keep working. Nothing else to do."

"Don't make police work your whole life, Perci. Don't end

274

up like me—old maid, no husband, no children. Are you interested in closing down the Mayfair Lodge?"

Perci was surprised. Indeed she was interested. "You read my report?"

"I've been getting complaints about that place since I came here. Just haven't felt politically strong enough to tackle it up until now. But now we've got Edison on edge I think he'll tell us some secrets, maybe some about Spatz that'll explain why he got pinned to that tree."

"I don't doubt it was Boyd did it," Perci said. "And for him to risk getting caught going to all that trouble, he must have really hated the man. I don't think Crozier and Dr. Spatz were strangers. I think the 'crucifixion' was a way of ridiculing a hypocrite."

"That's interesting. I understand the police in Elwell don't think very highly of Crozier."

"That's what Janet heard."

"Well, maybe we'll learn more when we get Crozier up here."

"What'll happen to him?"

"Probably depends on how much he's willing to cooperate."

"All right if I go see Milano? If Crozier gets to him, he might drop those stolen-car charges."

"As long as you don't tell him anything. We've got a long way to go before wrapping this up. Convincing ourselves is one thing; convincing a judge and jury is very different."

With the assistance of material from Boston, Janet Lucia quickly identified the two prints on Edison's revolver.

"Got a lot of points that say it's Lorraine Lord's thumb and her forefinger. She probably thought she'd wiped everything off. They commonly forget places."

"Want to do me a favor?" Webb said.

"Anything."

"Don't tell Charlie."

She didn't ask why. She probably knew.

It was around five when they left City Hall and drove across town to the TV station armed with an arrest warrant signed by Judge Kaplan.

"Agatha say anything to you about the Mayfair Lodge?" Webb asked.

"Says she wants it investigated."

"That interest you?"

"I might stick around for it," Perci said.

Lorraine wasn't at the station. She hadn't been there all day.

"If she doesn't show up pretty soon, or at least call in," the station manager said, "she's out of a job."

They found the senator's Cadillac in the parking lot outside Lorraine's apartment house. They found him in the hallway upstairs outside her half opened door. He was leaning on the wall, his chin on his chest. From twenty feet away, alerted by a sour odor, they saw a pool of vomit on the carpet in front of him.

He waved a trembling hand at the doorway. "In there. In the bathroom."

They found Lorraine in the tub, head back, mouth open, eyes closed, her face a pale gray. The water, which came just to the tops of her breasts, was saturated with blood. Webb felt for the carotid artery. She was dead.

While Webb was at the phone, Perci led Edison into the apartment, sat him in a soft chair.

"I came directly here from City Hall," he said, face in his hands. His fingers looked deathly white. "I told her what had happened. I advised her to turn herself in."

"You would have testified against her?"

"Of course. I can't imagine now why I hadn't seen it at the

time. All I could think about was Claire, even though I knew she wouldn't murder Sam."

"How long was Lorraine in the bathroom before you found her?"

"About an hour. She asked to be alone, said she wanted to take a bath. She always took a long time. Loved to soak and think, I guess. It didn't seem unusual. But after a while I got scared. I knocked on the door. She had locked herself in. I opened the door with a small screwdriver. And, you know . . . ?" He looked up, a strange pleading on his face. "I was shocked, but I wasn't surprised. You know what I mean?"

As Perci looked down at this frightened, defeated man, she reminded herself that she had wanted to see him suffer, to see him experience some of the pain he had caused Alicia Umber. She had called it retribution. She now admitted it was revenge she had wanted. But wanting something and witnessing it are different.

"Don't blame yourself," she said, putting a comforting hand on his shoulder.

He just sat there hunched over staring at the rug.

She left him alone for a few seconds. When he looked up, she said, "There's one thing I'm not entirely clear on."

He waited.

"When you dropped Dr. Spatz off," Perci said. "When you were there in the driveway, did you think something unusual was going on in the garage?"

"Lorraine did. She snapped off my headlights and insisted we wait, even opened the door so I wouldn't drive off. What tipped her was the way Sam acted when he got out of the car. She was always curious about their personal lives. She'd heard all the rumors."

"Did you see him come out the back door?"

"I saw him go into the garage. I didn't see what went on in there."

"You saw your sister come out?"

"She ran into the house."

"Barefoot?"

"Bare assed," he said.

Before going to a restaurant, Perci induced Webb to take her to the college. It took awhile but they finally located Vinnie in the gym playing one-on-one with a girl named Cindy.

"How you doing?" he said, sweat running off his face, holding the ball on his hip, Cindy waiting for him under the basket, hands at her sides, nice-looking girl.

"Just wanted to ask you to do me a favor," Perci said. "You know we found Boyd."

"Yeah, I heard. Smashed the front end of my car running from a trooper. And I heard about you. You okay?"

"Just a couple of nicks."

"I don't think Boyd did that. He's no good but he wouldn't shoot anybody."

"I'm sure it wasn't him. But I don't want you to drop the charges against him."

"My uncle won't let me."

"I know Boyd's your friend, but—"

"Naw, he was never my friend. He was just using me. I'm through with all that. The kind of guy he was . . . that's all behind me. Even this mess I'm in. I'll get out of it because I never did anything. All I did was act stupid."

"I think you'll be all right. And I look forward to seeing you in the NFL."

"Me too," he said.

She watched him dribble the ball, pass it to Cindy and break for the basket. The way the girl crowded against him, laughing, pushing him off, Perci suspected he'd have trouble changing at least one aspect of his old life. Women couldn't leave him alone.

"So what's going to happen to all these people?" Perci asked. She was following Webb back to their table from the salad bar. The fajitas would be ready in a few minutes.

"I doubt much will happen to Edison. Obstruction? I doubt they'll go after him. But I'd guess his political career is over."

"Think he might succeed Spatz at the college?"

"Not after this. No, I think he'll go back to making a lot of money practicing law."

"And Claire?"

"Big bucks from Sam's insurance. She'll probably move to Florida."

"I hope not."

"Hate the way it happened, but I think Cleeve College has benefited from all this. The Board can now pick a good president. The way things are happening, maybe abortion won't be an issue out there much longer. You never know."

"Or football, with Milano graduating."

"They'll settle down to the way things used to be—quiet little New England college. How about you?"

"Me?"

"You going back to Florida?"

The waitress brought the fajitas and a pitcher of beer. Webb filled their mugs.

"I think I might stay," she said. "Maybe we can stick that guy Steinmetz in jail and close down the Mayfair Lodge."

ABOUT THE AUTHOR

Jim Ingraham, formerly a college professor in New England, now lives in Florida with his family and spends his time writing and relaxing in the sun.